MAX BRALLIER

GALACTIC HOT DOGS™
REVENGE OF THE SPACE PIRATES
BOOK 3

Created by MAX BRALLIER

Illustrated by
RACHEL MAGUIRE, NICHOLE KELLEY,
STEVE YOUNG, and RYAN YOUNG

ALADDIN
New York London Toronto Sydney New Delhi

ALADDIN

An imprint of Simon & Schuster Children's Publishing Division

1230 Avenue of the Americas, New York, New York 10020

First Aladdin edition May 2020

Copyright © 2017 by Sandbox Networks, Inc.

Cover illustration by Vivienne To copyright © 2020 by Sandbox Networks, Inc.

All rights reserved, including the right of reproduction in whole or in part in any form.

ALADDIN and related logo are registered trademarks of Simon & Schuster, Inc.

For information about special discounts for bulk purchases, please contact Simon & Schuster Special Sales at 1-866-506-1949 or business@simonandschuster.com.

The Simon & Schuster Speakers Bureau can bring authors to your live event. For more information or to book an event contact the Simon & Schuster Speakers Bureau at 1-866-248-3049 or visit our website at www.simonspeakers.com.

Cover designed by Dan Potash

Interior designed by Rachel Maguire, Nichole Kelley, and Dan Potash

The text of this book was set in Good Dog.

Manufactured in the United States of America 0220 FFG

10 9 8 7 6 5 4 3 2 1

Library of Congress Control Number 2017942317

ISBN 978-1-5344-7803-9 (hc)

ISBN 978-1-5344-7802-2 (pbk)

ISBN 978-1-4814-2499-8 (eBook)

For Alyse and Blastie
—M. B.

To Declan, Jayden, and my dad
—R. M.

THE THIRD ANNUAL MILKY WAY GALAXY'S ORIGINAL HOT-DOG-SWALLOWING CONTEST!

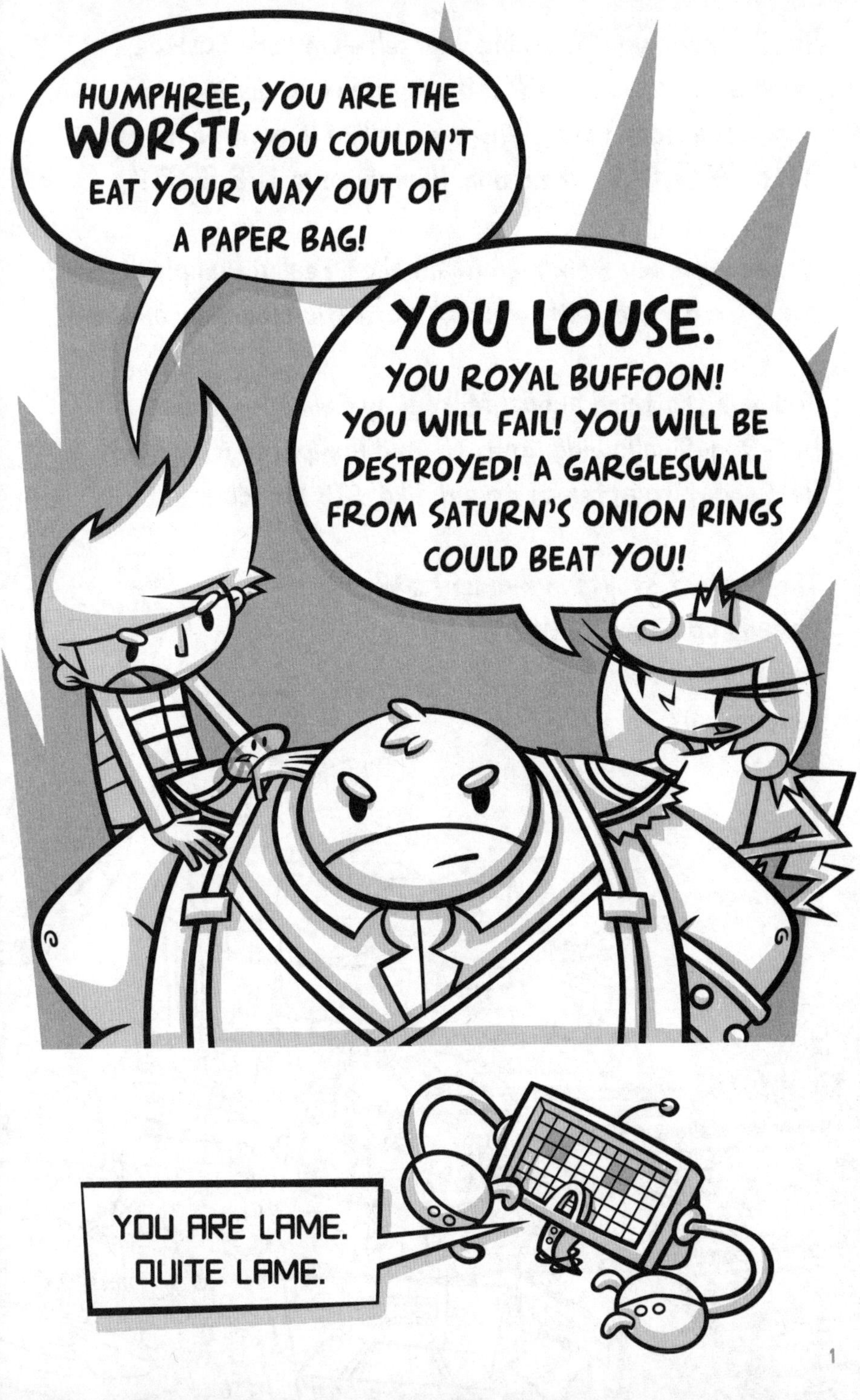
HUMPHREE, YOU ARE THE WORST! YOU COULDN'T EAT YOUR WAY OUT OF A PAPER BAG!
YOU LOUSE. YOU ROYAL BUFFOON! YOU WILL FAIL! YOU WILL BE DESTROYED! A GARGLESWALL FROM SATURN'S ONION RINGS COULD BEAT YOU!
YOU ARE LAME. QUITE LAME.

So ... maybe you're asking yourself—why are Cosmoe, Princess Dagger, and F.R.E.D. insulting and dissing Big Humphree right now? Why am I telling Humphree he's **THE WORST** when, duh, Humphree is **THE BEST**?

It's because my main man (main alien, really) Humphree needs some encouragement—y'know, motivational words and junk.

Today is the third annual Milky Way Galaxy's Original Hot-Dog-Swallowing Contest—and Humphree is competing. He's about to attempt to eat, like, 678 hot dogs.

The contest starts in moments. We're already up onstage. We're squeezing in our final few verbal abuses.

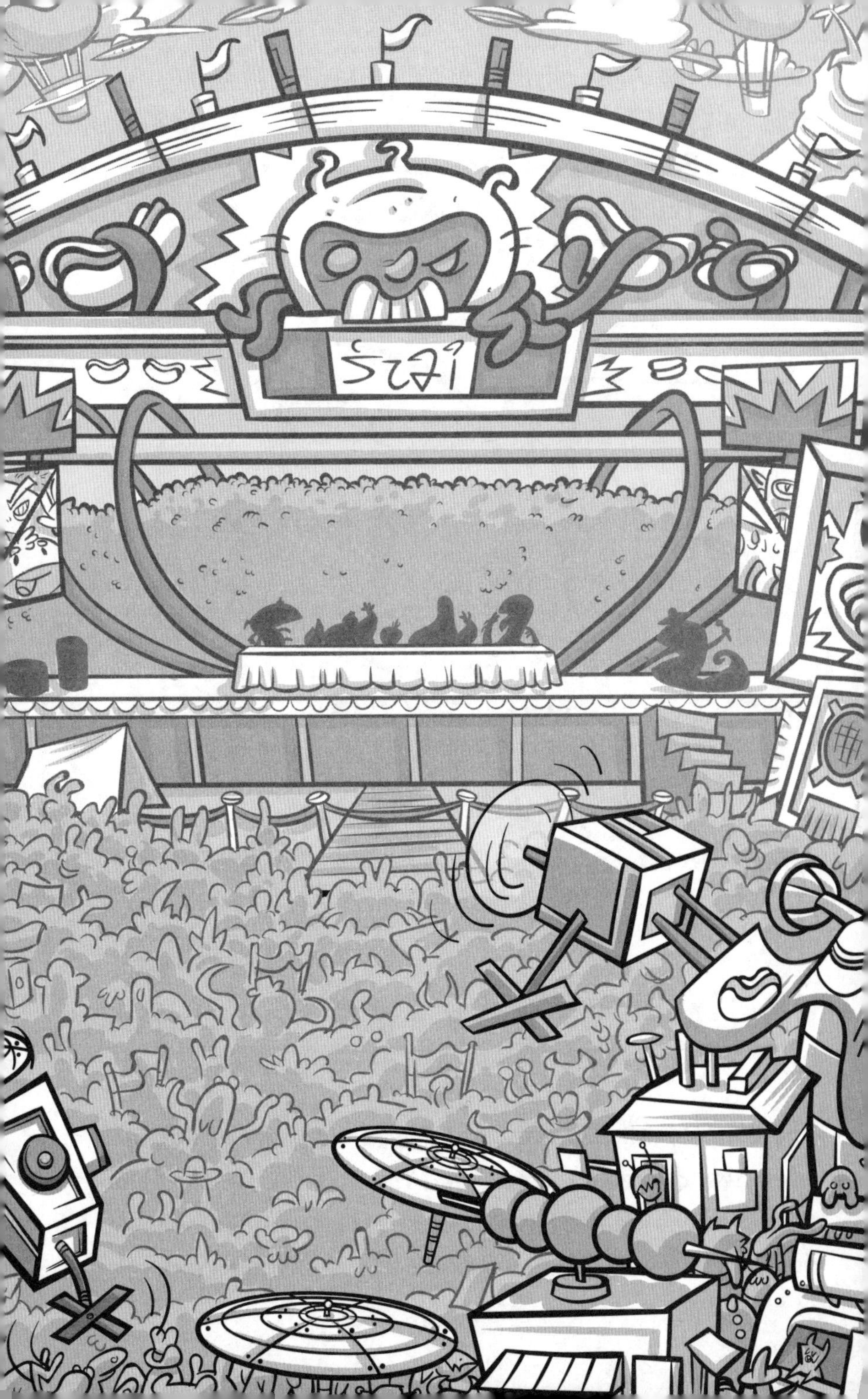

See, the one thing that REALLY motivates Humphree is being told he CAN'T do something. Two years ago, I told Humphree he was a sour-smelling, good-for-nothing schnitzel pit who probably couldn't even eat ONE slice of primo pizza. I said he'd never EVER, **EVER** claim the championship belt, and then...

The contest takes place on the beachy planet of Funnel Isle. I can hear the eager crowd and the booming of the famous rolo-zipper ride—but the loudest sound of all is right next to me: the thundering rumbling of Big Humphree's stomach.

Princess Dagger, the royal rascal, slaps Humphree on the back, then glances down at his gargantuan gut. "How long's it been since you ate, dude?"

Humphree groans. "A whole hour! I feel so weak..."

Just then Ozzkar Micc rushes past us to the front of the stage. Ozzkar is the competition's host—and he's an obnoxious slimeball. Word is, he used to host illegal robot karate matches. Not exactly a trustworthy dude...

YOU KNOW THE RULES!
WHOEVER EATS THE MOST
HOT DOGS IN THREE OFFICIAL SPACE MINUTES
WILL BE DECLARED **WINNER!**
NO PUKING ALLOWED!
IT IS **THAT** SIMPLE!

I've heard Ozzkar Micc's spiel before, so I start to zone out. Staring at the crowd, I think about me, a kid from Earth, now onstage in front of 10,000 aliens, about to cheer on my big buddy as he tries to break the galactic hot-dog-eating record. Weird world, huh? Weird UNIVERSE.

In the distance, near the boardwalk, I spot the other food ships. Each year, hundreds of flying food ships come from across the galaxy to sell food at the Milky Way Galaxy's

Original Hot-Dog-Swallowing Contest. Our ship, the *Neon Wiener*, is parked near the end.

I spot most of the usual food ship suspects: Big Early's Spaghetti Sandwich Stand, Dinko's Dollar Donuts, Singo's Sizzling Snaprats, and more. But something looks strange about the ships. Something is OFF, but I can't quite put my finger on it . . .

Then I realize that the sunlight is bouncing off the ships in a very weird fashion. It causes the ships to almost shimmer and dance like desert mirages in an old cartoon. It's almost like the ships aren't totally **REAL**.

"Hey, Dags," I say. "Am I crazy, or do those food ships out there look a little, like, **PECULIAR?**"

"You are crazy," Dagger replies, flashing me her happy, evil grin. "But now that you mention it, yup, the ships look, like, **FAKE.**"

"But do you think they're, like, undercover evil?" I ask.

See, Princess Dagger is kind of an expert on being evil . . .

Princess Dagger (aka the royal rascal) is the #3 in our trio—and she's a unique case. See, Dagger is EVIL. She has evil genes! There's evil in her blood, inherited from her evil mom. Her mom is Evil Queen Dagger, and she rules the galaxy with an evil iron (and probably spiky) fist.

A little while back, Princess Dagger kidnapped herself onto our ship. She just straight-up hijacked the *Neon Wiener* and basically forced me and Humphree to hang out with her.

She begged us to let her stay on board the *Neon Wiener*—so we let her hang. Her mom was not pleased—but whatever! Now Princess Dagger is one of us, no matter what.

9

"Are you prepared?!" Ozzkar Micc shrieks, and my mind zips back to the moment. The crowd roars with approval.

Ozzkar Micc's voice is booming as he announces the whos and whats of the contestants, none of whom I've ever heard of. Glancing at the other contestants, I realize that these dudes are gnarly ROUGH looking. They don't look like professional eaters: no, they look like someone sprung them from jail just for this contest. Not the type you'd want to meet in a dark Jetway . . .

The crowd roars even louder as Ozzkar Micc comes to the grand finale, shouting, "The Bronkle, hailing from the planet Bronkellia! Eight feet tall and weighing 1.1 tons, the gigantic guy, our returning champion, the great Biiiiiiig Humphreeeeeeeee!"

Humphree pats his belly. Dagger and I clap, cheering for our main man.

"SO . . ." Ozzkar Micc shrieks. "FUNNEL ISLE, I HOPE YOU'RE READY! THE CONTEST BEGINS IN 10 . . . 9 . . . 8 . . ."

And the audience takes over, counting down the seconds. And I join in, because I love this—I love the crowd, and I love the sun and the beach, and I love just how BIG this event is, and more than anything, I love my buddies—and I'm so happy that I get to be up here with them . . .

And then—**BOOM**—the contest begins!

The tabletop slides open with a whoosh. A robot arm thrusts upward, holding a doggie—and Humphree starts eating . . .

THE SuMBIOS . . .

2

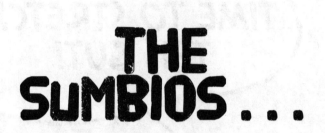

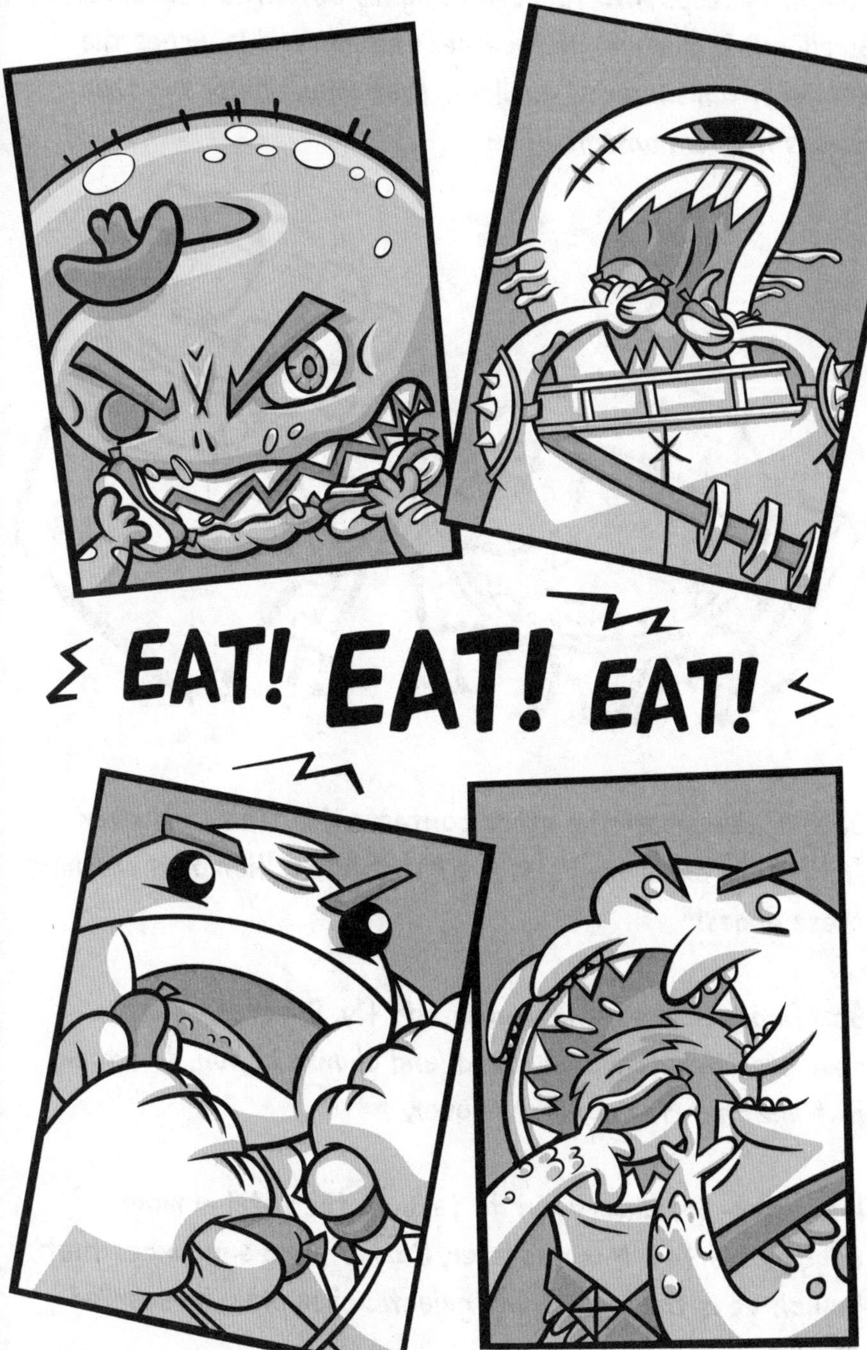
EAT! EAT! EAT!

Humphree leaps into the lead using his patented "Squeeze 'N' Swallow" technique. He squashes the bun and launches the doggie into his mouth, swallows that in one gulp, and then chases it down with the bun ...

Dagger glances at the other contestants. "This isn't even a fight!" she exclaims. "This is a MASSACRE. Humps is crushing these dudes!"

Scarfing increases, and wiener bits fly. Spectators are showered in ketchup, mustard, and chunks o' bun. And then, just like that, the contest is over.

Inspector-Bots hurry out to tally up the total number of doggies scarfed. Minutes later, Ozzkar Micc announces that Humphree is the winner and galactic champion: he scarfed down 692 hot dogs.

"Yes!" I exclaim. "Nice work, Humps! With the prize money, we can kick back and do nothin' but chillaxing."

Dagger groans. "We've been chillaxing for MONTHS. I need some action! Some adventure! Some action and adventure!"

Ozzkar Micc bangs on the microphone and a hush settles over the crowd. His voice booms: "We are honored to have a special guest presenting this year's championship belt. Here she comes now!"

Squinting against the sun, I spot the championship belt—it's made of glimmer globs that sparkle like diamonds. Two hands hold the belt high, carrying it toward the stage . . .

My shoulders stiffen. Something feels **OFF** here. Goober tightens around my wrist—something has him nervous too.

Oh right! Goober! It's time for some backstory and junk...

See, Goober is the rubbery, elastic blob that is forever wrapped around my wrist. Goober is symbiotic and lives off my adrenaline—that means he can't leave my side or he'll die! But it's worth it, 'cause Goober is frappin' rad and can turn into all sorts of awesome junk, like...

PREVIOUSLY IN
GALACTIC HOT DOGS...

GOOBER THE HAMMER!

GOOBER THE FIST!

GOOBER THE ANNOYING PAL WHO NEVER, EVER LEAVES!

GOOBER THE FART DAMPENER!

Suddenly, Dagger elbows me. The crowd is parting, and I see who this special guest is. I just about swallow my tongue . . .

It's space pirate Rani Zonian.

I stare into her eyes. They chill me to the core. They remind me of some of the worst moments of my life. And immediately, I know why she's here.

She's come to take Goober. . . .

HUMPHREE, EARTH-BOY-GREETINGS. LONG TIME NO SEE. I'M FINISHING WHAT I STARTED THREE YEARS AGO—DELIVERING THE SUMBIOS TO THE GENERAL.

Suddenly the other contestants are rising, yanking blasters from beneath the wiener table, forming a semicircle around us. I realize why I didn't recognize them: **THEY'RE PIRATES, TOO!** This entire contest was one big trap!

My eyes are drawn to the distance. High in the sky, purple clouds shift, and neon sunbeams shower the food ships. And that's when I see they're not food ships at all . . .

They're small pirate ships: jump jets. And rising up behind them is the mother ship.

Space pirate Rani Zonian is taking no chances today. She has brought an army with her.

Rani taps her sword against the ground. "Humphree, it's taken me a long time to track you and the boy down."

Very slowly, Humphree stands. Calmly, coolly, he wipes hot-dog crumbs from his shirt.

AND IT'S GOING TO TAKE _YOU_ EVEN LONGER TO CATCH US, MY CAPTAIN ...

You could slice the tension with a lightsaber. And if I had a lightsaber, I would totally do that. Of course, if I had a lightsaber, then I'd be a Jedi and this would be _Star Wars_ and life would basically be AMAZING.

But it's not amazing. In fact, right now it's super not good and is only about to get worse.

I feel Dagger jab me in the side, eager to know what's up ...

COSMOE, **WHO** IS THIS AWESOME-LOOKING CHICK? I **WANT** TO HANG OUT WITH HER!

LONG STORY, DAGS. I'LL EXPLAIN WHEN WE DON'T HAVE BLASTERS POINTED AT OUR HEADS. BLASTERS AT THE HEAD IS NEVER A GREAT TIME FOR EXPLAINING STUFF.

A sudden, piercing shriek cuts through the air. It's Rani's familiar—a strange spider on her shoulder that screeches like a bird. All pirate captains have them: they're like space versions of pirate parrots, back on olden-days Earth.

"No more chitchat," Rani growls. "You are surrounded. You are unarmed. And you, Humphree, are most likely very full."

I hear Humphree's stomach roll. It's not a nice sound. Rani is right—Humps's belly is definitely jam-packed.

Humphree leans over and lifts a hand to his mouth. "Cosmoe," he whispers. "When I make my move, you run. And you don't stop running. It's YOU and GOOBER she really wants."

"No way," I say, shaking my head. "We all split together."

"WILL SOMEONE PLEASE TELL ME WHAT'S HAPPENING?" Dagger says, practically exploding.

"Silence!" Rani barks. "Humphree, hand over the Earth-boy, and I may forgive your previous betrayal . . ."

Humphree glances down at me and smiles—a smile that says, "You and I both know, kid, that I'll never make that deal."

That's when I know this standoff has come to an end. There's no point in chatting. And Dagger agrees . . .

"Okay," Dagger says. "This pirate lady is radical looking, and I'm crushing on her. But no one—NO ONE—talks to us like this. It's time we exited. Humphree, get ready . . ."

Dagger's eyes flash, her hand curls into a fist, and she socks Humphree in the belly—

Humphree whips his head from side to side like a lawn sprinkler, showering the nearby pirates in puke. The nastiness sprays the first rows, and suddenly the onlookers are fleeing—the entire crowd is one stampeding mass.

Leaning over, gasping for breath, Humphree says, "Princess! You punched me in the gut!"

Dagger shrugs. "It worked! Room to breathe—although it smells like hot-dog puke—and room to fight!"

Goober circles into a boxing glove, and—**POW!**—I uppercut
the nearest two pirate villains. Dagger, whirling, kicks the
nearest in the jaw and his head snaps back.

"F.R.E.D., fire up the *Neon Wiener!*" I shout, and F.R.E.D.
zooms ahead, speeding above the fleeing crowd and the
rushing pirates.

The air turns hot as pirate vessels hover toward us. They're
blocking our escape path to the *Neon Wiener.* Massive
cannons are cranked, swiveling and spinning, targeting us.

"If we can't get around these pirate ships," I say, eyeing the
closest ship, "we'll have to go right over them . . ."

AWESOME LADY PIRATE

I throw a quick glance up at the closest pirate ship, and then it's go time: I fling my arm forward and Goober whips through the air like a zip line come to life. I feel Humphree and Dagger grab hold of me, and we're all suddenly yanked off our feet. "We have to battle from ship to ship!" I shout. "It's the only way we can get to the *Neon Wiener*."

Goober carries us screaming upward, toward the pirate ship, and then we're scrambling over the side . . .

I peer down the length of ships. F.R.E.D. has the *Neon Wiener* hovering at the end of this long row of ships. Just have to keep moving, keep jumping, keep battling—that's how we get home.

It's like a videogame—some sort of side-scrolling, platformer thing.

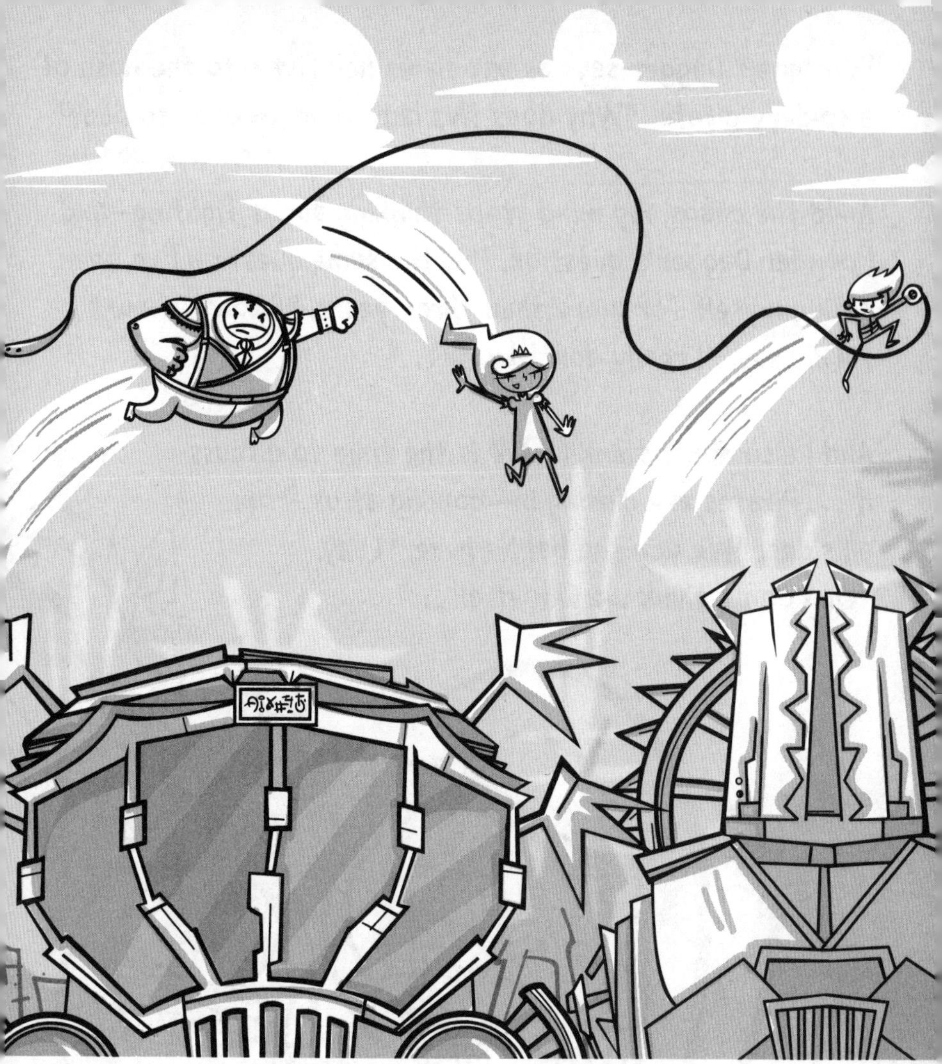

My feet hit the poly-wood deck as I land on the next ship—and then my stomach flips as the pirate vessel soars upward, then plummets down. One moment, flying high, the next, free-falling.

With only one ship to go before reaching the *Neon Wiener*, we leap into a storm of pirates . . .

"Cosmoe," Dagger says as she slams her fist into the nose of a spidery pirate. "Why does this lady want Goober so bad?"

Amid the chaos, my mind stops thinking about fighting—and I ponder Dagger's question. It's the same question I've been asking myself for more than three years. "I don't know," I finally say. "I really don't know . . ."

And I also don't think **NOW** is the time to discuss it . . . Pirates are closing in—coming at us from all sides. "We win the battle here," I say. "Or I don't think we win at all . . ."

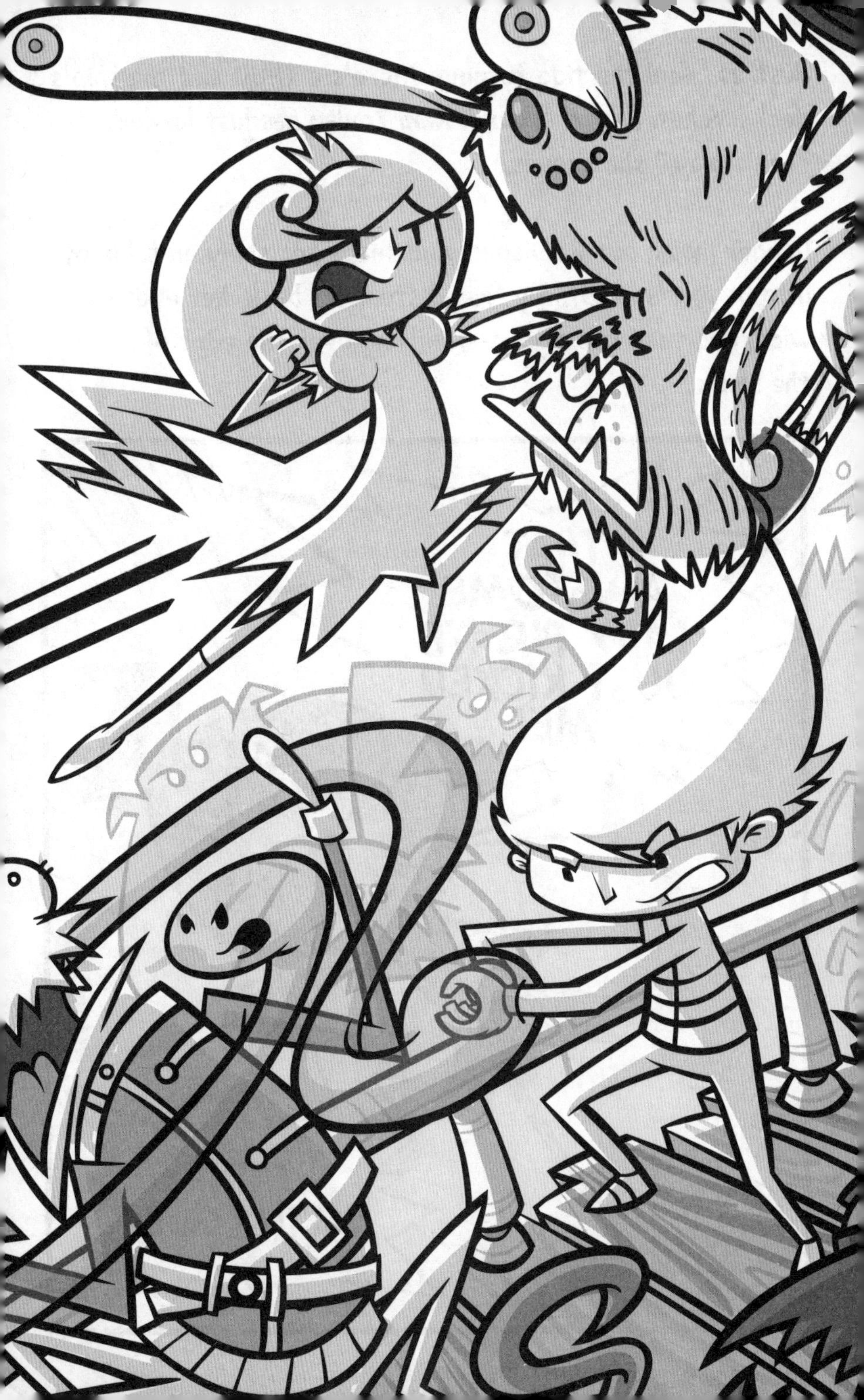

Just as I feel the tide turning, there's a THUD and the ship's deck lurches. I whirl around. Rani Zonian has just landed. "Let's play," she growls.

Dagger leaps, but Rani spins and snaps her shiny metal boot into Dagger's chest. My friend stumbles back, her eyes go wide, and then she's gone—tumbling over the edge of the ship . . .

Fear floods me—Dagger just went overboard! But I race to the ledge and look down—and I watch Dagger do four backflips, two double spins, and a twirling twist before sticking an A+ landing. I swear, the princess is part cyber-cat.

Doors whoosh open. A rush of space pirates swarm from the lower hold, charging onto the decks.

"Humphree, behind you!" I shout.

But it's too late. A massive thud-hammer slams into Humphree's noggin, and he drops to his knees, eyes doing the loop the loop.

"Over the side with him," Rani orders.

Humphree fights and resists, but there are simply too many—and he's just too dazed. Humphree stares into my eyes—and then, just like that, he's thrown overboard.

"NO!" I cry out. I race toward the edge of the ship. Humphree is crazy heavy—he can't crash to the ground! He'll be splattered!

But Rani slides in front of me, blocking my path. Pirates close in from all sides.

"HUMPHREE!" I cry out. "ARE YOU OKAY?" I hear nothing . . .

An instant later, Dagger bellows from below. "I caught Humphree! He's okay! Now get out of there, Cosmoe!"

I whirl around. Rani reveals something: a strange, see-through box. It glows magenta.

The box causes Goober to shrivel, curling tighter around my arm. I feel his fear, and it courses through me. I glance down. "Uh, hey, Goober—whatcha doing, buddy? Not a good time to be shriveling. Big fight happening. Stuff's going down."

But Goober just trembles like Jell-O. And then Rani is there, opening this strange box and then slapping it shut on my wrist, covering it, and just like that . . .

-CLICK-

GOOBER RENDERED USELESS!

My heart jackhammers inside my chest. High above me, I can feel the heat from the pirate mother ship's tremendous thermal engines.

I throw a quick glance over the side of the ship. Far below, I see Humphree and Dagger. They stare up at me—but they might as well be a world away. I'm alone here. And my weapon, my power, my friend, MY GOOBER is gone.

"You're coming with me now, Cosmoe," Rani says. There's a *TAP TAP* as her sword hits twice against the deck, and then...

SPLURT!

The familiar on Rani's shoulder suddenly LEAPS! I try to close my eyes, try to look away, but it's too late...

HE'S NOT "THE SUMBIOS"... HE'S MY FRIEND

4

A short scream escapes my lungs, but then I'm silenced. Silenced by this wet, foul, odorous creature that covers my face. I feel its spidery tentacles probing my mouth, choking my tongue.

I try to scream **"GET IT OFF! I'M FREAKING!"** but the words just come out like blubber sounds.

I can't see, but I can hear. I hear Humphree and Dagger, shouting, telling me they'll come for me, telling me they'll rescue me. I hear footsteps: Rani's footsteps, and my own, clink-clinking up a metal gangplank.

I'm being led to the mother ship: the *Looting Star.*

A **WHOOSH** as the ship's door opens. I recognize the sound. The galaxy is full of doors that move and slide and spin and spiralize—but this sound is unique. It creaks as it glides open, the exact same way it creaked three years ago.

TAP! TAP! Rani Zonian's sword hits the floor, and her familiar unsucks itself from my face. It springs back, returning to the captain's shoulder. The door shuts behind me, and I hear the creaky sound once more.

"Your door still needs oil," I say, wiping slime from my lips and nose.

Rani chuckles at that. Wonderful. I got a laugh out of a villainous space pirate. I'll be polishing my stand-up act next.

CARL, WELCOME ABOARD MY SHIP, THE *LOOTING STAR.*

"I remember the ship," I say. "No welcoming needed. And don't call me Carl. I go by Cosmoe now."

Rani coolly lifts one leg and leans on her sword, taking a load off. I'll give the scoundrel this: she knows how to pull off the bad-but-cool look. After a moment, she asks, "Are you scared, Cosmoe?"

"No," I lie.

"Good. There is no need to be. I'm a pirate. A businesswoman. Not a monster. The deal is for the sumbios—"

That word—SUMBIOS—it gets my blood bubbling, roiling over the standard Earthling 98.6. "His name is Goober!" I bark. "He's not 'the sumbios'—he's my FRIEND."

The spider-familiar stiffens, like it's just itching to pounce again. Rani calmly pats it on the head. "All right, GOOBER," she says finally. "The deal is for Goober, not for you. You will be set free."

"Goober's my friend. You just want to take him?" I ask.

"It's a big galaxy," Rani says. "It's full of disappointment. Now come, enough chitchat."

Rani steps through a door—there's another WHOOSH. This one not so creaky, and I follow her toward the ship's deck.

The deck is teeming with pirates: all different, but all similar.
I recognize some species: Pulsaes, Amaruuks, and M'lesei.
I spot metal among the pirate skin-bots.

They glance over as I enter. A few grin, happy to have me
aboard—knowing they're now one step closer to their big
payday. Grease drips from the crew, and some have the
stink of fried energy on them. I nearly gag as I pass one
particularly wretched sailor.

Space pirates are a filthy bunch: they spend months and years cruising the cosmic seas, and they only stop at port after a successful raid.

The galaxy is full of 'em, but none as legendary as Rani Zonian: She found Black Spine's lost treasure! She defeated the Evil Queen's most famous warship! She's **SERIOUS.**

And as she leads me through the ship, I have to admit, I'm in awe of the way she commands her crew . . .

WORTH A PILE OF SPACEOS, YOU ARE.

"Slytheris, step away!" Rani barks, and the creature quickly wriggles back. "Double engine vacuuming duty for you. Speak to the prisoner again, and you walk the plank."

I chuckle to myself. Rani remembers what happened the LAST time a crew member got too friendly with me. Things went bad . . .

I trail Rani down a dark hall and down even darker steps. "You've been a busy boy since I last saw you," she says. "Destroying Ultimate Evils, shutting down monster circuses."

"Us Earth-boys," I reply. "We just got a knack for adventure."

I remember this walk like it was yesterday: at the bottom of these steps is the prison block. My skin starts to crawl . . .

"The person who's paying you for Goober. Why do they want him?" I ask. I remove the attitude from my voice, because I want a real answer, no hoater-crud. Also, because anything I can do to slow my entry into the cell is fine by me.

"I didn't ask," Rani says. "Not my job to ask."

"But you're a pirate!" I exclaim, suddenly exasperated by this whole frappin' thing. "Your job is to live by your own unbending pirate code. You follow no one's orders!"

Rani flashes a devilish smile. "When the money is right, all codes are a bit bendable."

We come to a stop at one dark, shadowy cell. I recognize it: the same cell that I was in last time. It makes me tremble . . .

A lump builds in my throat. "What if I don't go in?" I manage.

Rani lifts her sword an inch from the ground, and her familiar stands at attention. "You won't like what happens."

I'm supposed to simply step into this horrid cell, all on my own. There are no guards here. Because Rani knows the awful truth: without Goober, I'm no threat at all.

But is that TRULY the awful truth? Without Goober, am I REALLY nothing? Just a useless human butt? There's only one way to find out ...

With no warning, I suddenly lower my head and barrel toward Rani. She easily sidesteps, jerking out a boot, hooking me as I blow past her ...

I crash to the floor. Before I can get back to my feet ...

CLANG!

Rani slams the metal bars shut. Her eyes narrow, like she's studying me. "At least you tried to resist," she says. "I'll give you that, Cosmoe. Even without the sumbios, you tried. Now, I suggest you sleep—we're traveling to the distant systems."

With that, she turns and disappears down the dark hall.

I push myself back to the corner of the cell. I try to breathe, to keep myself from freaking. And as I inhale, I suck in the odor of the cell.

Three years later, and the cell's stink hasn't changed. Smells, scents—they're good at bringing memories charging back.

I stare out at the galaxy, feeling alone. Lost. Feeling like I did when I sat in this same cell, years earlier ...

BACK IN
THE DAY . . .

Time jumps around in my mind, moving in herky-jerky leaps and bounds. Moments. Images. Smells. Emotions.

Suddenly, it's five years earlier, and I'm pulling myself from the wreckage of the Brayer and Brothers circus tent. The circus was my home. And it collapsed. My ears were ringing, which was just fine—it kept me from hearing the screaming all around me.

And then I was lying in a hospital bed. The room smelled of antiseptic and the lights above me were buzzing. My left arm was broken. It was the same arm that, someday, would be covered in Goober.

A man and a woman from the state were sitting across from me, telling me things, but I barely heard them speak. Their voices were muffled and distant.

The woman said, "Carl, I'm afraid I have some bad news. Your parents both died in the accident."

I didn't respond. Somehow, I already knew.

The man said something about arranging for a foster home. Then something like "Chin up, son. It'll get better," and I wanted to jump from the hospital bed and drive my skull right up into his chin.

I waited for them to leave before I cried—and when I did, the tears came in giant, heaving, shaking sobs.

Again, time leaps forward. The foster home. A dark building with the sour odor of vinegar and decay.

My broken arm was still in the cast—it was broken in three places, and it was taking its precious time to heal.

I didn't like the kids there. They pushed me. They poked me. And the fifth time I was pushed, I used the cast like a club and I hit back. A boy tumbled to the dirt and when he lifted his head, blood was running from his nose.

After that, the kids didn't push me so much at the foster home.

I didn't really blame them, though. Everyone in the home was there because something bad happened. They were there because their life didn't turn out the way you want a life to turn out.

Some sulked. Some lashed out. Some fought. Me? I buried my nose in stories ...

CARL, WHAT ARE **YOU READING?** TALES OF SPACE? **THIS GARBAGE WILL ROT YOUR MIND! LIGHTS OUT!**

Ms. Gradwohl ran the home, and she was basically a demon.

The books and magazines and comics were my father's. The man and woman from the state brought them to me: a trunk loaded to the brim with adventure stories. He loved all of that stuff.

My father was a natural adventure dude—I mean, it takes a natural adventure dude to stick your head in the mouth of a lion for a living, and that's what he really was: a lion tamer.

I read every single comic book: X-Men, The Rocketeer, Spider-Man, Silver Surfer. When I was done, I got a library card—and I snuck out during the day and I read more and more.

That's how I "escaped." That's how I "left" the foster home. That's how my mind "left" Earth.

I hated Earth. Earth took my parents. It took them, and it kept them. They lived inside it—beneath the surface, in wooden boxes.

Earth is an awful place, I think.

I left Earth first through books, but then I dreamed of leaving it for real: escaping to space, like the adventure stories ...

It was a damp September night. I had the window cracked. I love the rain odor. The rain hides you.

It was past midnight. I shared a room with six other boys, but they were asleep. Ms. Gradwohl says "lights out" at nine, but if I sat at the window, there was just enough moonlight for me to read.

Outside, fireflies danced, and I watched them—every spark, glowing in the blackness like UFOs. And then another spark, much bigger ...

It streaked through the sky. A comet? An asteroid? E.T.?
I didn't know what it was, but it had my heart leaping.

It disappeared behind a cropping of trees, far beyond the
home, and I expected the ground to rumble. I expected to see
an explosion of light. But that never came.

Quick but quiet, I crossed to the door. I heard the TV—
Ms. Gradwohl, downstairs, watching her programs. Awful
game shows and late-night infomercials.

I quickly threw on a sweatshirt, glanced around the room
to make sure everyone was still asleep, then opened the
window. Moments later, I was creeping across the roof,
leaping to the old oak tree, climbing down.

The grass was tall and whipped against my legs as I raced
toward the trees. I dashed through the cropping and came
out the other side. And then I saw what had crashed—and
nothing would ever be the same...

It looked like a snail, without its shell house. Or like a giant, gently pulsing booger. Whatever it was—it was **ALIVE!**

I should call the police, I thought. Or the government. Or Steven Spielberg or J. J. Abrams or **SOMEONE!** But I didn't.

Instead, I crouched down, edged over the smoldering lip of the crater, and slid into the hole. There was an odor that I can only describe as Sour Patch Kids swimming in Elmer's Glue.

And then I did something crazy. I don't know why. Now, three years later, I still couldn't tell you why. But I reached down and I touched the thing, and . . .

I shrieked.

But after a second, I realized there was no pain.

This strange, swirling being at my wrist suddenly seemed scared—I don't know how I knew it, but I just **KNEW** it. I felt what it felt.

Was it a he? A she? An it? A nothing? An everything? I didn't know, but I just knew it was now **THERE** on my wrist.

Suddenly I was showered in bright light, blasting down from above. The air itself seemed to tremble and rumble. Trees shook and the grass fluttered and waved. The air crackled with electricity and my hair stood on end.

It was a spaceship. A real one. A **BIG** one. It hovered above the field, suspended in the air. A door opened, and a plank extended—like the gangplank on an old pirate ship from the movies.

A figure appeared in the doorway, the lights dimmed, and I saw her stepping down.

YOU SHOULD NOT HAVE TOUCHED THE SUMBIOS, EARTHLING. NOW YOU ARE PART OF SOMETHING **MUCH BIGGER** THAN YOU.

I didn't resist. I didn't run. When she brought me aboard the ship, I just WENT—practically sleepwalking, like I was in a dream.

Space pirates oohed and aahed. But not at me—not really. They oohed and aahed at the strange rubbery thing on my wrist.

FINEST TREASURE THIS PIRATE SHIP HAS EVER CLAIMED!

THE GENERAL WILL BE SO PLEASED!

NOT A TREASURE. A PRIZE.

I caught words and phrases. I shouldn't have understood them. These creatures were all speaking a different language—but I sensed the words coming THROUGH the thing on my wrist and then somehow traveling into my brain. I understood EVERYTHING.

I was brought to a cell: the exact same cell where I sit, now, three years later.

The ship blasted off, and I raced to the small porthole window, throwing my hands against the wall, pressing my face close, watching planet Earth shrink and shrink and shrink away until it was just a tiny blue marble, floating in blackness. Until finally, I couldn't see it at all.

And that's when I heard the footsteps. Heavy footsteps. Footsteps that must belong to a creature that weighed about a ton.

HEY, SHORT PANTS. I BROUGHT YOU SOME FOOD. I'M THE CHEF ON THIS HUNK O' JUNK.

A LITTLE
GOOBER

The chef's name was Humphree—although you probably figured that part out already.

Twice a day he brought me food. I tried to eat, but I could barely keep it down—my earthling stomach wasn't used to this alien weirdness. I thought the food was bad at the foster home—but this, man, this was just CRUEL.

Every once in a while we'd fly near some star and the cell would be flooded with light, but besides that, it was always dark, and it was tough to keep track of time.

Finally, on what might have been the fourth or fifth day, the chef brought me, like, the pirate version of a pupu platter. He even opened the cell door. And we talked . . .

SO WHAT DO YOU EAT ON EARTH?

BETTER STUFF THAN THIS. BUT THEN AGAIN, ROADKILL WOULD BE BETTER THAN THIS.

"You watch it," Humphree said. "On my planet, if you offend the chef—the chef makes YOU the next meal."

I looked at Humphree, suddenly nervous. But he just laughed and slapped me on the back so hard I spit out the weird ear-looking thing I was eating. I didn't complain.

"You're telling me Earth food is better than this?" Humphree asked as he stabbed his thick fingers into the platter and plucked out something crispy.

"You bet," I said. "I traveled the whole country with the circus, so I got to eat foods from all different places. But I'll tell you, the best food . . . HOT DOGS!"

"Huh? Hot dogs?" Humphree asked.

I leaped to my feet. Humphree smiled as I exclaimed, "Hot dog! It's like a sandwich . . . sorta. But with this delicious round meat in it. Long meat. I mean—it's just a hot dog. You can't describe a hot dog. A hot dog is a hot dog."

Humphree chuckled, dug into something that looked like wet popcorn, and said "You're all right, short pants."

After that, Humphree began to come every day. He'd eat breakfast with me, and he'd tell me about the pirate life. And I'd tell him about life on Earth, and I'd try my best to be brave.

I cheered up some, knowing that at the end of every long day in the cell, Humphree would be coming.

And while I waited, I got to know the rubbery blob on my wrist. I talked to him. I sounded like I was going crazy, but I figured SOUNDING like you're going crazy was better than ACTUALLY going crazy—and I was afraid if I didn't acknowledge this thing, I would lose my mind.

I noticed stuff about it. The most important: it had a face. Just a simple little smile and two dots, like eyes. But it could frown, smirk, and smile—all the important expressions.

And when I was feeling particularly down, it seemed to notice—and it smiled to cheer me up. We passed an asteroid field, and the ship shook and shuddered, and I felt— I SENSED—that the thing was scared.

Looking down at it, I made a decision. I said, "You're a weird little goober, but you can stay as long as you want. You just need a name . . ."

I'LL CALL *YOU* **GOOBER.** BECAUSE THAT'S WHAT *YOU* ARE.

A LITTLE GOOBER.

It was the seventh or eighth day when Humphree returned and I asked him what I'd been wanting to ask him.

And the moment I asked, he sighed. His sigh sounded like a Buick with a bad engine—a rumbling from his belly.

> HUMPHREE, CAN *YOU* LET ME OUT OF HERE?

> I CAN'T, SHORT PANTS. IF THE CAPTAIN EVEN CAUGHT ME TALKING WITH YOU, I'D PROBABLY BE WALKING THE PLANK.

"Walk the plank?" I asked. "They do that in space?"

"Yep. And Rani Zonian won't hesitate."

"But pirates are BAD. I mean, pirates are COOL, sure. Jack Sparrow. Blackbeard. Cool dudes, in the movies. But in real life—you're **BAD**."

Humphree quickly shook his head. "No. No, I'm not."

"Yes, you are! You're a pirate. Your captain stole me from my home! I'm being taken against my will! That's bad!"

"I'M NOT BAD!" Humphree suddenly roared, and his voice boomed like thunder in the small cell. I instinctively squirmed back.

Humphree stomped out of the cell. And he didn't come back for a while after that. Days and nights went by, and there was no Humphree.

I'd lost him. Just like I'd lost everyone else.

But then, in the middle of the night, he returned, shaking me awake. "We need to get you out of here. I found out where they're taking you. It's bad. Worse than the usual pirate bad."

"How?" I said, still half-asleep, watching Humphree turn a key, unlock the rusty door, then creep down the hall.

WE'RE STEALING A SMALL JUMP JET. EVERY PIRATE SHIP HAS THEM, FOR SHORT SOLO-JACKINGS.

I followed Humphree through the guts of the ship, tiptoeing past snoozing scoundrels and recharging bots. A spiral door spun open, and we stepped into a small interior dock—and I saw it.

The jump jet.

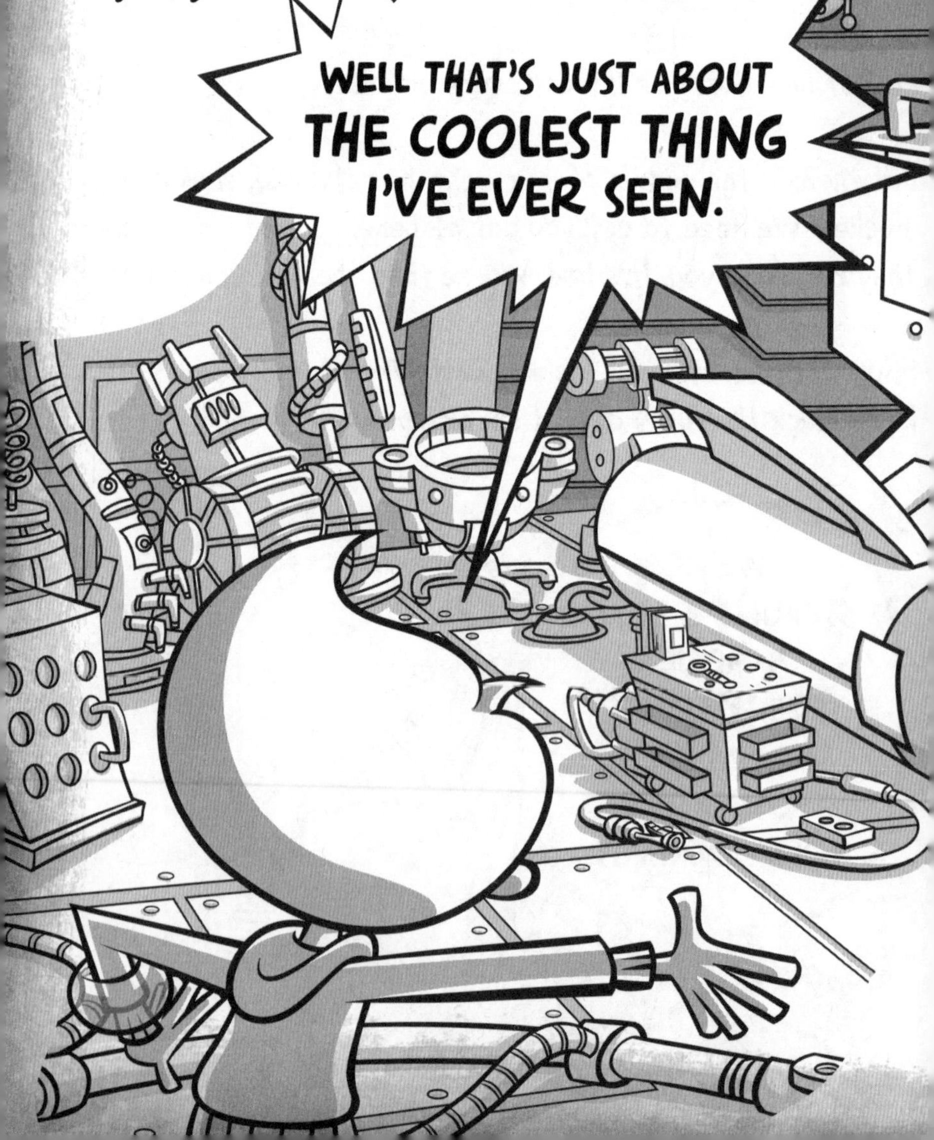
WELL THAT'S JUST ABOUT
THE COOLEST THING
I'VE EVER SEEN.

Humphree pulled a set
of ship keys from his pocket, and they
jangled in the stillness. And then we heard another sound.

TAP. TAP. **TAP. TAP. TAP. TAP.**

And then, before I could do anything, the pirates had seized Humphree. Three of them gripped his massive arms.

Rani glared at Humphree for a long moment. "You'll walk the plank. I have no other choice. You've BETRAYED us."

Humphree sagged, and his head dropped. When he raised it again, he was looking at me. "I'm sorry," he said.

And it was weird.

I didn't feel scared. I felt angry.

I felt rage from my head to my toes. From my toes to my arms. From my arms to my hands ...

My HAND. My **WRIST**.

And as I felt the anger, so did this strange, rubbery BLOB on my wrist. So did GOOBER. And before I knew it, my whole body was tingling, pins and needles. And suddenly, I just sensed it. I felt something.

UNHAND HIM!

A LOTTA GOOBER

Rani raised her hand and took a slow, cautious step forward. "Carl, please, calm down," she said.

"Let me go!" I shouted. "I want to leave! I don't want to be your prisoner! I don't want to be on this ship!"

Rani spoke softly, "Just relax and—"

I would not relax. I refused. And something happened. Goober grew warm around my wrist, and then hot, and then . . .

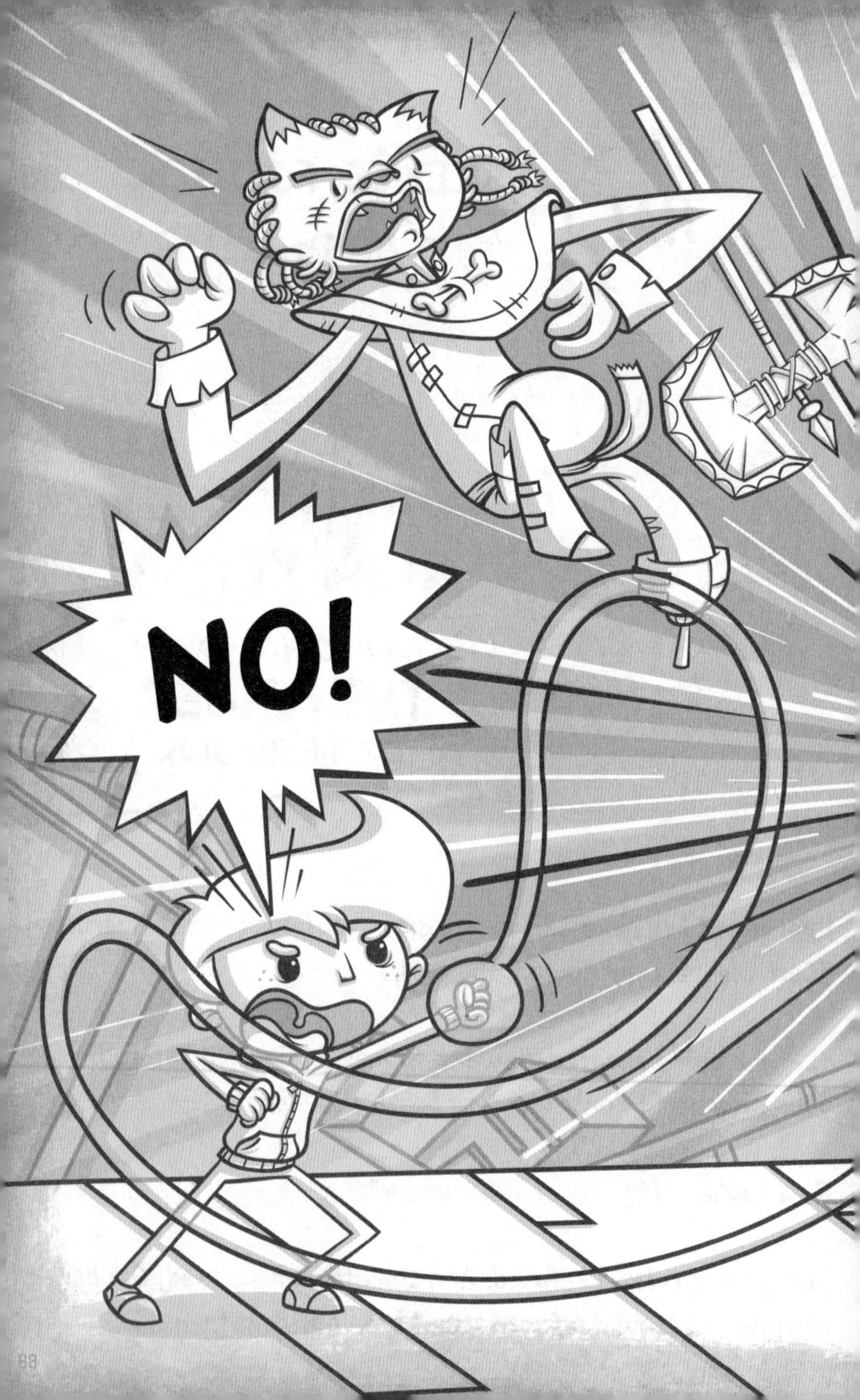
NO!

I didn't
know how I did
it exactly, but I did it.

Goober felt my anger. And I felt Goober's
power. I controlled him, and he controlled me.

When all was said and done, three pirates were
slumped on the floor—out of commission. Rani
took a slow, scared step backward . . .

"Come on, kid. **NOW!**" Humphree barked, and I raced
toward the jump jet.

"What did you do?" Humphree exclaimed, a mix of awe, shock, and seriously impressed-ness on his face. I followed him inside the ship—the ship that would soon become my home. Though at that moment, all I knew was I was terrified and there was blaster fire erupting behind me.

"I'm not sure WHAT I did!" I shouted. "But it's getting us out of here!"

Inside the cockpit, Humphree flipped toggles and thrust a knob forward. Flames erupted from the rear thrusters as the engine began to heat up. I raced to the window—where I saw the pirates retreating into the air dock. And I saw one face watching me—Rani Zonian.

I thought I'd never see her again. And for three years, I didn't ...

Rani is banging against the cell bars.

Slowly, I rise. I get a quick glance out the window, and what I see is a planet unlike any other.

It's trash. Literally. All of it. And that rings a bell. Trash planet. But I'm too groggy to remember why...

The gangplank lowers as the *Looting Star* touches down. The first thing that gets me is the smell. It's like a tidal wave of awfulness rushing up. A foul flood of rot.

I catch the sound then: whirring. I glance around—and out of the corner of my eye, I glimpse F.R.E.D.! He's here! He's on board. I feel a grin practically explode onto my face. Maybe all is NOT lost.

BE GOOD, AND THIS WILL BE OVER SHORTLY.

YOU'LL BE BACK ON BOARD, AND I WILL DELIVER *YOU* TO EARTH—SAFE AND SOUND.

GENERAL KRAX VON GRUMBLE RETURNS!

8

Rani leads me down the gangplank.

The landing platform is compacted trash, from a thousand different worlds. Stepping off the gangplank, I catch a glimpse of a flattened Dr Pepper can.

And then a glimpse of the creature who has brought me here.

Oh. Smudge. It's him. It's General Krax von Grumble.

COSMOE THE EARTH-BOY. **I'VE MISSED YOU.** HAVE YOU MISSED ME?

I don't respond to Krax's question.

"Many years late, Rani Zonian," General Krax says, "but you have finally delivered the blob."

Rani steps around, inching in front of me. "I've only just landed. Not delivered. I'll deliver when I see the spaceos."

Great. Just great. Another fine mess, Cosmoe. I'm in the middle of a complex hostage-negotiation-situation thing. A high-stakes trade—Goober for a bunch of spaceos. And of course, Goober includes ME.

But why Goober? I didn't know why they wanted Goober way back when, and I still don't know . . .

Krax signals, and two of his Rumblers suddenly appear behind him, lugging a massive chest. I can practically smell the gold inside. "Send the boy and the blob over, and the chest is yours."

Rani tightens her fingers around my upper arm. "The deal was for the sumbios and the sumbios only. The Earth-boy is not to be sold or traded. Remove the blob here, the deal is done, and we go our separate ways."

"Hey, do I get any say in this, or . . . ?" I ask.

"NO!" they both bark.

Right. As I figured.

Krax says, "I cannot remove the sumbios here. Extracting it from the boy is a long process. Trial and error. I cannot promise the boy will even survive . . ."

I hold up a finger. "If I could interject—I'd like to make clear that I am NOT okay with that. Really, definitely not okay."

I expect Rani to shove me over, but she justs taps her sword against the ground. I wait for her familiar to do something bonkers, but instead I hear whirring, buzzing, cranking, and heavy footsteps.

I glance behind me. A dozen pirates trudge down the plank, all of them carrying massive blasters. Above us, pirate cannons suddenly begin jutting out of the side of the ship. All of them pointed at Krax.

With the mighty pirate weaponry behind her and her crew on either side of us, Rani's lips turn to a grin. And she says, very slowly, very clearly, "Then we have no deal, Krax. You know the pirates' code: A BROKEN DEAL IS NO DEAL, AND THOSE WHO BREAK DEALS SHALL BE DEALT WITH."

Krax chuckles softly. He snaps his fingers and calls out, "RUMBLERS!" And they appear—they appear by the hundreds. Along with junk cannons, junk blasters, and other junk weaponry.

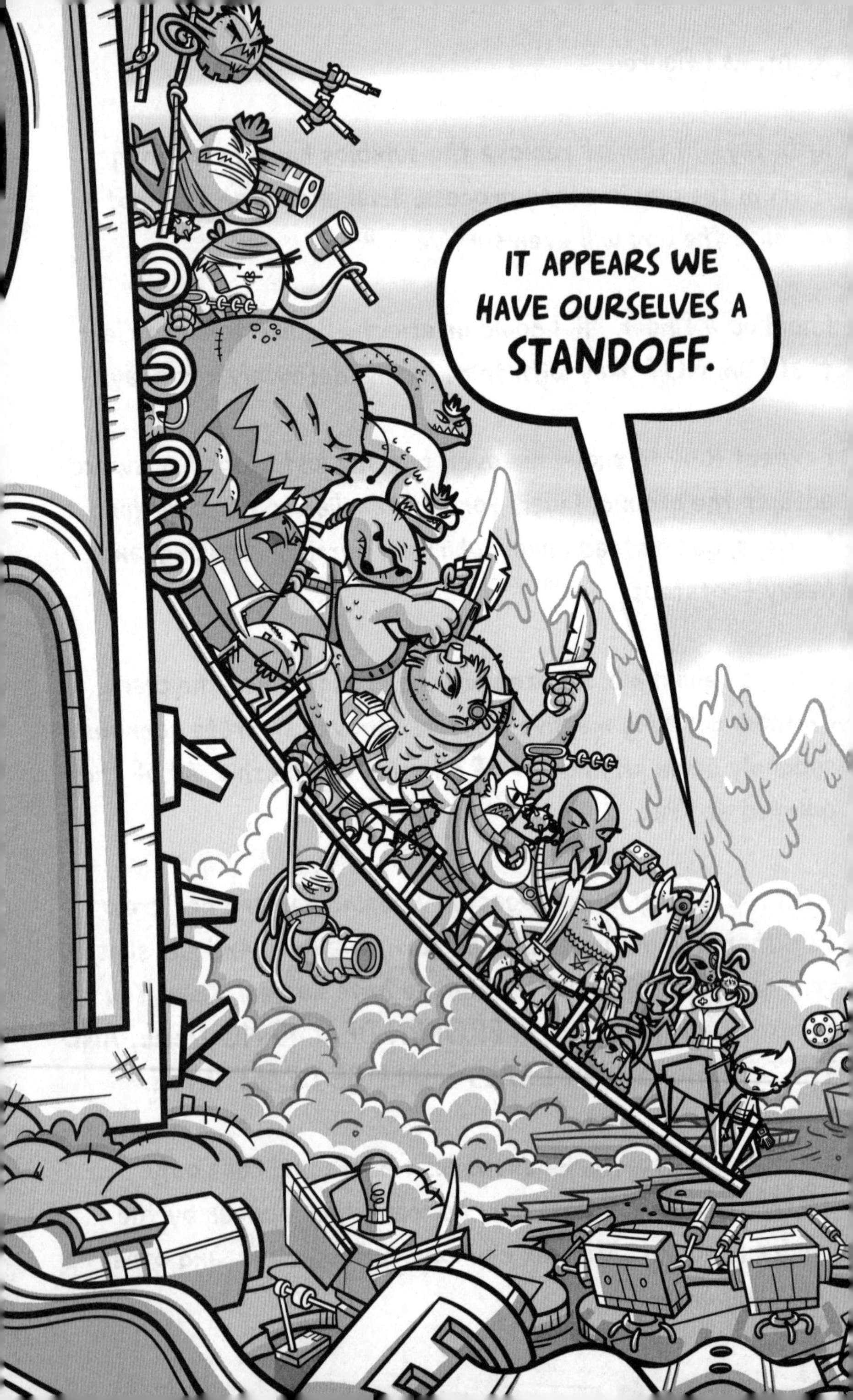
IT APPEARS WE HAVE OURSELVES A STANDOFF.

YOU CAN CALL IT A STANDOFF, BUT MY JUNK CANNONS WILL TURN YOU ALL TO DUST.

I swallow. Not from fear, but because I feel a sneeze coming on. And I know the slightest movement, even a sneeze, could set both these villains blasting.

And I also know Rani's pirate pride. It will be hard for her to budge or give in.

So I decide I'll settle this myself. "I'll go," I say as I jerk my shoulder away and step forward. "Humphree and Dagger will save me. You'll see. And I prefer that than seeing everyone here blown to bits—myself included."

Across the platform, I hear Krax chuckle. "Smart boy!" he calls out. His voice is a thick, nasty growl.

The Rumblers carry the chest across the dock. They drop it, and a pair of pirates drag it up the gangplank into the ship. The other pirates follow.

Soon, the engines are whirring and small bits of trash swirl on the landing platform. Rani grips the side of the gangplank, watching me.

And then the engines fire and the *Looting Star* blasts off . . .

I turn from watching the ship, and I see Krax looming over me. "That is life in space," Krax says. "No one can be trusted. No one can be counted on. All you have is yourself. Well, in your case, you and the sumbios—but I'm afraid you won't have him for very long. Now come, boy. We've work to do."

A large elevator made of compacted trash rises, and I follow Krax inside. Again, I'm reminded of how useless I am. How helpless I am without Goober.

Krax talks, but I barely listen—I'm too focused on the smell. The walls are cramped and wet and all of it, every bit, is made of garbage.

IT WAS SEVEN EARTH YEARS AGO WHEN I LEARNED OF THE SUMBIOS'S POWER—

GOOBER. HE'S MY FRIEND. HE HAS A NAME. GOOBER.

Krax chuckles in that cruel way that creeps can chuckle. "Yes, GOOBER. I employed Rani Zonian to retrieve it. But you know what happened after that, don't you..."

My curiosity is genuinely piqued. I know bits and pieces—but not all. "I do. Partly."

"The creature resisted capture. Flung through space. Landed on Earth, where you found it. Rani Zonian was to deliver you to me, but you escaped. I thought I had lost you forever..."

"When I encountered you in the Mutant Worm Wrestling arena, I had no idea YOU were the boy who had ruined my plans." He finishes his sentence with a wave, and the elevator door opens. Looking out, I immediately regret my decision to simply hand myself over to Krax...

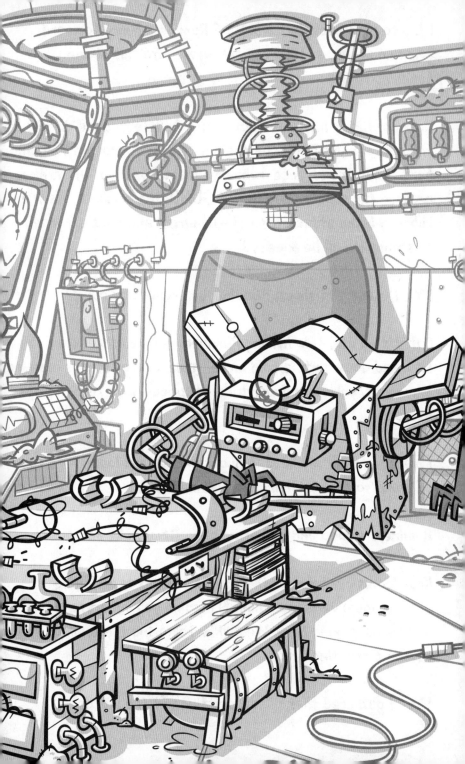

I try to step back, but a pair of Rumblers hurry forward, gripping my arms. They're yanking me into this buzzing, humming room.

Krax continues his spiel. "But then you defeated me during the now famous Battle of the Ancient Evil. I thought long and hard about the strange, rubbery weapon on your wrist. And I realized the sumbios had been FOUND. The sumbios was the rubbery being attached to YOUR wrist. And now, after all this time, it will be mine . . ."

"No, it won't!" I shout. "Goober will never be yours!"

But it's no use. Two hulking Rumblers rip me into the air. I'm slammed down onto a cold metal table. Energy straps ensnare my wrists, ankles, and waist. I'm trapped—with zero hope for escape . . .

I manage to lift my head. A huge, empty tank looms. It's full of some sort of bubbling, neon-blue liquid.

Rumblers swoop and bob around me. They poke and prod.

Krax looms over me, so that I'm staring up at a flipped, upside-down version of him. "I assume you understand what's happening here. We will be removing the sumbios," he says in a taunting growl.

"Yes, I gathered that," I say, spitting out the words.

"There are a few different ways we may go about it. If one doesn't work, we'll try the next. And the next. And then the next," Krax says with a grin. Turning to the bot in charge, he says, "If everything is ready, you may begin . . ."

The bot leans forward and grips the lockbox. I feel Goober bubbling inside.

The moment the creep opens the box, I'm going to whack him and smack him with Goober. Goober might just do it himself. They don't realize what they're messing with here.

The box opens with a CLINK and I'm about to unleash Goober havoc and destruction, but—

ZAP! Electricity rushes through me. Krax chuckles. "Do not try it," he says.

The electricity calms down, subsiding, and the lockbox is removed entirely. I breathe, sucking in air.

I watch the bot in charge walk to the wall. His metallic hand reaches up and grips a large switch. "No . . ." I whisper. "Please don't."

But he does.

The bot pulls the switch, and it's suddenly a whole terrifying Frankenstein thing—and I feel . . .

PAIN.

Pain unlike anything I've ever felt rushes through me. It's like my nerve endings are on fire. It's like my blood has been replaced with lava.

Goober throbs and pulses and bubbles on my wrist. I feel Krax and his minions trying to pull Goober away from me. I clench my fists. I kick my feet.

But it's useless.

The pain is so strong that, finally,
I can do nothing but scream . . .

Sleep.

I beg for it.

I suck the pain inward, and my eyes shut, and I find sleep.

And as I drift off, I continue to remember my past. I remember my first time aboard the *Neon Wiener*...

MANHATTAN WIENERS

As soon as we had put some distance between ourselves and the *Looting Star*, I started checking out this funky little jump jet's cockpit. And I was IMPRESSED ...

Humphree groaned. "Kid, kid, calm down. It's MY TURN to ask the questions. I'll start with the BILLION spaceo question," he said. His thick finger pointed at Goober. "What is THAT?"

I shrugged. "All I know is, I kind of like him. Honestly, I hoped YOU'D know what he—or she or it or whatever—is . . ."

"I'm just the chef," Humphree said, waving his hands in protest. "I got no idea WHAT Rani wanted that thing for . . ."

Right. RANI. And I remembered that I wasn't out here to have fun or cruise or spend my time jaunting around spaceships and poking at stuff. I was LOST IN SPACE.

I looked over to Humphree, and he had the same look on his face—dumbstruck. He lifted his big hands and lowered his big head and whacked his knuckles against his skull. "Why did I do that? Freeing you! Leaving my ship! Stupid, stupid!"

"Never would have happened if you didn't kidnap me."

"Kidnap you?" Humphree exclaimed. "I didn't kidnap you!"

I glared at him. "Are you MAD? YES. YOU DID."

"My CAPTAIN did."

"Uh, you're a **PIRATE**," I said. "On a **PIRATE SHIP.** That makes you responsible for all **PIRATEY ACTIVITIES** occurring, thus!"

"And I thought it was going bad," Humphree said. "So I helped you escape!"

"That's not how it works! If you punch someone in the nose and **THEN** realize punching people in the nose is bad, that doesn't unpunch the first nose!"

Humphree suddenly erupted. He pounded the dash, set it to autopilot, and stomped out of the room.

I didn't go. I sat. I was in a spaceship. A cockpit. *Millennium Falcon*—style. Knobs and dials and buttons and digital readouts and **ALL THAT.** But I couldn't enjoy it ...

I was so **LOST.** I knew—I KNEW—I COULDN'T tick off Humphree. I'd only spent a few days in that cell, but Humphree was a friend. The closest thing I had, at least.

I sighed and stood up. My body felt heavy. I wasn't sure if it was the strange gravity of interstellar space or if I was just reluctant to move. My legs were heavy, herky-jerky things ...

I found Humphree inside a small storage room. He was flipping through cabinets and drawers and yanking open panels. "What are you doing?" I asked.

"Looking for food! That's what I do when I'm stressed. Or when I'm happy. Or sad. Or bored. Or not bored. I eat. So I'm trying to find something, but there's nothing good. Argh—just . . ."

"How about a hot dog?" I said. "It's comfort food."

"What's comfort food?" Humphree asked, still sort of half-barking, but not all the way roaring now.

"It's, like, a food that makes you feel **RIGHT** inside," I said. "A rainy day, you eat it. Or after you fail a test at school. Or after you do something super-embarrassing and everyone sees."

"Or after you rip off a deadly space pirate and steal her greatest prize with no plan or anything?" Humphree asks.

YEP. **DEFINITELY** COMFORT FOOD TIME.

Humphree slammed the cabinet shut. "Well, there's not any 'comfort food' in here!"

And suddenly I was hungry too. My stomach was flipping from the spaceflight and my legs were like noodles. I staggered back and slumped into a chair. Humphree hurried over, and he set his big alien paw on my shoulder.

"Hey. Hey, kiddo," he said. "It's all good. Sorry I yelled. I just need some food. And I think you do too. So let's get you a hot dog, huh? Some—uh—COMFORT FOOD."

Looking up at him, I asked, "For real?"

He nodded. "For real. I'm hungry. And hey—if it's good enough for you, it's probably good enough for me."

And then I didn't feel down. The sadness and the freaked-ness was gone, and feel-goodness came like a wave, rushing over me, and I was leaping to my feet, exclaiming, "Then . . . SET COORDINATES FOR PLANET EARTH!"

I then, of course, realized that I had no idea how spaceship navigation worked. "Wait, Humphree, is that how it goes? Do I just say, like, set coordinates and we go, or no? Is that not the way it all goes down?"

Humphree chuckled, even though I could see he didn't really want to. "You're not far off. Come on. I'll need a copilot."

I almost instantly blacked out as Humphree threw the ship into hyper-leap. It was my first time flying turbo-speed in a jump jet, and it's a bit rough on the old noggin. Brain rattling, really.

When I woke up, we were zooming toward New York City. And that was fine, because I figured if there's one place on Earth where **NO ONE** will question a giant, eight-foot alien, New York was that place.

We came in screeching, the ship splashing down and then skipping across the Hudson River.

Humphree wrestled the controls, managing to get the ship up on land. Leaving the ship, we got a **TON** of funny looks—no surprise there—but I think most people thought we were filming a movie or something.

I took Humphree to the first dirty water dog stand I could find . . .

THREE DOGS, PLEASE, WITH THE WORKS.

I'LL HAVE 248. PLEASE.

Humphree was chomping his way through the wieners when I noticed we were drawing more and more weird looks, so I led us to the nearest park.

Between monster-sized bites, Humphree said, "Short pants, I'm sorry I got so angry before on the ship. I just get grumpy when I'm real hungry."

"It's okay," I said cheerfully. "I do too."

Humphree burped. Loud. I think I heard a window shatter on the Empire State Building.

"So this is where you're from, huh?" he asked, looking around, eyeing the skyscrapers.

"Sorta," I said with a shrug. "Earth. But not the big city, like this."

We were quiet for a while after that. I took my time eating my third hot dog and drinking an orange soda. Humphree finally slowed down once he got to his, like, 189th hot dog.

After a bit, I said, "So what are you going to do now?"

Humphree shook his head. "I don't know. Rani's going to have a price on my head. A serious one."

"Can you go home?" I asked. "Like where you grew up? When you were a kid?"

"Ha. Short pants, I didn't leave my home planet on good terms. But you know, all this mess aside—let me tell you something..."

THESE ARE THE BEST THINGS I'VE EATEN IN MY ENTIRE LIFE!

THE REST OF THE GALAXY? THEY DON'T KNOW WHAT THEY'RE MISSING!

The moment Humphree said that, I heard a sound. It was the familiar tune of Mister Softee. I spotted the ice-cream truck rolling to a stop on a winding road that ran through the park.

And that's when it started clicking. A plan was forming and the noggin knobs in my head were turning . . .

"Humphree," I said. "What if we SHOWED the rest of the galaxy what they're missing?"

"What do you mean?" he asked, chomping, hot dog bits flying.

"You're a chef, right? So we buy a whole mess of uncooked wieners and grill 'em up! We could take that ship, turn it into a flying food truck, and we could sell them!"

"Flying food truck?" Humphree asked.

"Sure! We fly around space, go to places where aliens hang out, and we SELL hot dogs!" I exclaimed.

Humphree's eyes lit up for a moment, and I could see he was diggin' the idea. But then his frown dampened. "But, short pants, this is your home. You're BACK now. You got that Goober on your arm, sure—but you're back and you're safe. I won't tell anyone you're here, pirates' honor. You're home."

I thought that over. He was right. Sort of . . .

I DID have Goober on my arm. And I'd have to deal with that—definitely needed a way to hide the little guy. Like extra long gloves or something. Or mittens. A big wraparound scarf for my hands? Not sure. Something. But even then ...

Did that matter? WAS this REALLY my home?

Earth had hurt me. A lot.

And man, I didn't have much interest in getting hurt any longer.

EARTH ISN'T MY HOME. NOT ANYMORE ...

And with that decisive declaration, we got to work! We trekked across the city, buying every single hot dog we could get our hands on. Grocery stores, delis, bodegas—we went EVERYWHERE.

Walking back to the ship, dragging nine shopping carts worth of wieners, I said, "So what do we call our new business venture?"

Humphree shrugged. "I'm not creative. We're selling hot dogs to the galaxy. Maybe ... Galactic Hot Dogs?"

"That works," I said. "And what do we call the ship? It says *Neon Wing* right now, and—" I began grinning. I knew EXACTLY what to call it.

I borrowed a can of spray paint from the local graffiti heads, and pretty soon I had made the ship WAY more hot dog appropriate. It wasn't perfect, but it would do for now ...

Humphree opened the door to the ship. Which was good, because more and more people were starting to gather around. I wasn't eager to see Humphree chatting it up with the NYPD. "You ready, Carl?" he asked.

I paused. After a moment, I said, "One thing. I'm not Carl. Not anymore. On Earth, I might have been Carl. But not any longer."

"Well, up there, in the cosmos, what should I call you?" Humphree asked.

UP THERE IN THE COSMOS, YOU CAN JUST CALL ME COSMOE.

And that was it. We were partners. We had a business. We were slinging wieners. It was that simple. And it didn't take long for it to take off.

Our first stop was a liquid slide park, and we sold HUNDREDS of hot dogs. It was great. It was perfect. It was—

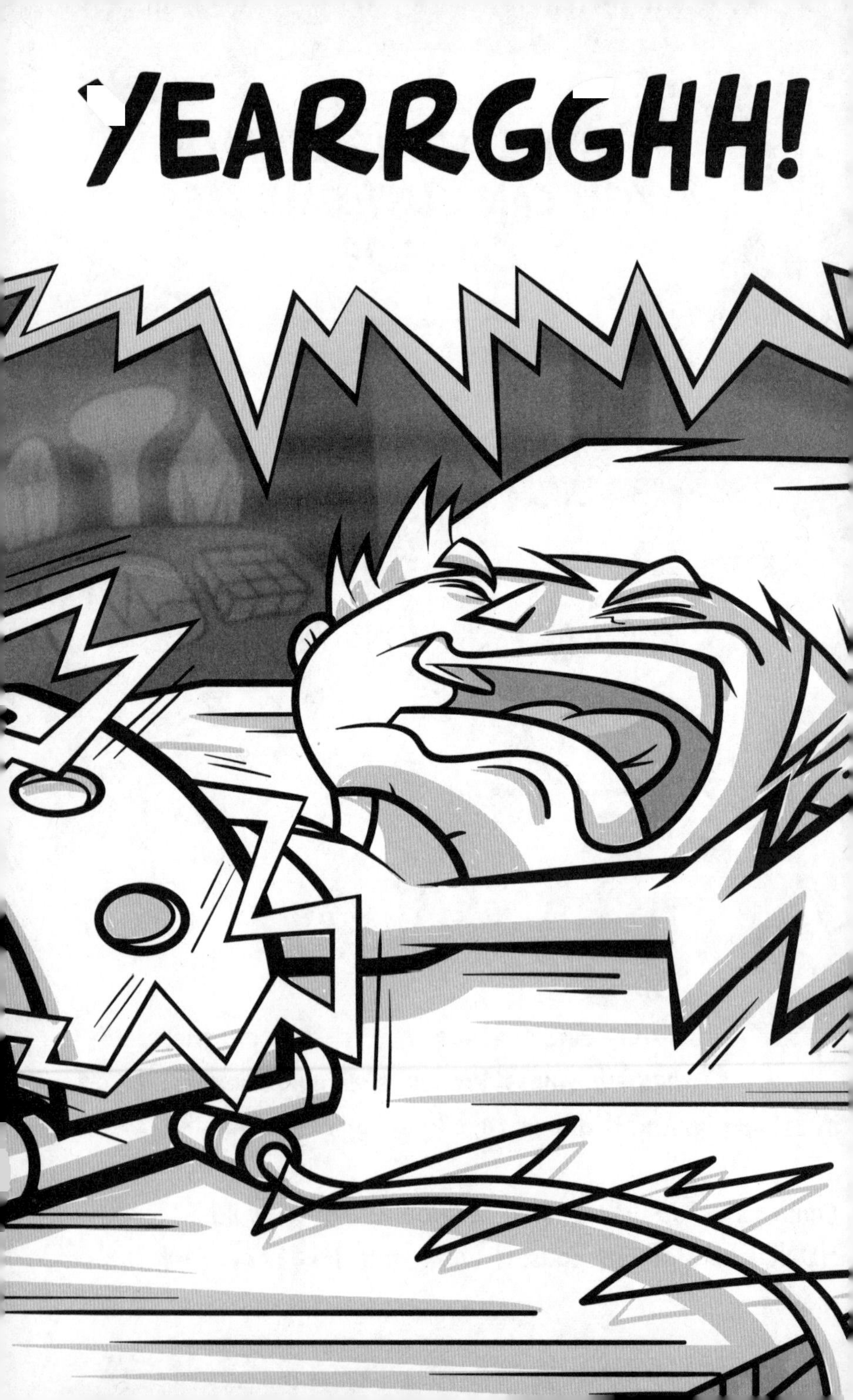
YEARRGGHH!

Sharp, stinging pain brings me tumbling out of my lovely little peacetime flashback, waking me up with a snapping jolt. I immediately realize that something is wrong.

A piece of me is missing. Goober is gone . . .

COSMOE DISCOVERS AN INCREDIBLE SMELL

10

Goober isn't far away. Somehow, I know it. There's a seventh sense, of sorts, linking me to the rubbery little guy.

The mad-scientist bot looms over me, poking at my bare arm. I want to show my teeth, maybe try to chomp on him quickly—but I don't. Instead, my head swings to the side.

Goober. **THERE.**

My rubbery buddy is floating inside a large sort of extraction tank. He flips and flops around, and then his tiny black-dot eyes focus on me ...

I don't even realize I'm doing it, but I reach out, trying to touch the tank, and—

ZAP!

The electro-restraints. Pain rips through me, blasting down my spine. I flop back onto the table.

The feeling of pain is strong.

But this feeling of loss? This feeling of Goober-less-ness? It's more than simply strong—it's frappin' overwhelming.

Behind me, the elevator door zips open. I hear heavy footsteps, followed by the growl of General Krax. "Wonderful," the general says. "The sumbios has been removed. And it only took five days."

I catch a glimpse of the mad-scientist bot nodding. My mind begins racing. WAIT, HOW LONG DID KRAX SAY? FIVE DAYS? DID HE SAY **FIVE DAYS?**

It felt like hours. Or like less. Like NOTHING. The neurotoxin they gave me must have been STRONG. But there's no time to think about that. I have questions that need answering. Questions like ... "WHY DID YOU TAKE GOOBER?!"

I roar the words, craning my neck, staring up at Krax.

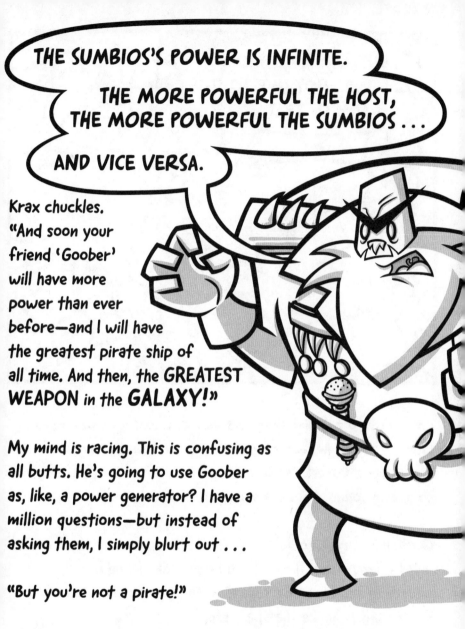

THE SUMBIOS'S POWER IS INFINITE.

THE MORE POWERFUL THE HOST, THE MORE POWERFUL THE SUMBIOS . . .

AND VICE VERSA.

Krax chuckles. "And soon your friend 'Goober' will have more power than ever before—and I will have the greatest pirate ship of all time. And then, the **GREATEST WEAPON** in the **GALAXY!**"

My mind is racing. This is confusing as all butts. He's going to use Goober as, like, a power generator? I have a million questions—but instead of asking them, I simply blurt out . . .

"But you're not a pirate!"

He looms over me. I can smell the badness on his breath. "But I will be. In fact, I will be more than just a simple pirate. I will be **THE CORESKY KING! AND I WILL WIELD A WEAPON UNLIKE ANY OTHER!**"

107

I'm about to tell him that he's a lunatic and his mom maybe didn't tell him he was special enough and that I have zero idea what a Coresky King is when I hear a sudden plopping and splashing sound. My eyes shoot to the tank.

Goober is thrashing back and forth. He appears to be having a total freak-out. His rubbery body is like liquid metal, morphing and changing. I want nothing more than to help my friend and to make that pain stop.

My buddy thrashes again violently, and then there's a sudden, loud **ZZZ-KRAK!** The lights flicker and flash and the room hums and cracks with energy.

Krax whirls, eyeing Goober, and I catch serious concern on the villain's face. "Rumblers!" he barks. "Remove the boy immediately! He cannot remain in the presence of the sumbios. Take him to—"

But before he can finish, there's a snapping BZZ-BANG! Every single light in the room BURSTS. For a moment, it's pitch-black. But then, the emergency power kicks in, and . . .

My arms are freed from their restraints!

Red light flashes and fills the room as a pair of doors zip open. I hear a familiar swoop and buzz, and I turn to see . . .

"F.R.E.D.!" I exclaim, swinging my legs over the table. "Good timing! C'mon, we need to get Goober back!"

"I AM HAPPY TO HELP, COSMOE."

I quickly charge toward the tank, ready to throw my entire body into it in, hoping to break the glass. But Krax suddenly slides over, blocking me.

He snarls and raises his electro-zap bat. I've tangled with that weapon before, and it's less than fun.

I lock eyes with Goober, the frustrated and apologetic look on my face telling him I can't save him now, but I **WILL** be back. I **PROMISE**. And I hope he understands ...

Krax roars, **"YOU'RE NOT GOING ANYWHERE, BOY!"**

A super-charged bolt of electricity zips past me, and blows a hole in the wall. That hole is going to be my way out of this joint . . .

"F.R.E.D., come on!" I shout, running toward the smoking hole.

"There's no escaping my planet!" Krax roars, aiming, about to fire again. But it's too late. I'm dashing, leaping, diving . . .

I plunge through darkness. Falling, tumbling, plummeting at top speed, surrounded by nothing but pitch-black nothingness and the hot stink of garbage. The only light comes from F.R.E.D., who follows, jetting through the gloom behind me.

"F.R.E.D.!" I shout. "This is a LOT of falling! I'm not looking forward to landing!"

And then, suddenly, dim light below. Rising up toward me. Fast. Faster. And, oh no—

SMASH!

After being spun, whipped, and zipped through a long, endless fall, I finally land. In a hunk of hot garbage.

THE SMELL. I thought it was bad before. But now it's something else entirely. Like it's marching through every pore in my body.

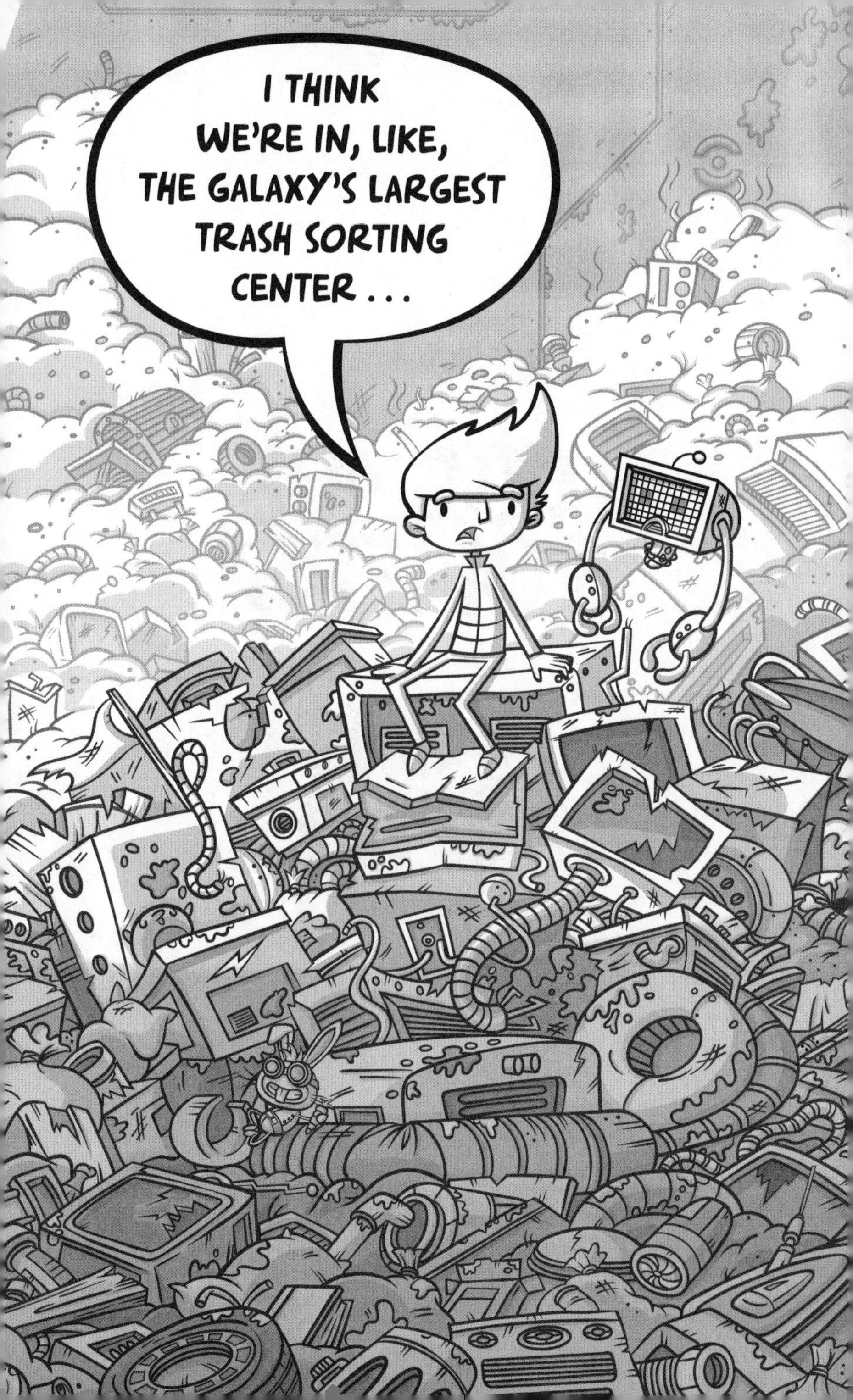
I THINK WE'RE IN, LIKE, THE GALAXY'S LARGEST TRASH SORTING CENTER . . .

COSMOE POWERS!

I pull my shirt up over my nose, trying to shield myself from the stink. I want to rest, but I'm not convinced that Krax won't follow me down the garbage chute. That would be a total Krax move.

After catching my breath—an act that almost makes me barf—I begin tramping down the massive heap of trash. I hear something that sounds wet and slithering, and I pick up the pace.

I'm getting the sense that there's stuff ALIVE in this heap of garbage—and if the original, CLASSIC *Star Wars* taught me anything, it's that creepy and scary stuff lives among gnarly old trash. Yep, that's right: I'm talking about the nasty eyeball thing that yanked on Luke and pulled him under.

I wander through a maze of garbage for hours, tramping across trash until my feet are sore and my shoes are practically falling off.

Suddenly, F.R.E.D. zips ahead, raising his arm, pointing.

Squinting, I see a sign: EARTH-BASED WASTE SORTING.

Earth trash. Great. Just like me: Discarded, useless, rejected.

I stumble through a door into a room that's as big as a baseball stadium. Near the edge of a towering pile of Earth garbage, I spot a heaping mound of juice boxes. I collapse . . .

After catching my breath, I sit up, wiping the sweat away. My wrist brushes across my forehead, and I instantly realize—and remember—Goober is not there.

My buddy. My friend. He's been stolen. He's gone.

And not just Goober. Everything. **EVERYONE.** I got no Humphree. I got no Dagger. I got no ship. I got no hope . . .

It's all been taken from me . . .

The realization hits me harder than a Humphree uppercut. I'm trapped, lost, stuck—deep inside a garbage planet, surrounded by nothing but cold rubbish and angry enemies.

"COSMOE, WHY ARE YOU NOT MOVING?" F.R.E.D. asks. "WE SHOULD BE PROCEEDING."

"What's the point?" I say, dismissing F.R.E.D. with a flip of my hand.

"YOU MUST BE THE HERO, COSMOE," F.R.E.D. replies. "AS ALWAYS."

I'm not a hero! I was only a hero when I had **GOOBER!** I'm like Iron Man! I don't have any special FOR-REAL powers! Without my suit, my weapon—I'm nothing!

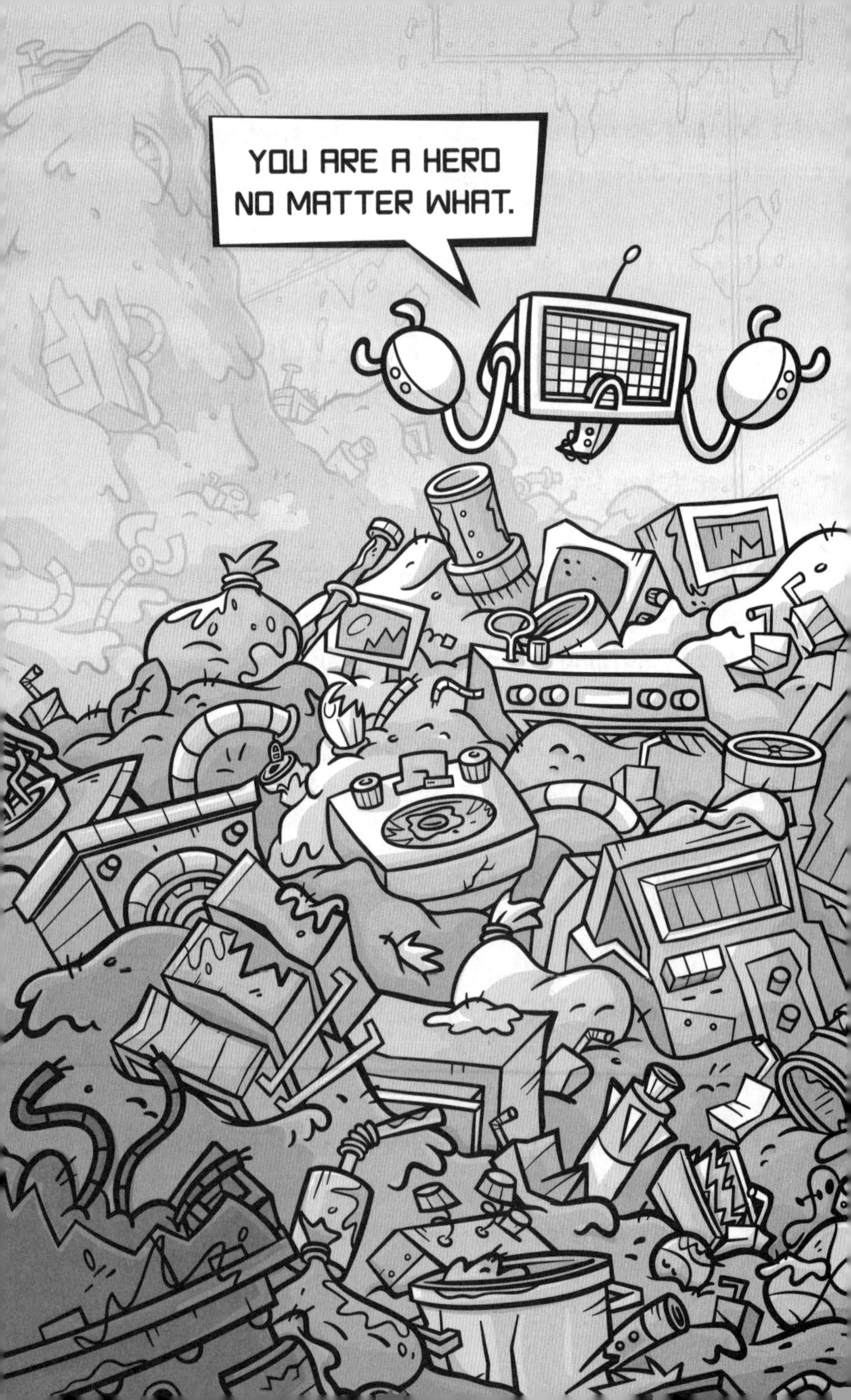
YOU ARE A HERO NO MATTER WHAT.

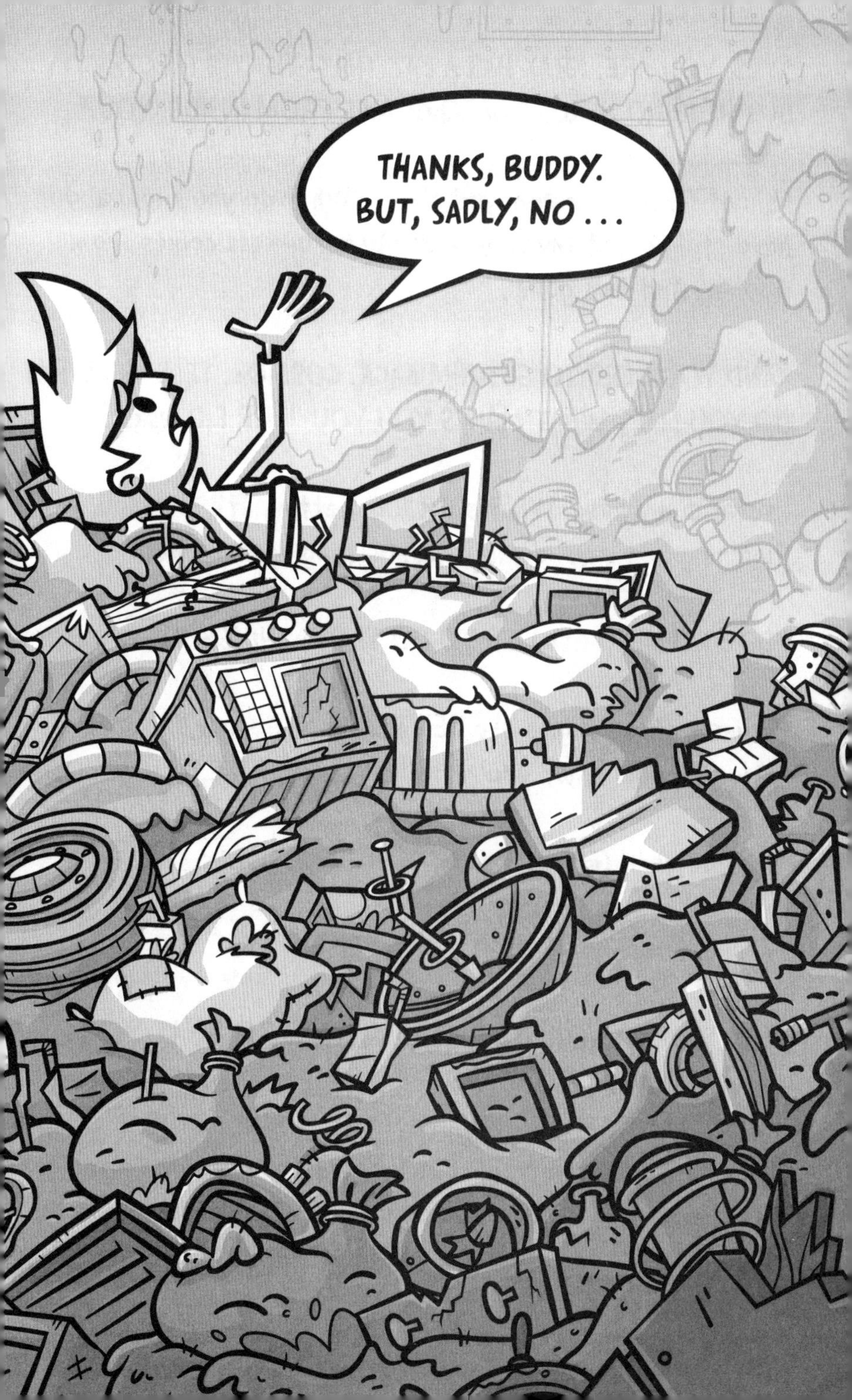
THANKS, BUDDY.
BUT, SADLY, NO . . .

"YES, YOU ARE. KRAX HAS A BAT THAT SHOOTS ELECTRICITY. BUT HE IS NO HERO. A HERO COMES FROM INSIDE. YOU."

I shoot F.R.E.D. an annoyed glare. "What do you know about hero stuff? And anyway—me? My hero-ness comes from Goober. And he's gone . . ."

"AND YOU NEED TO GET HIM BACK, COSMOE. TELL ME, WHAT DO YOU LIKE? WHAT MAKES YOU YOU?" F.R.E.D. asks.

I scratch my head. What's F.R.E.D. getting at? "I dunno. Punching bad guys, dumb jokes, burping, videogames."

"DO YOU NEED GOOBER TO DO THOSE THINGS?"

"I mean, those things are BETTER with Goober," I reply. "I don't know what you're talkin' about, F.R.E.D."

"Do you need Goober to be you?" F.R.E.D. asks.

I shrug. "I dunno—"

"NO. YOU DO NOT. SO JUST BE THE HERO THAT YOU ALREADY ARE, COSMOE."

I sink back into the trash. I look down to my wrist. Nothing. But then I look at the trash beneath me. Old wires. A winter glove. A deflated football. EARTH TRASH, JUST LIKE ME. And suddenly—

YOU'RE RIGHT!
I **USED** TO HAVE GOOBER POWERS,
BUT I NEED SOMETHING NEW. AND
WE CAN BUILD IT, HERE!

The words come pouring out of my mouth now. I can't speak fast enough... "Instead of Goober powers, they'll be like... Cosmoe powers! ME versions of all my old Goober tricks! Goober shield, Goober whip, Goober punch, Goober hammer, Goober bat!"

Catching my breath, I look around. I see Earth junk at my feet, and other Earth junk, piled high—a whole gigantatorium's worth.

"I'm not smart with science and building, but I've read a million space adventure stories and I know all about kicking butt. And you, F.R.E.D., you know EVERYTHING about everything! So let's search this junk and get building, buddy!"

And with that, we get to work. We begin building, crafting constructing. Creating the **ULTIMATE** Cosmoe...

'80S VIDEOGAME CONTROLLER + FISHING REEL + OOZY GARBAGE PIT SLIME =

WASTE WHIP!

VACUUM NOZZLE + KITCHEN UTENSILS + HAIR-SPRAY CANISTER =

SCRAP BLASTER!

WINTER BOOTS + SLINKY + SPINNING EGG BEATER =

PUNT OF POWER!

ANCIENT ACID-DRIPPING AA BATTERIES + NUCLEAR SLUDGE + TENNIS BALLS =

GARBAGE GRENADES!

SOON . . .

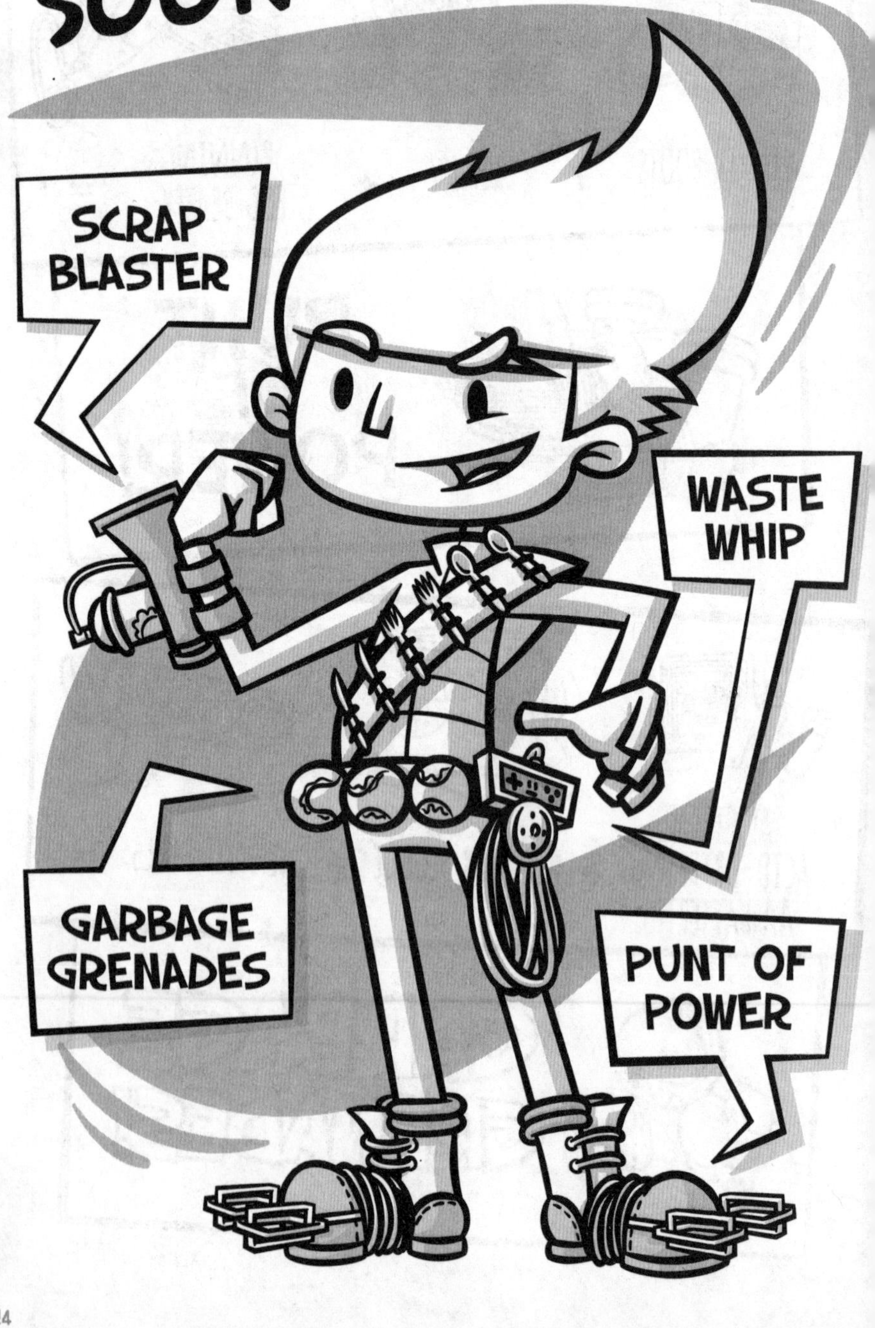
SCRAP BLASTER
WASTE WHIP
GARBAGE GRENADES
PUNT OF POWER

I'm admiring my many weaponized gadgets when F.R.E.D. says, "COSMOE, I DETECT A SMALL, SHORT-DISTANCE SPACECRAFT ON THE SURFACE OF THE PLANET. WE CAN ESCAPE WITH IT."

"You mean you found a way off this joint?" I ask happily.

"CORRECT," F.R.E.D. replies.

I grin. "Then lead the way, buddy!"

F.R.E.D. whirs ahead. His GPS guides and steers us down empty alleys and around dark corners. We move upward, away from the core and toward the surface.

But as we get farther away from the GD9 ship's center, it becomes harder to avoid Krax's army of Rumblers.

The ship is crawling with the junky, scrappy villains. And as we turn a corner, I hear a squad of the robo-heads speaking. Their robotic trash voices sound like an old, out-of-tune radio—but the message is clear ...

A Rumbler says, "You heard the boss. Krax says we find the Earth-boy and we dispose of him. No mercy!"

I gulp.

Two can play at that game. Time to put my Cosmoe powers to use ...

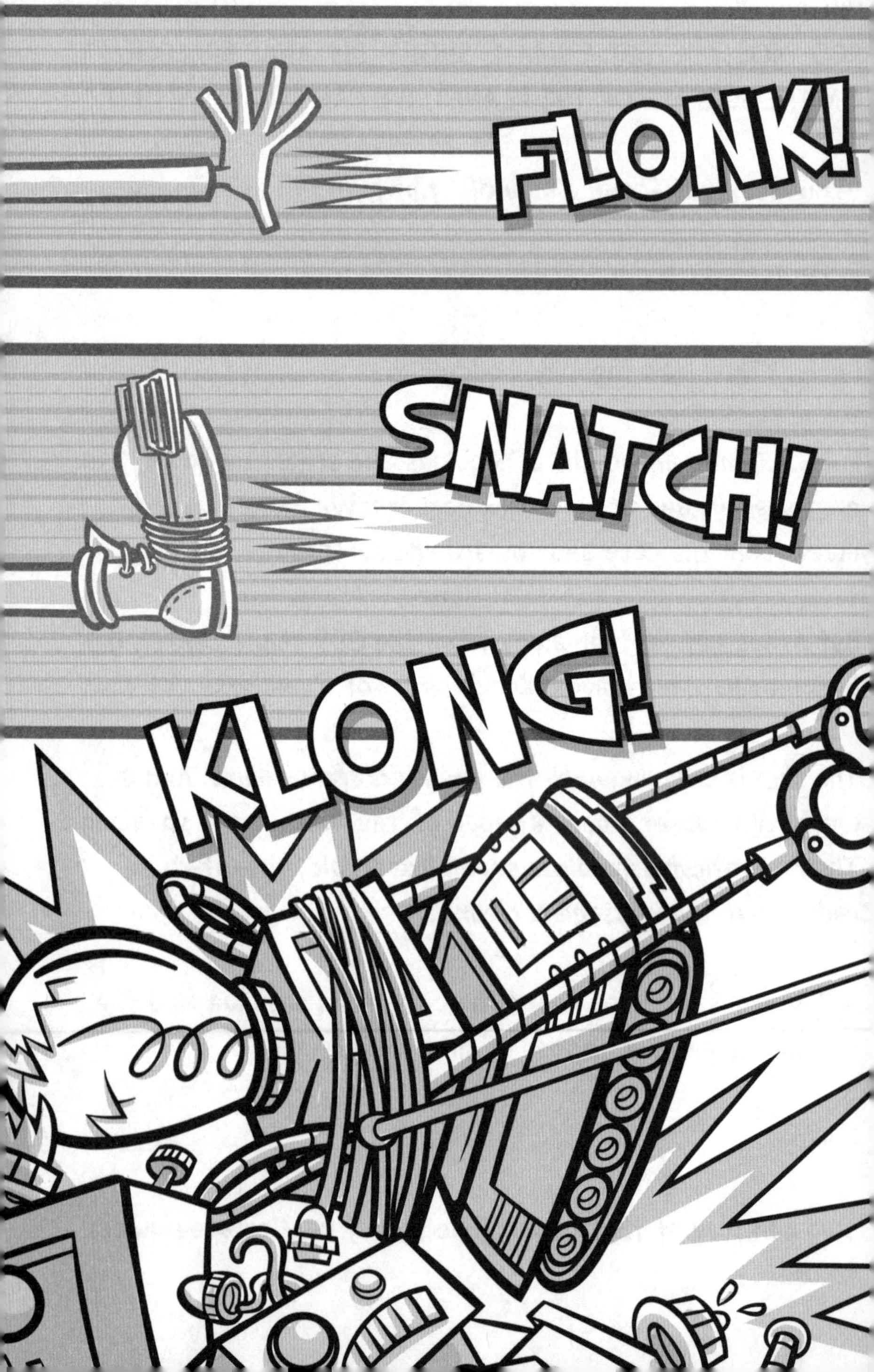
FLONK!
SNATCH!
KLONG!

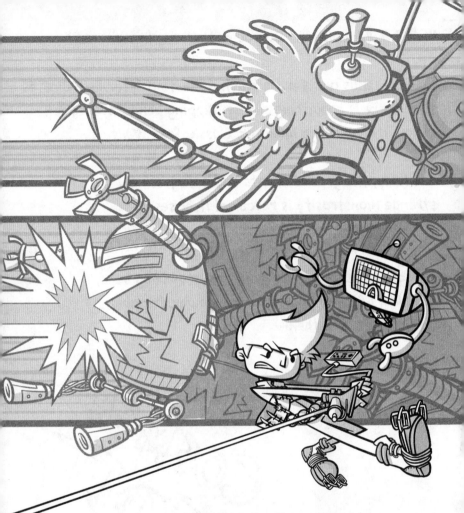

I dispatch a dozen Rumblers as we
trek through the recesses of the ship. I'm
stomping away from a pile of bolts when F.R.E.D.
says, "COSMOE, WE ARE CLOSE TO THE SPACECRAFT."

FANTASTIC! At last! I'm just beginning to speed ahead,
when I catch a whiff of something. It's the same odor I
caught back in the first garbage room. The slithering,
wet-smelling thing . . .

"F.R.E.D.," I whisper. "Do you detect any life-forms?"

F.R.E.D. sends out a pulse blast. An instant later he indicates that there is something sliding, slipping beneath our feet. I knew it. A garbage monster. Classic *Star Wars* . . .

Suddenly, the ground erupts and a disgustingly strange monstrosity is revealed! It hisses, flashing jagged, rotten fangs.

I practically shriek. Fear sends me stumbling back, fumbling with my Cosmoe wrist power, tripping on my laces. And then—

COSMOE BOLT BLAST!

The bolts whip through the gruesome beast and small green bits of ooze explode from the thing's neck. A second later, it howls and disappears beneath us.

"Whoa," I say, looking down at my hand, crazy impressed by my Cosmoe powers. "Goober can't even do that ..."

And then we're racing ahead, sprinting through a spiraling door, and hurrying out onto the landing platform. Time to get outta here ...

REUNITED!

12

The ship sparkles in the dim, dull light. Coming out of the dark guts of the planet, I suck in the surface air—it's not perfect, but it's better than that giant trash bucket interior.

"Let's go, F.R.E.D. Quickly!" I race ahead, my feet pounding the compacted trash surface of the landing platform.

But then, suddenly, a sound. An awful sound. A hollow BOOM followed by a high-pitched shrieking and a fearsome howl. Something zipping across the landing platform.

KRAKA-BLAM!

The ship explodes in a furious eruption of flame. It's gone—and with it, all hope of escape ...

I hear footsteps stomping across the platform. I smell his smoking weapon. Krax ...

YOU BUILT SOME CUTE TOYS, COSMOE. BUT **THEY'RE NOTHING** COMPARED TO MY TOYS.

Krax stands far across the platform, his electro-zap blaster propped up on his shoulder. That thing's been upgraded since I last tangled with him, and now—apparently—it can fire frappin' warheads.

Just as things are extra hopeless, I feel tremendous heat at my back—and not the flames from the explosion. Energy. A ship.

Krax's face hangs for a moment, then I watch it twist into a furious, foul expression of rage.

I turn ...

The *Looting Star*? Rani? What's happening here?

I'm not exactly dying to return to Rani or get back aboard that blasted ship, but right now, ANYWHERE is better than here.

And then, squinting, I spot someone else...

Rani is with Humphree and Dagger! How can that be? Where did they come from?

Wait! Has Rani kidnapped my buddies, too? Man, will this foul pirate ever STOP kidnapping people?

Hmm. No. My buds are waving. Dagger and Humphree look relieved and happy to see me. I mean, they COULD have blasters to their backs—like, Rani is forcing them to look happy and relieved to see me and it's really all just a classic Rani trap.

But, ehh, no. Dagger would never stand for a blaster at her back.

Yep, this is a rescue. A real-deal rescue. And just in time . . .

Suddenly, Dagger cups her hands to her mouth. From atop the ship, I hear her scream, "COSMOE! RUN!"

I glance back at Krax. His lips curl into a growl. I flash a grin and throw him a taunting wave.

Cranking and whirring echoes across the platform. The *Looting Star*'s huge cannons are spiraling, opening, and jutting through the side of the ship. "F.R.E.D.," I say. "Life is about to get hot."

And it does. Very hot.

There's an eruption—a massive volley of pirate armory, fired downward. The entire world seems to explode around me as the platform is rocked by explosions.

"We're coming!" I cry out. With that, I'm racing toward the *Looting Star*, eyes on my friends, and F.R.E.D. whirring behind me.

Explosions cause the landing platform to shudder and shake beneath my feet. The *Looting Star* jerks in my view, jumping about as I run harder and faster than I've ever run before. I'm speeding toward the edge of the landing platform, no chance of slowing or stopping, and then—

I LEAP.

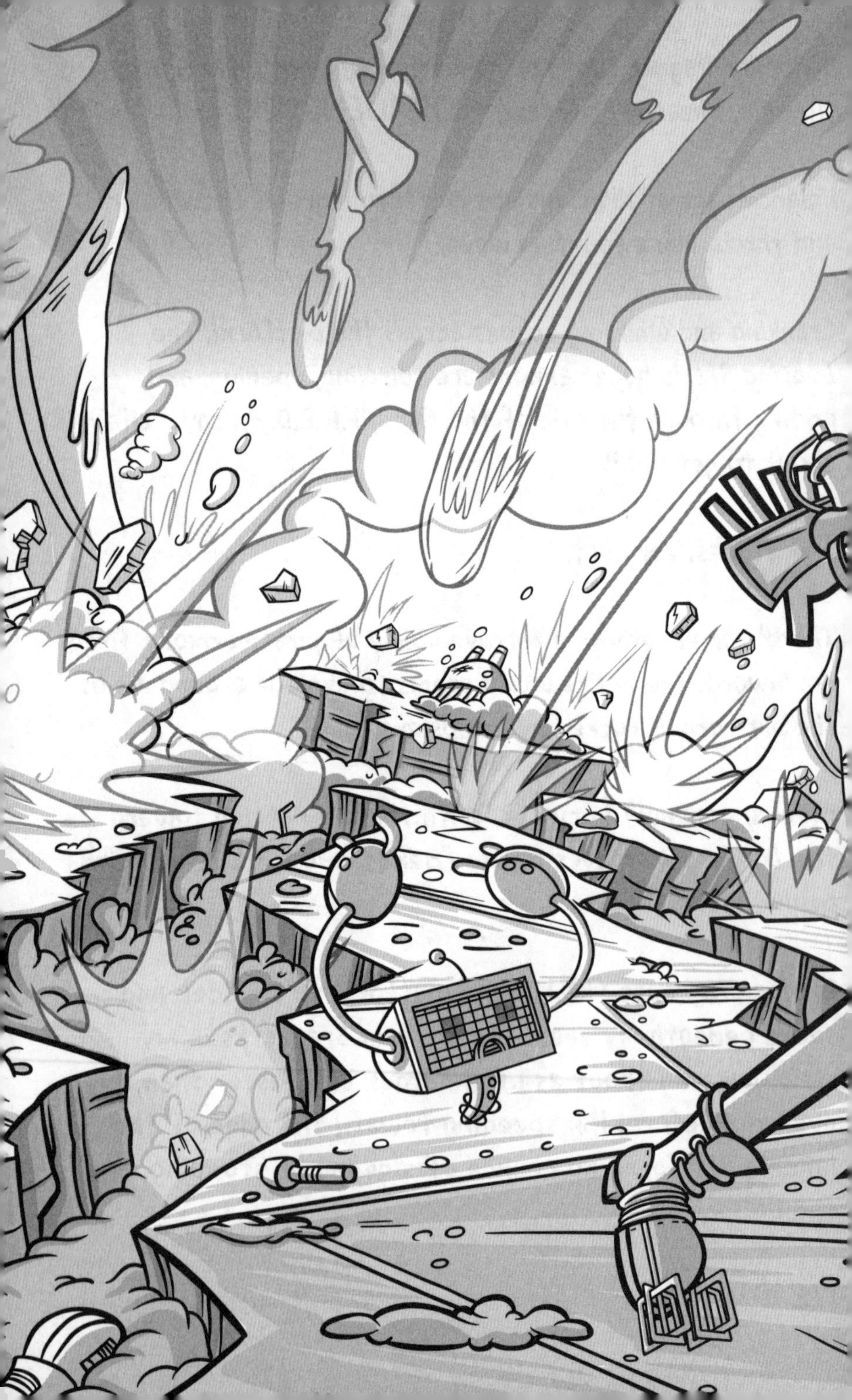

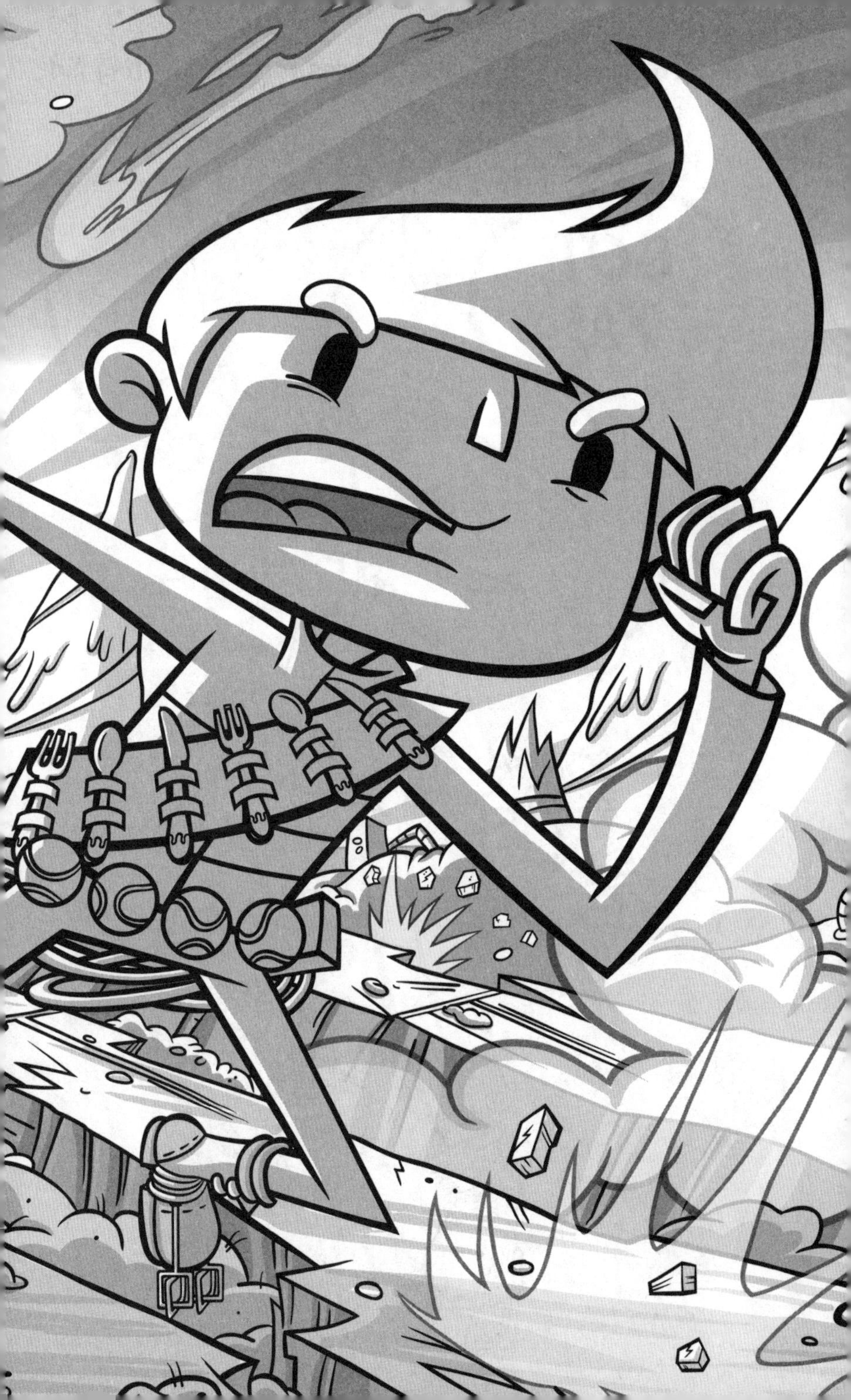

I fly toward the ship. Humphree hurries forward, jutting out an arm.

"Humphree! Dagger!" I exclaim. "Where did you guys come from?!"

"No time for chatting or celebrating!" Rani barks.

She's right.

Krax's junk cannons are returning fire. The *Looting Star* lurches as a rocket explodes against the hull. The next blast jerks the ship to the side.

"We need to leave. Now!" Rani barks. She leads the way, all of us hurrying inside, dashing down the metal steps, into the ship.

Behind us, over the rumble of the engine and the powerful roar of the rear thrusters, I hear a shout.

A promise.

It's General Krax, saying he's not done with us. Saying he will have his revenge.

And that's just fine. Because I'm not done with him either. He still has Goober . . .

THE CORESKY KING . . .

We're sitting in the captain's quarters. Rani, Humphree, and Dagger are staring at me, blank looks for a moment, and then they exchange uncertain glances.

"What?" I ask. "What's going on? Why's everyone acting like we're on the same side all of a sudden?"

"We came to an agreement," Rani says simply.

I want to ask more, but the temperature in the room is a little bit—ah—COLD, so I let it go.

"Fine," I say. "Anyway . . . here's the deal. And hold on to your shoulder squids, 'cause it's bad . . ."

I point to my bare wrist: **"GOOBER IS GONE!"**

Humphree and Dagger are about to speak, probably about to say a bunch of sweet and sympathetic things, but there's no time for that. "Don't start," I say. "More important is **WHY** he's gone. Goober is apparently like a big rubbery **BATTERY**. And Krax is going to use him to power something—some sort of great big weapon."

"Good luck defeating that," Rani murmurs.

KRAX'S PLANS ARE **NOT** MY CONCERN. WE ARE PIRATES. PIRATES LIVE OUTSIDE OF THE NORMAL SYSTEMS OF THE GALAXY. **WE FOLLOW NO RULES.**

SWOON!

"What do you mean 'good luck'?" I say. "You have to help us stop him! That's why you came back!"

Rani chuckles. It's a cruel sound. "We only came back because Krax broke our deal. Now that you have been retrieved, the deal is complete. It is that simple."

I glance at Dagger, shooting furious laser beams of anger with my eyes. Fine, okay, I get it: she thinks Rani Zonian is radical and awesome and all that—but c'mon! The lady kidnapped me! And now Dagger's staring at her like she'd happily ditch me and Humps for, like, two hours of hangout time with Rani. I want to scream, STOP SWOONING, DAG!

But more than just that, there's the issue of—y'know—the **ALL-POWERFUL WEAPON.** The all-powerful weapon that I know, like, nada about. Zero idea what it could be!

My mind races as I contemplate the awful possibilities, straight-up bad-news-bazookas possibilities . . .

Yeah, this all-powerful weapon is def life-endingly bad. But before I can argue my point, the door whooshes open and a mob of pirates stomps in. They don't look particularly pleased...

I do a covert whisper to Humps. "Hey, buddy, all this walk-the-plank stuff—you guys really do that? In space?"

Humphree shakes his head. "There's no real PLANK. See, the pirate is forced to climb inside an energy cannon, they are then fired out into space, destined to float there forever—or until they run out of oxygen..."

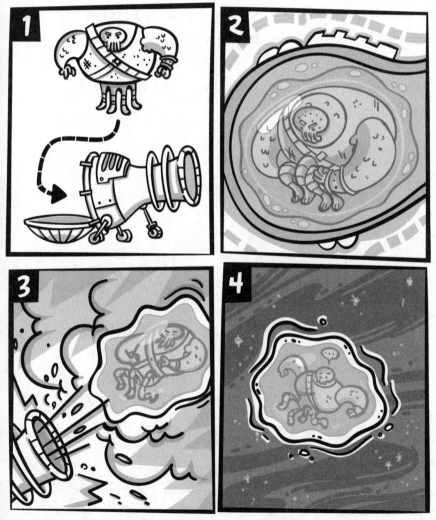

"He walks!" Slytheris barks. "The pirates' code demands it!"

"You'll walk the plank before I do!" Humphree roars. "You were going to send an innocent boy into the arms of General Krax! I never saw 'sell kiddos' in the pirates' code!"

"You're no pirate!" another growls.

Humphree nods proudly. "You're right, I'm not! I'm a hot-dog slinger and you'd better believe it!"

Dagger shoots me a nervous glance. "We need to do something, Cosmoe..."

"I know. The truth should be enough..." With that, I burst to my feet and SLAM my fist against the table.

WHY ARE WE ARGUING WHILE KRAX THE CORESKY KING IS OUT THERE?

Suddenly a cold silence seems to suck the air from the room. I glance from face to face. I see shock and terror.

Humphree says, "Did you—did you say—"

"The Coresky King?" Rani says, finishing his sentence. There is visible, HORRIFIED fear on her face.

"Um. Yeah," I say with a shrug. "That's what Krax said. He said Goober was going to allow him to become the Coresky King."

"It can't be!" one pirate exclaims. "The boy lies!"

Rani stomps across the room, forcing me back, slamming me into the wall. "Krax said those words?" she growls. "Are you CERTAIN he said the words 'Coresky King'?"

"Yes. I'm certain."

She glances to F.R.E.D. "Does the boy lie?"

F.R.E.D. simply says, "NO."

Rani staggers back, like she just got the wind knocked out of her. She collapses into her captain's chair. "I gave him the sumbios," she says. "Me. Oh, what have I done . . . ?"

Dagger groans. "Dudes, can someone PLEASE explain . . . ?"

It feels like the lights in the room have lowered, and everything is going dark. Humphree leans forward, gravely serious. "The Coresky King was a legend..."

"No, not a legend," Rani says. "REAL. The Coresky King was the space pirate **KING**. His powers were supernatural. He dominated pirates. Turned them into slaves..."

Dagger waves away that notion with a flick of the wrist. "Pshht. My mom would crush any pirate king."

Rani looks down at Dagger. I can see her thinking. "I now realize, young princess, it is in fact **QUITE** good that we have you with us. I believe we may need you..."

Dagger flashes me a confused look. I just shrug.

"But there hasn't been a Coresky King in a thousand years," one pirate adds. "No one would attempt to become the Coresky King unless they had an unimaginable power..."

"Krax said he would wield a great weapon," I say. "Oh, and he **ALSO** said he was going to build the greatest pirate ship in the history of the galaxy. If that matters."

"Pirate ship?" Rani asks curiously.

"He must be using all that trash to construct some sort of vessel..." Humphree says.

"And Goober is the ship's power source," I say.

Rani stalks the room. "There is one more thing he needs. All pirate captains have a 'familiar.' You've met mine," she says, patting the squishy little blob. "Its name is Spootnik."

"I met him face-to-face," I say, not hiding my displeasure.

"Pirate captains share power with their familiars," she says. "Their familiars make them stronger, and they make their familiars stronger."

"Like Goober!" I say.

Rani nods. "For Krax to become the Coresky King, he must first retrieve the previous Coresky King's familiar."

"Well, where is it . . . ?"

"It is still with its previous master—on the boney skeleton of the previous Coresky King. It now drifts through space," Rani says. "So . . . that is where we must go."

With that, Rani turns and marches to the bridge . . . I don't follow. Instead, I simply lean back, shut my eyes, and get some much needed NON–MAD–SCIENTIST–TABLE sleep. And as the *Looting Star* jets across space, I'm quite happy that I'm NOT rocked by flashbacks . . . I've told my story—all that's left now is to see how it ends . . .

A crackling on the ship's intercom snaps me awake. It's Rani. "Cosmoe, Dagger—come to the bridge."

When I enter, Dagger is already there. I walk in midconversation, with the princess saying, "You said you might need me. I don't understand. What's this got to do with me?"

Rani smiles. "There is a legend. And you are part of it..."

Before Dagger can respond, the ship is lurching and shuddering as it comes out of hyper-leap. Our eyes go wide... Rani points. "That is the carcass of the old Coresky King. Somewhere down there is his familiar. We must retrieve it before Krax does."

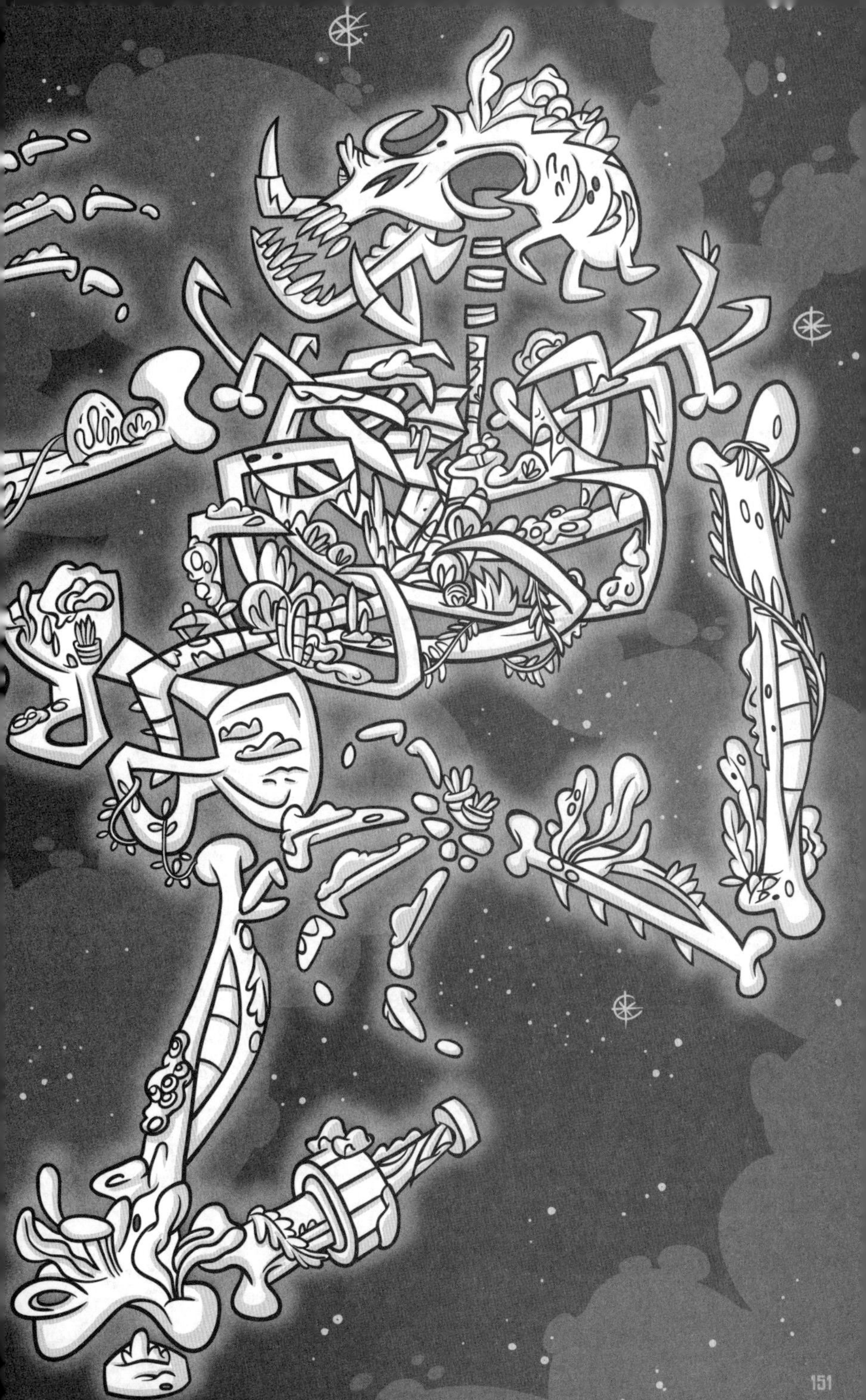

Rani spins the wheel, pulls back on the throttle, and the *Looting Star* descends. After touching down, she orders the rest of the crew to remain with the ship.

The gangplank lowers, and Rani stomps down. "Come," she says. "We don't have much time. This will be General Krax's next stop . . ."

Our party sets out: just myself, Rani, Humphree, and Dagger.

"How long has this big ol' skeleton been here?" Dagger asks.

"A millennium," Rani says. "Long enough that life has begun to grow. Long enough that it holds secrets . . ."

We trek across the surface of this strange celestial body. The air is damp and thick as we march through the trees. Huge, hideous bugs skitter along branches and dart beneath the brightly colored undergrowth.

"It's so **BIG**," Dagger says. "How can this be the body of a PIRATE?"

Rani draws her sword, using it to hack through the plant life. "The stronger the Coresky King becomes, the larger it becomes," she says. "Every time it plunders gold, every time it steals a ship—it grows in size. And this Coresky King was the greatest in history."

The being's odd body stretches out ahead of us. Rani sighs and takes it in. "I can lead us to the Rib Cage Bridge. But then, Princess, it's up to you . . ."

"But I'm telling you I don't know anything about any of this!" Dagger says.

Rani shoots Dagger a sly glance. "You see, young Princess, it was your family that destroyed the Coresky King. And the legend says that only a descendant of the Dagger family can find his familiar . . ."

"Why did the Dagger family have the Coresky King, ah—killed . . . ?" I ask Rani.

Rani says, "The Coresky King became so powerful that the Dagger family—the princess's great, great, great, great, great, greaty-great-great-grandparents—decided it could no longer exist. It was a threat. So the entire might of the Dagger army was sent to destroy it."

Dagger sucks in a sharp breath of air.

"And now we walk across the Coresky King's skeleton. All that remains is the pirate king's familiar. Come," Rani says. "Quickly, across the bridge . . ."

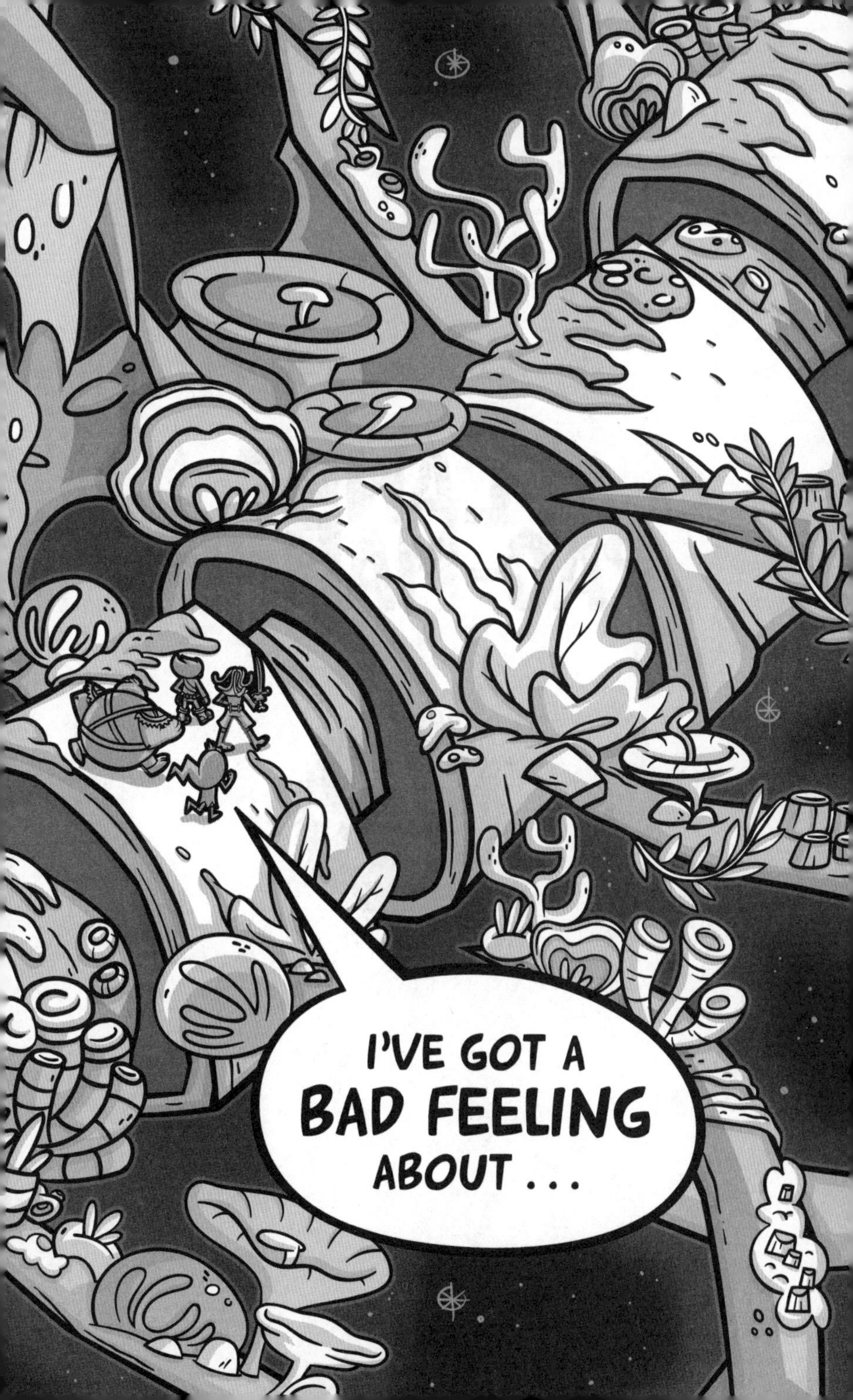
I'VE GOT A BAD FEELING ABOUT . . .

PLANET PAC-MAN?!?

14

The jungle grows thick and dark as we leave the Rib Cage Bridge behind us. Trees loom, casting eerie, dancing shadows.

Suddenly, Dagger races ahead. "Holy butts," she says. "I feel something . . ."

"Dagger!" I cry out. "Hold up!"

I speed after her, following a short trail of broken branches. Rushing through the brush, I nearly plow into her. And I realize we've found it . . .

Dagger inches closer to the door. Something appears to be etched into the stone. It's a language and a script that I don't recognize.

Rani and Humphree come crashing through the brush behind us. Rani steps toward the door, running her hand over it. "It is the original language of pirates. It says . . ."

ONLY ONE OF EVIL BLOOD
CAN CRACK THIS PIRATE'S CODE.
SPEAK THE WORDS OF ROYALTY—
ONLY THEN SHALL YOU GO.

"Maybe we need to speak some Elvish," I say, grinning. "Y'know, *Lord of the Rings*? How they get into the Mines of Moria?"

Blank looks, all around. "Whatever," I grumble.

Dagger coughs into her hand. "Uh, guys. Cosmoe's weird Earth jokes aside, the problem is . . . I don't know any ancient words of the royal fam or whatever."

Humphree groans. "Dagger, you should have paid attention to all your evil schooling!"

"Just a tiny bit of studying, Dags!" I exclaim.

Dagger roars, "Oh, shut up, Cosmoe! And you too, Humphree! You can't just throw me in here and expect me to know what to do, you armpits! Both of you can SHOVE OFF!"

Suddenly, I catch a sound. A slight rumbling. "Did you guys hear that?"

"Hear Dagger screaming?" Humphree asks. "Hard to miss."

"No," I say as I inch toward the ancient door. "I think IT moved. I think the door, like, budged a bit."

"But I didn't say any special words," Dagger says.

And that's when it hits me. "Wait!" I exclaim. "Your family's evil and REALLY mean! So they said a lot of mean stuff. Maybe that's the 'words of royalty'! Talking like a big jerk. Dagger, say more vile stuff!"

Dagger shrugs, and then—

YOU STUPID, UGLY, GOOD-FOR-NOTHIN' #$*% $%&#! @^&* @*!$% *$!#^@ DOOR!

Hot smudge, it's working! With each awful utterance, the door inches open. Ancient bits of rock crumble.

"Wow, you're good at that," I say.

Dagger grins. "I had lots of practice at the contest, telling Humphree he stunk at eating hot dogs."

"Steel yourselves, crew," Rani says, inching forward.

I have my Cosmoe powers ready. Humphree raises his fists. Dagger grips her blaster. And then, the door swings open fully—revealing a very small, very dumb-looking bird . . .

"Wait," I say. "That doofy little thing is the big, bad familiar?"

Even Rani, holder of knowledge of all things piratey, is looking a little confused. "I—ah—I guess so," she says.

We slowly step into the dark cave. This odd little bird creature looks at us, nothing but dumb dullness on its face.

Suddenly there is darkness behind us. And a strange electric smell in the air. Rushing back outside, peering up, I see what looks like a solar eclipse.

And then a powerful rumbling that shakes EVERYTHING. The Coresky King's carcass shifts beneath our feet.

This is no eclipse.

It's Krax.

And he wasn't using the junk to build a **NEW** pirate ship. No. Not at all.

His planet **IS** the ship . . .

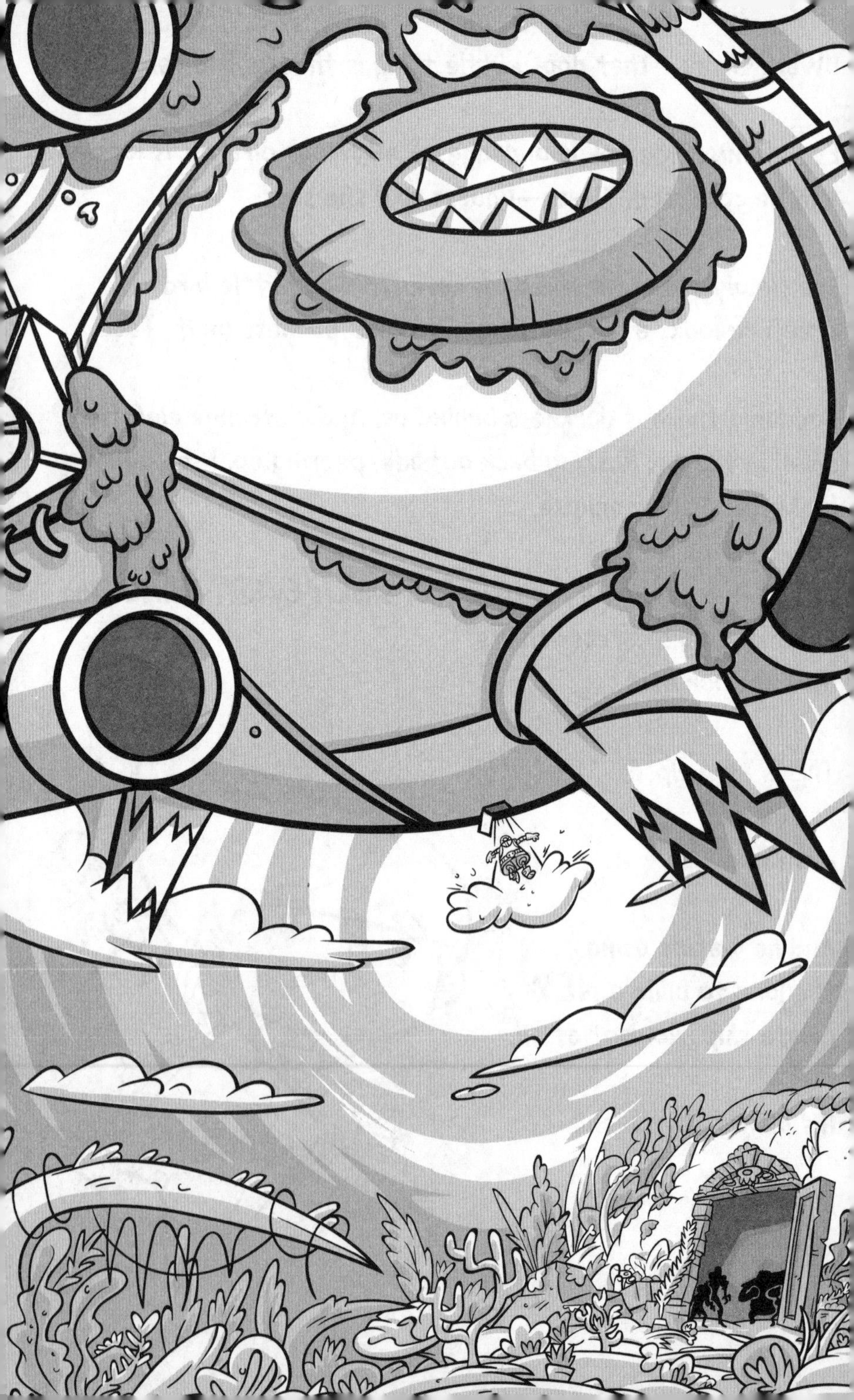

The planet-ship drifts closer. Frozen with terror, we watch as a figure appears—just a blip, first, and then it grows larger. It's Krax, himself.

"What do we do?" I ask.

At least, I **THINK** I ask—it's hard to know for sure. I'm so scared, so freaked out, that I'm not sure my mouth is working.

I watch as Krax—jetpack-powered—descends.

Krax now speaks directly to the doofy bird. "Hear me, familiar! I am the new Coresky King. I am YOUR servant! And you are MY servant! Together, we will feed off each other. Together, we will rule over all space pirates."

"Really?" I say, still not believing that doofy thing can be all that special. "That dinky bird?"

The bird begins hopping out of the cave toward Krax. Its little feet carry it across the ground, then its little wings help it up through the air.

Krax bends down and extends an open hand . . .

Rani draws her sword. We all step forward—no one is
sure **WHAT** to do, but all of us are sure we have to do
SOMETHING.

Krax grins wickedly as the familiar hops up his arm. And my
heart slams inside my chest and my hair stands on end as the
doofy little bird-creature begins to change.

It grows, morphs, and mutates! It begins wrapping around
Krax, tentacles flying—and as it does, Krax grows . . .

Krax's space suit shatters! He doubles in size, turning
full-on monstrous!

This foul new version of Krax lifts into the air, headed for his planet-ship GD9. But his jetpack doesn't fire. The familiar— the bird!—has given him wings, and the power of flight.

As he approaches GD9, the side of the ship begins to open. It's transforming—chunks of trash and metal shifting and sliding. I swallow hard.

Dagger shrugs. "At least we're still alive! I'm surprised he didn't execute us. Or zap us. Or chop us up."

I shake my head. "I don't think he's done . . ."

The side of the planet-ship opens. It looks like a **MOUTH**. A ferocious, giant mouth, made of junk! It reminds me of, like, Pac-Man. And that's when I realize . . .

"It's not **JUST** a planet and it's not **JUST** a ship!" I exclaim. "The planet is a ship and the ship is a weapon!"

"**THAT** is the **ALL-POWERFUL WEAPON** he was talking about!" Humphree exclaims. "A junk planet that will devour anything in its way!"

Rani Zonian instantly understands. "It will grow bigger and stronger as it goes!"

I can't help but be impressed. "I mean, he did say that he was going to build the most awesome pirate ship in the history of pirate ships—and that **IS** pretty awesome."

"Well, what now?" Dagger asks.

And at once, we're all screaming the same thing:

"RUN!"

LAST GASP
OF THE
LOOTING
STAR

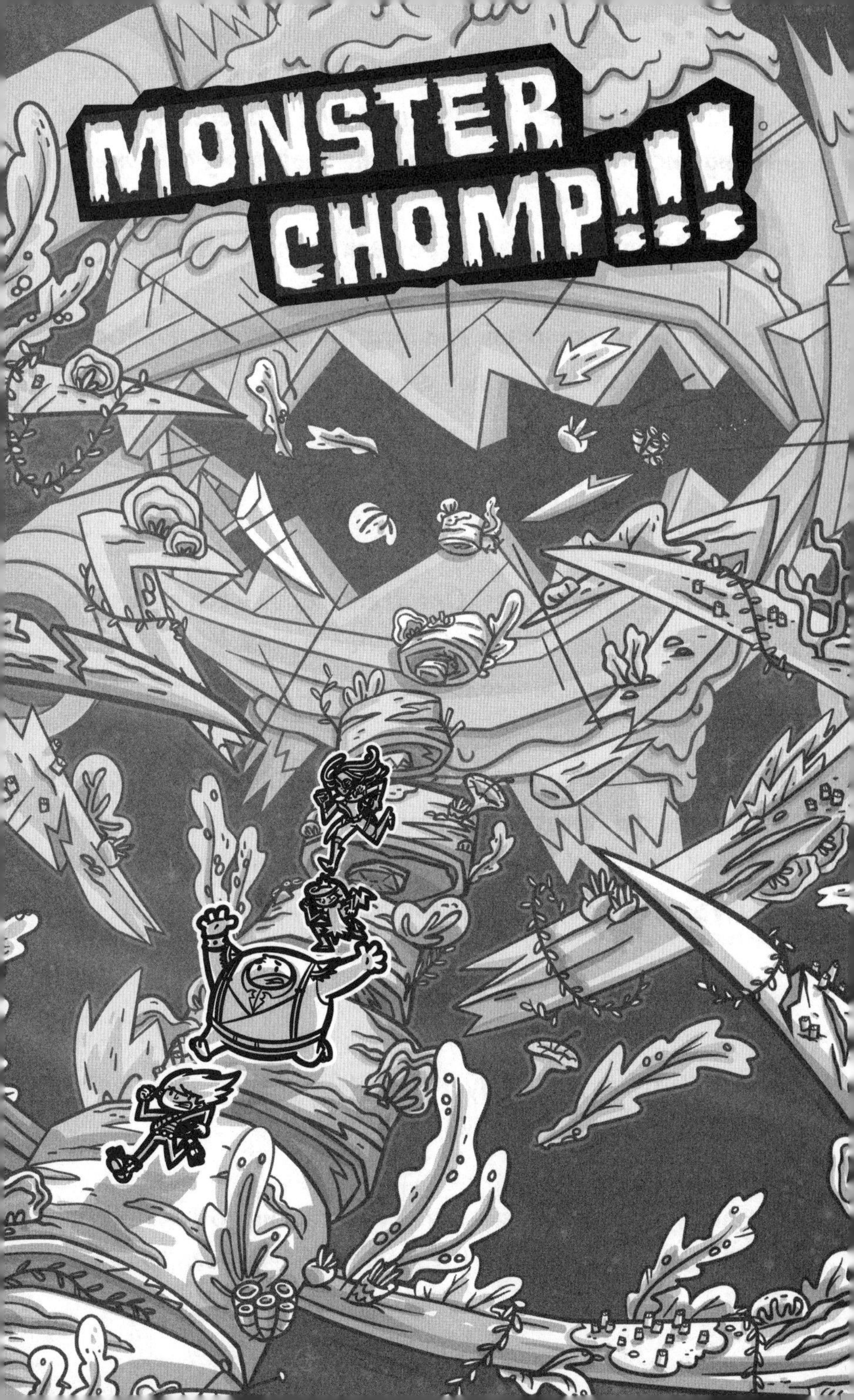
MONSTER CHOMP!!!

The ground quakes, shuddering and shattering, as we race back through the thick jungle. The sound is deafening. I hear gnawing and gnashing—chewing—the shattering of bone.

I want nothing more than to be back in the *Neon Wiener.*

We dash up the gangplank and into the *Looting Star.* "Get her started!" Rani hollers to her crew.

"What's happening?" Slytheris shouts. And then, through the main deck window, he sees . . .

The ship rocks and shakes. One tremendous lurch sends me stumbling into the wall. My face bounces off the porthole window—and for a moment, I can't help but watch . . .

Through the window, I see Krax's planet-ship devouring the husk of the old Coresky King. Every bit of it is chomped and devoured, and as it eats the old Coresky King, the planet-ship GROWS . . . It's taking it, adding to its mass.

"We need to get out of here—now!" I bark.

The *Looting Star* is already lifting off, rotating, jets beginning to fire. But Krax is not done.

Whirling, I grab Humphree. "We're not going to take off in time!" I cry. "Krax's planet is going to eat us! We have to get off this ship!"

"Off the ship?" Slytheris barks, stomping forward. "Are you mad!"

He reaches out to grab me—but he's suddenly gone, disappeared, as the ship is bitten into and the wall disappears . . .

The *Looting Star* snaps in half! Pirates hang in the air and then are instantly swallowed.

"My crew!" Rani exclaims. "No . . ."

"Rani! Come on!" I shout, screaming over the roar of the destruction. "We have to get to the *Neon Wiener!*"

"I will not abandon my ship or my crew!" she barks.

I snap back, "Your ship is sinking and your crew was just eaten!"

"Then I'll go down with the ship," she says.

"And then what?!" I cry. "Every other pirate in the galaxy will become Krax's slaves! You need to **WARN THEM!**"

Rani looks at me for a long moment. **TOO LONG.** At last, she stomps past me. "Blast. Come on!" Rani barks.

The ship is plummeting back toward the surface of the great skeleton. My stomach lurches as we race down the ship's narrow halls.

Everything is crumbling and collapsing around us. Finally, we burst into the hangar. The *Neon Wiener* sits peacefully. Dashing inside, I think, MAN OH MAN, I NEVER WANT TO SET FOOT ABOARD A PIRATE SHIP AGAIN . . .

"The *Looting Star*'s power is down!" Humphree barks. "I can't open the hangar doors!"

"We don't need hangar doors," I say.

"How do you plan on flying out without opening the doors?" Rani barks.

"Just hang tight. As soon as that big planet chomps again, we escape!"

And then I hear it. The mouth opening and preparing to bite down. My knuckles are fleshy white as I grip the thruster. Here we go . . .

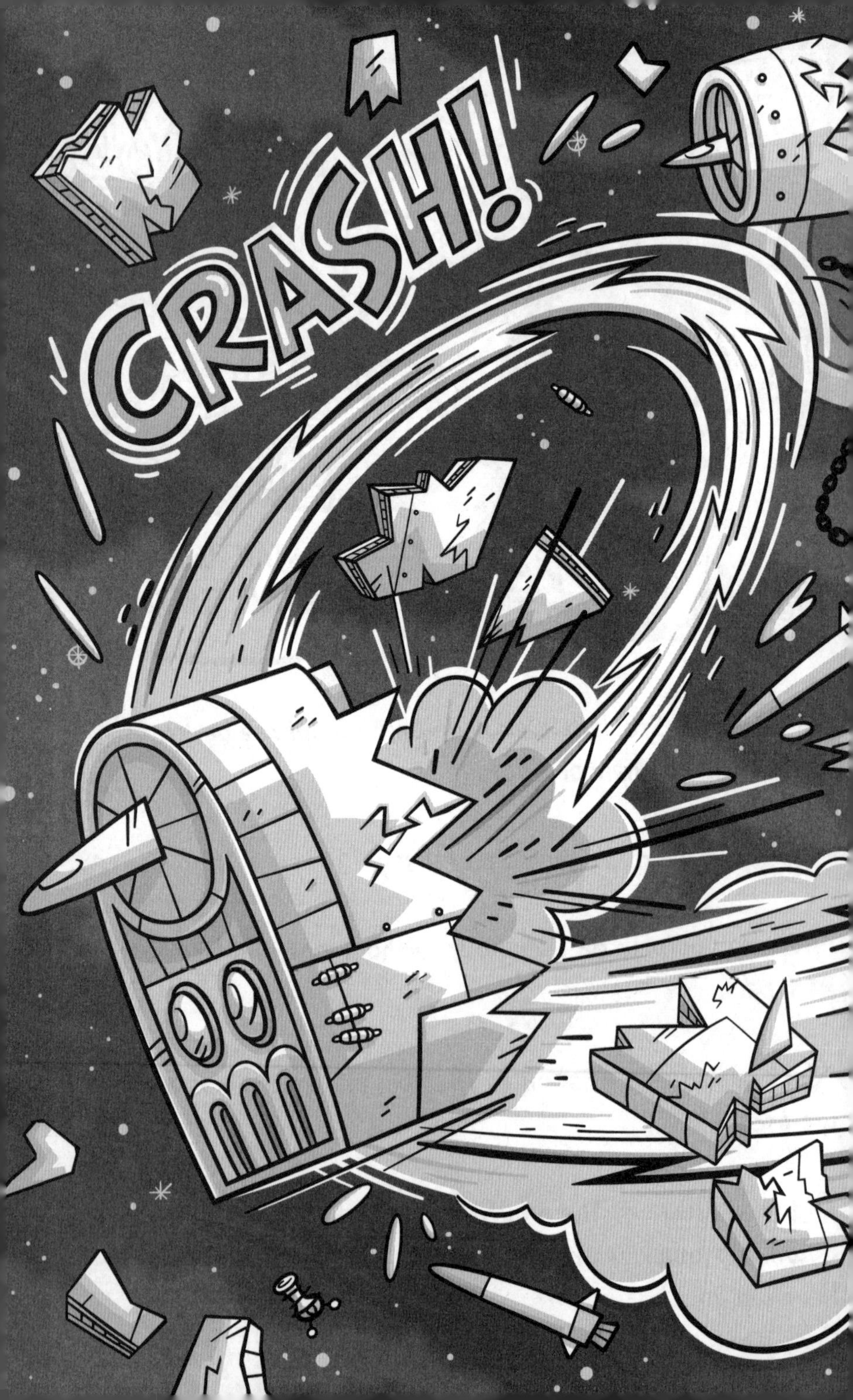
CRASH!

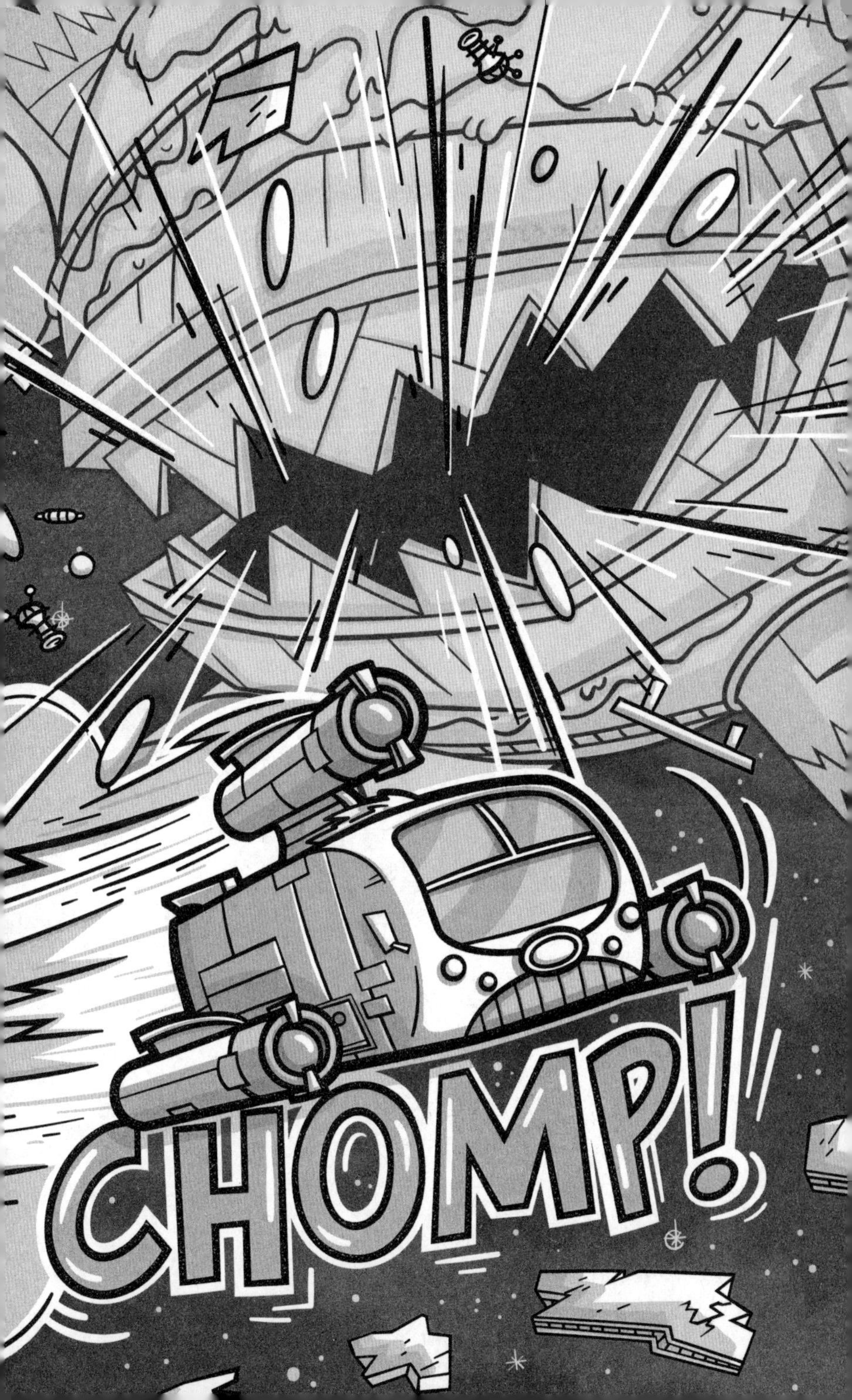
CHOMP!

IT'S ALL OF OUR FAULTS!

16

I pull away from the window, but Rani remains. "My ship," she whispers. "My family. My crew. MY LIFE. All gone . . ."

The look on her face—I imagine it's not much different than the look on my face, years ago, when everything I had was lost . . .

Suddenly Rani is stomping across the cockpit, jabbing a finger at Humphree. "If you hadn't freed the boy, this never would have happened!"

Humphree's throat starts rumbling, and I know he's getting angry. He stabs a finger back at Rani. "You're the one who kidnapped the boy!"

I groan. "The boy? Really? I'm 'the boy' now?"

"COSMOE!" Humphree barks, enunciating my name all distinct and clear. "Rani, you took COSMOE."

"That was years ago," Rani says. She whirls around, and her hair SNAPS against Humphree's face.

"This wouldn't have happened if you hadn't taken him!" Humphree barks. The tension in the rear hold of our ship is growing faster than mutant plant life.

"It wouldn't have even begun if HE hadn't touched the sumbios," Rani says, suddenly spinning and barking at me.

"Wait ... Me? ME? I'm getting blamed now! Goober crashed in my backyard!" I say.

"Doesn't mean you had to touch Goober!" Rani says. "Do you touch EVERYTHING in your backyard?"

"I mean, sorta," I say with a shrug. "I liked to explore. But y'know—I don't HAVE a backyard anymore, 'cause you TOOK ME."

"Once you touched it, we had to," Rani says.

"Nice try," I spit back. "But you only TOOK me so you could hand me over to Krax!"

"But Krax wouldn't even know about Cosmoe if DAGGER hadn't hijacked our ship back when," Humphree says. "That's how he found us and realized you had Goober!"

"Yeah! And Dagger released the familiar!" I exclaim.

Just then Dagger strolls in. "Huh? You're talking about me? Wait, you're BLAMING ME? She told me to open the special familiar door!" she says, pointing at Rani.

"She's a pirate!" I scream. "You always do what pirates tell you to do?!"

"Cosmoe, YOU thought it was a good idea!" Dagger says.

And then Humphree jumps in to defend Dagger, and then for some reason Rani is defending me, and I'm shouting at Humphree, and Dagger's screaming at me, and Rani is screaming at EVERYONE, and I realize, man, it sounds JUST like I'm back in the orphanage.

Everyone arguing. Everyone fighting.

"Guys, please! Stop pointing fingers at each other!" I cry, but that just seems to make it worse, so finally I bark out—

"NO, Y'KNOW WHAT? KEEP POINTING FINGERS! EVERYONE! KEEP 'EM UP! AND LOOK!

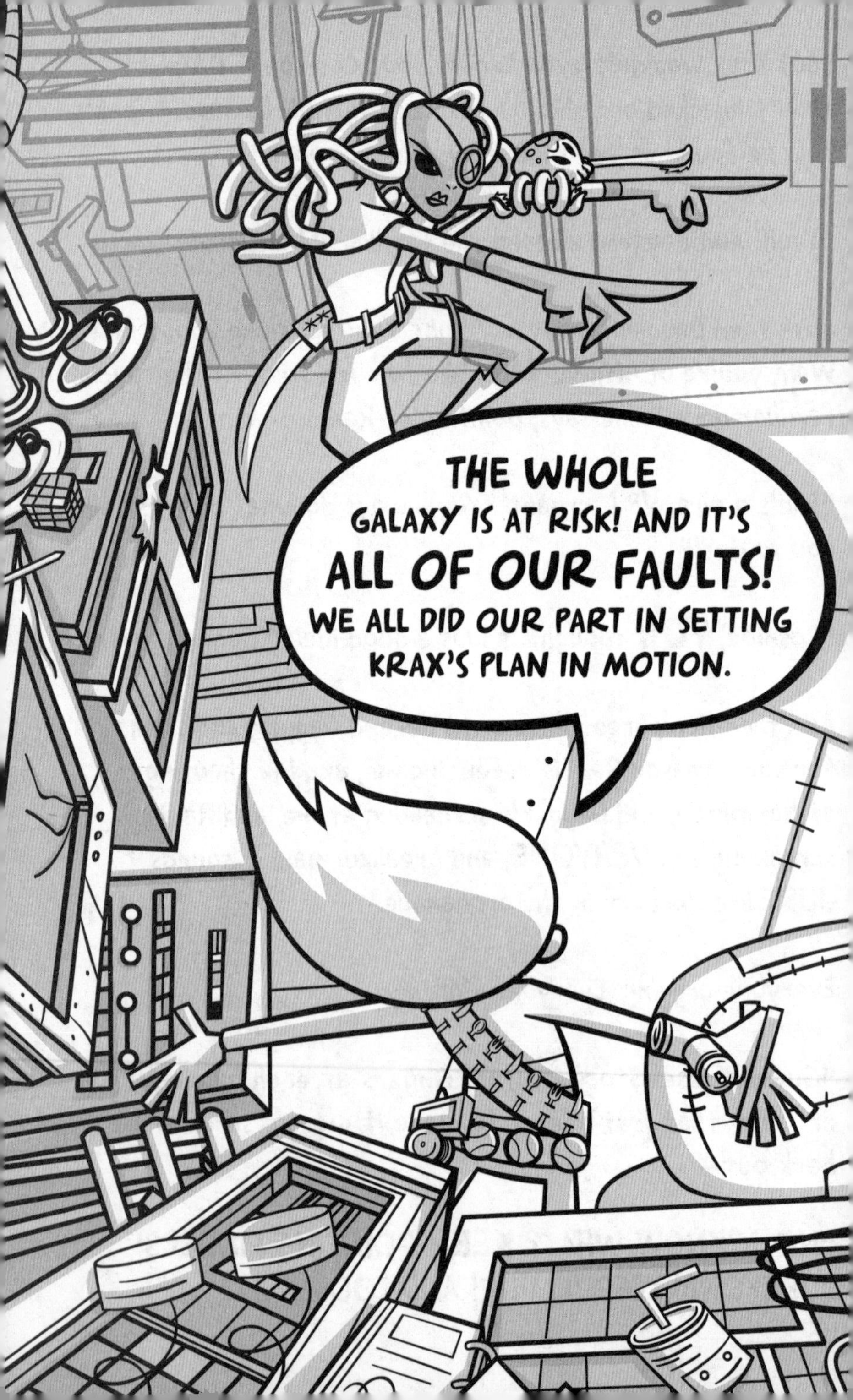
THE WHOLE GALAXY IS AT RISK! AND IT'S ALL OF OUR FAULTS! WE ALL DID OUR PART IN SETTING KRAX'S PLAN IN MOTION.

Softly, movie-star dramatically, I say, "So that means..."

Blank stares, all around. **STILL.** Just a circle of blank gazes.

"Really?" I say. "No one can finish that sentence?"

Humphree sighs. "So that means we all need to stop Krax..."

"That's right! Us wieners, us pirates, us royal rascals! Together, **WE** need to defeat that big lug and his planet-ship!"

I'm still getting blank stares. My motivational words are, so far, less than motivational.

"LOOK!" I say, pounding the panel and sending a bowl of coco-crisps flying. "I never wanted to be in space! Actually, pause, not true—I dreamed all about it. But I never asked to be KIDNAPPED into space. But here I am! And here we ALL are. A bunch of dumb aliens, dumb me, and an awesome robot pal. And we're the only ones who know about Krax and his giant planet-ship. So no more arguing. Tell me... **WHAT ARE WE GONNA DO ABOUT IT?"**

And suddenly, Humphree and Rani Zonian lock eyes. "Pirates Cove!" Humphree says. "**THAT'S** where Krax is going. He wants us to kneel. He wants the pirates to kneel. But they won't—"

"My home," Rani says. "The home of ALL pirates. It's the one place where pirates are safe. It's where their families stay. There is a truce. We need to warn them—because Krax will kill them all if they don't pledge fealty..."

"Then that's where we're going," I say. And with that, I quickly shove them all out of the cockpit—I'LL be doing the flying. Rani glares. As I begin to close the door, I quickly say, **"AND OH, JUST REAL QUICK, BY THE WAY, NONE OF THIS IS MY FAULT WHATSOEVER,"** and before they can all explode at me, I've shut the cockpit door and I'm steering us to Pirates Cove...

I feel Dagger shaking my arm, waking me up. I wipe crust from my eyes and look up. "What's up?" I ask yawning.

"Looks like you got some rest," Dagger says.

"Just enough. F.R.E.D. took the wheel for a bit."

Dagger leans forward, setting a hand on the dash. "You awake enough to see something pretty frappin' cool?"

"Don't say 'frappin'.' That's my word."

"Well, are you ready to see something MILK SHAKE COOL? We're here. Pirates Cove . . ."

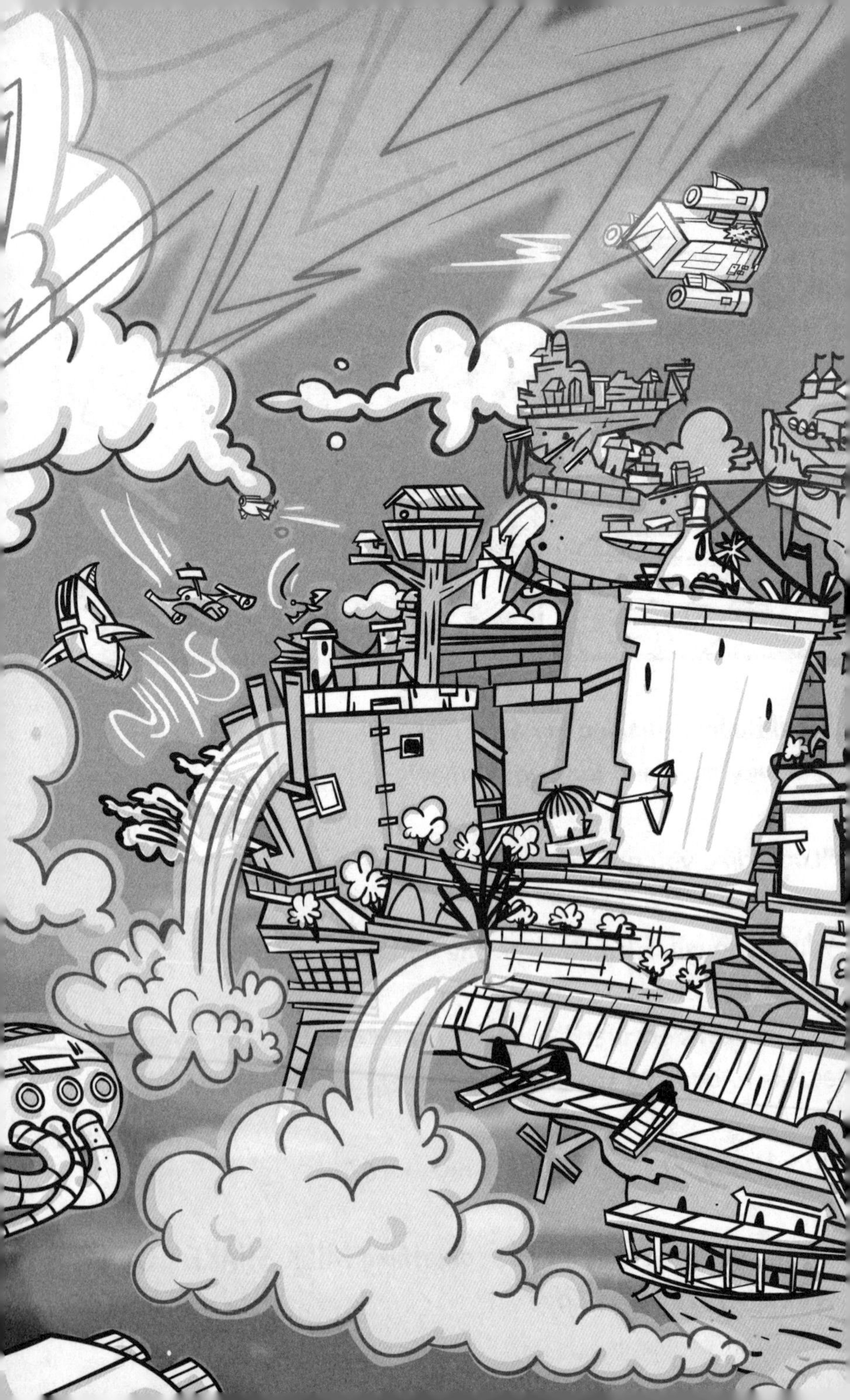

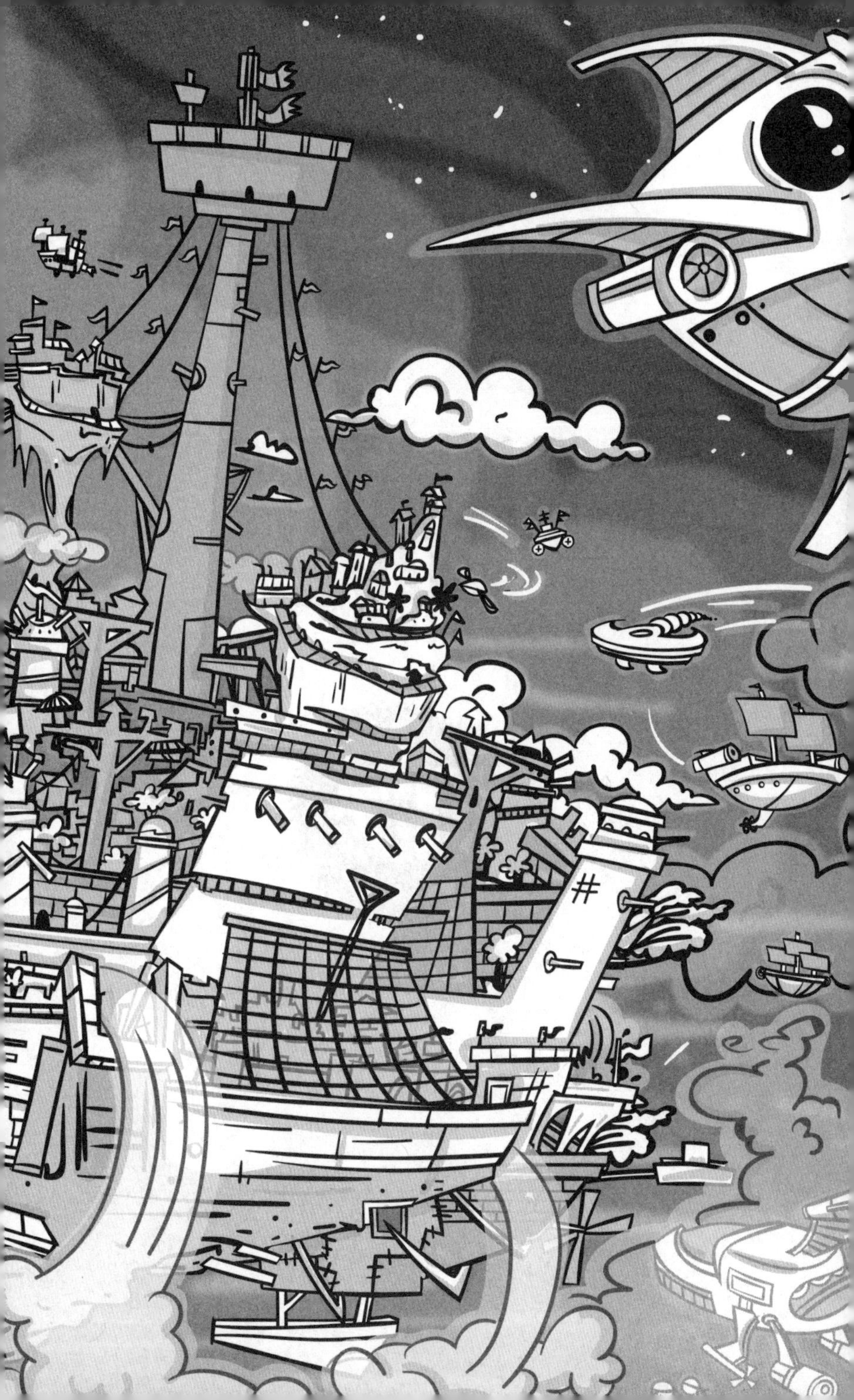

PIRATES COVE

We dock the *Neon Wiener* at one of the hundreds of landing platforms that dot the outer ring of Pirates Cove. Exiting the ship, I eye Rani. "Well, now what?"

"Now we tell these pirates that Krax is coming," Rani says. "And we hope they believe us ..."

Entering the city, I look up in awe. This strange mixture of port and city and home is immense—and it's teeming with curiosities.

Huge trees tower over us, built of metallic trunks but sprouting leaves of orange and blue.

SO THIS PLACE IS EXTRA RADICAL AND FANTASTIC, HUH?

BEYOND.

Rani leads us down tight, curving streets, toward the center of the cove. The whole vibe reminds me of the Rainforest Cafe, but with way more weaponry and shadier-looking dudes.

But it's not ALL shady. We pass families. Children. **HOMES.**

Shops are stacked high upon another, alongside a hodgepodge of stands selling electro-riggers and astro-anchors.

Pirates call out, offering fusion blasters at cut-rate prices. We slip through narrow alleys, then out into a vast, open-air market . . .

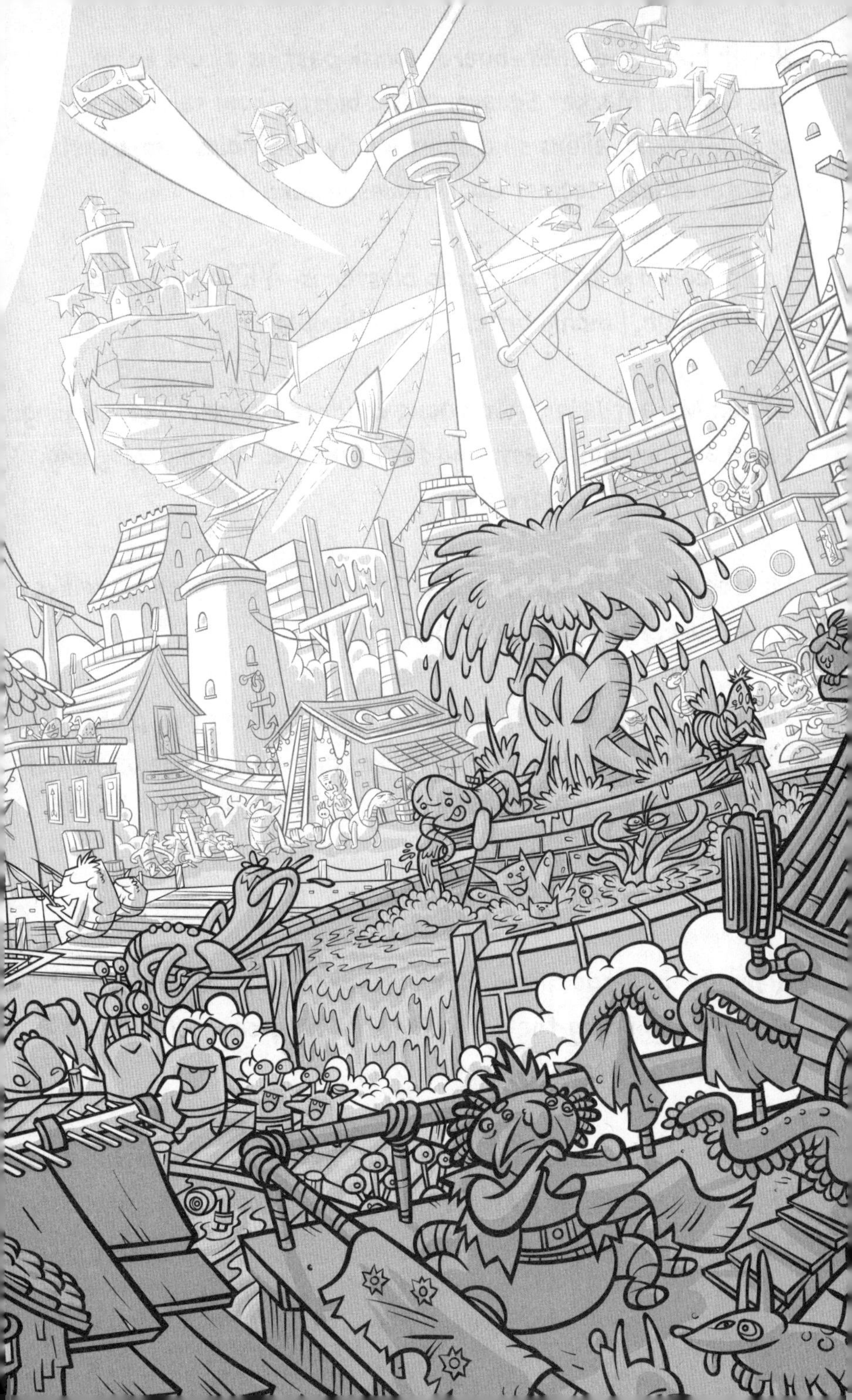

Hover bikes and drift-boards whisk past us as we enter the Central Market Square. Music blasts from saloons, and seedy-looking aliens sing along loudly. Unwholesome, beastly creatures lean against doorframes, eyeing us.

I gulp, confirm that my scrap blaster is—YES—equipped. Still, though, I inch a bit closer to Humphree.

But an instant later, two young children run past me, giggling. I spin as they dash past. And then a father chasing, laughing, calling after his children.

Pirates aren't totally terrible. Some are, sure—some are like pure, pure, PURE badness. But not all.

"Humphree," I say. "We can't let Krax destroy this place. We MUST convince these dudes there is a real, bad-news threat on the way. We need to convince them to fight! But how?"

"That should get us started," he says, pointing.

Glancing up, I spot Rani. She has hurried ahead and is in the midst of climbing the towering, spinning central mast. It is, I realize, the peak of Pirates Cove.

A short gasp escapes Dagger's lips. She elbows me in the side. "Man, is she cool or WHAT?"

I don't respond. Because the answer is yes—but I have no interest in encouraging Dagger's little crush.

"She's climbing the Black Mast ..." Humphree says, impressed.

And when Rani reaches the peak, her voice booms. It is the powerful voice of the most legendary space pirate captain in the galaxy ...

Each word echoes off the market stalls, the lean-to houses, the storefronts. Rani's voice grabs the pirates' attention. "Many of you know me," Rani calls out. "You know me for being true to the pirates' code and true to my word."

A few pirates murmur in agreement. More pirates shuffle into the square—thousands now, watching her.

"Believe me, now, as I tell you the unbelievable," Rani continues, her voice echoing nearly throughout the entire city-cove. "A new Coresky King is coming. He's coming **HERE!** And we only have hours to prepare . . ."

In an instant, the mood of the pirates changes—a 180 flip. Some pirates laugh. Others curse Rani. A general feeling of annoyed disbelief.

"The captain of the *Looting Star* has lost it!" one shouts.

"The captain of the *Looting Star* is no more!" Rani barks in response. "The Coresky King DESTROYED my ship. He DEVOURED my crew. The Coresky King—General Krax von Grumble—has taken **EVERYTHING** from me."

Murmurs. A few of them maybe, possibly believe her. But "a few" is not enough. To mount a defense? To defeat Krax the Coresky King? It will take more than "a few"—it will take every last stinkin' buccaneer.

"On it!" Dagger says cheerfully, and she's quickly sprinting ahead, using her evil acrobatic skills to scale the Black Mast.

At the top, she shrieks—her voice sharp in the air. "I am Princess Dagger, heir to the throne of evil! And what Rani says is true! I freed the familiar. General Krax has what he needs to rule you all! You can fight him here, now—or he'll rule you dudes forever. Me and my buds will help. But we can only stop the jerk together. So what's it gonna be?"

Princess Dagger gets their attention. Royalty tends to do that. And not only that—the daughter of the actual QUEEN of Evil.

When Dagger finishes there is silence throughout the square. Silence that I realize is a grim understanding of the situation—of the truth...

And the tide turns...

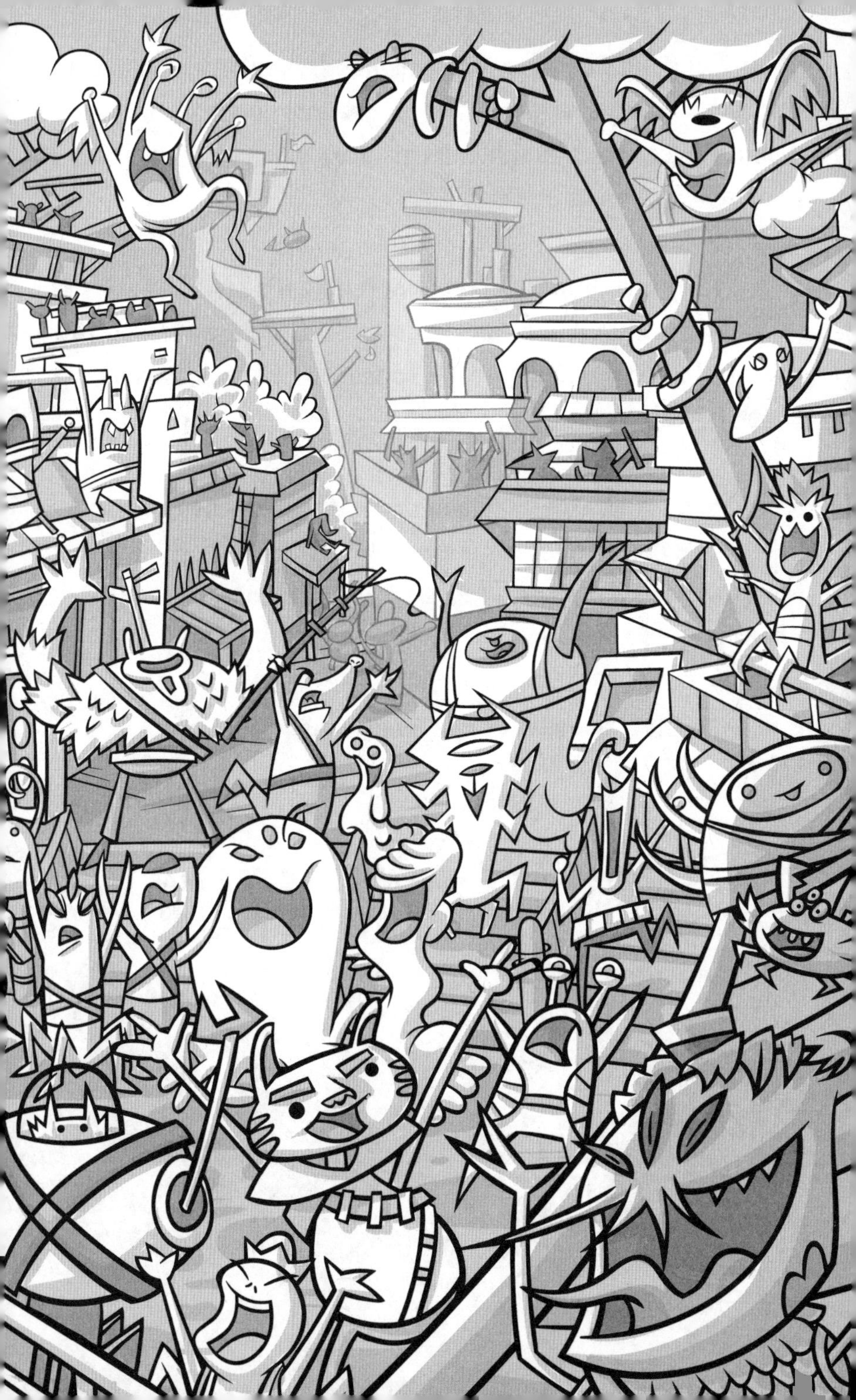

Soon, Rani and Dagger have descended. Rani gives orders and instructions. Pirates hurry off in groups. Hundreds will man the outer cannons, and hundreds more take to their ships, to pilot a first line of defense.

After they've outlined a plan, I catch Rani's eye. She nods for us to follow. We move quickly down four dark alleys, finally coming to a stop at a sort of spaceified tiki hut named Lunar Louie's.

Rani orders a fizzing, bubbling drink, then knocks it back in one hard slam. "The pirates are with us," she says. "But now? Now we need a plan to DEFEAT Krax the Coresky King . . . There is very little time."

And with that, she swings her head in my direction. "Me?" I ask.

WELL . . . AH . . . THE WAY I SEE IT, IT ALL COMES DOWN TO GOOBER. I NEED TO RETRIEVE THE LITTLE GUY. THAT'S THE ONLY WAY TO STOP KRAX. AND TO DO THAT, I NEED TO GET INSIDE KRAX'S PLANET-WARSHIP . . .

Rani shakes her head. "Any ship that flies close—Krax will either blast out of the sky or swallow whole."

Suddenly a short, round pirate comes jogging over. "Captain, the ship is ready."

Rani flashes a mischievous grin at me and Humphree. "Do not be mad. But I had some alterations made to your *Wiener* vessel."

Rani is suddenly, again, marching across Pirates Cove, and we're all following. "Hey!" I bark again. "Slow down. What did you do to the *Neon Wiener*? What did you do to my ship?!"

"Hey, short pants, **OUR SHIP**," Humphree says, jabbing me in the side.

"Right, right. **OUR SHIP**. What did you do? Reminder, lady—we **SAVED** you in that ship. You'd be Krax planet-food if it wasn't for the *Neon Wiener*."

But turning the corner onto the docking platform, I see what she's done. And I have very few complaints . . .

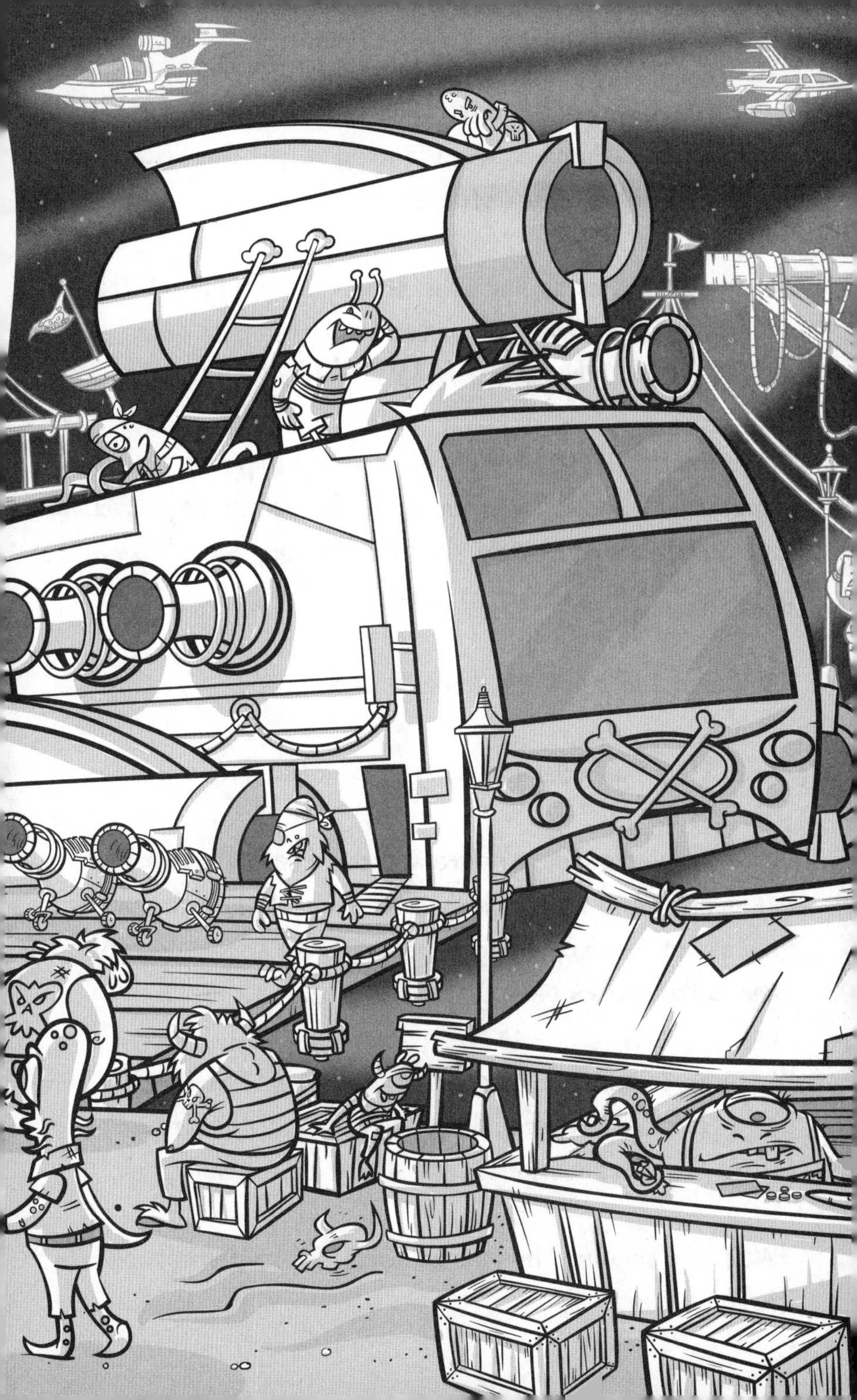

"So . . ." I say. "The *Neon Wiener* is a pirate ship now . . . Radical. But we've still got to figure out a way to get INSIDE Krax's planet-ship weapon. We need to get Goober back—that's the only way we stop him!"

Dagger scrunches up her eyes, thinks for a moment, then exclaims, "IDEA! What if we send every ship at once? Just like, **WHAM**, y'know, SO MANY SHIPS!"

Rani shakes her head. "We'll need every ship just to defend the cove! And even **THAT** won't be enough to slow Krax for long. He's claimed himself the Coresky King. So he'll want our allegiance. He'll want us to kneel."

"So . . . couldn't you just kneel?" I ask.

"Kneel?!" Rani exclaims, looking at me like I've lost it.

"Well, only, y'know, temporary-like!" I say. "To catch him off guard! And then, quickly, just unkneel—hop to your feet. I'm talking knees on the ground for like 7 seconds—tops. And then, whoop, back on your toes," I say.

"Cosmoe," Rani says, with an annoyed sigh. "He doesn't want us to LITERALLY kneel. Although probably that, too. He wants full surrender. Flash the white holo-banner."

"Wait one second," Humphree says. "Short pants's idea isn't **THAT** crummy."

"Surrender?" Rani barks, suddenly stomping toward Humphree, jabbing a finger in his chest. "Mention that thought again and I **WILL** make you walk the plank, Humphree."

Humphree's eyes suddenly flash. A lightning bolt of thought. I see the big BINGO going off in his head. "You've been itching to make me walk the plank for a long while, Rani."

Rani snarls. "What of it?"

Humphree grins. "Well . . ."

THAT'S EXACTLY IT. KNEELING AND THE PLANK. RANI, YOU'RE GOING TO BE VERY HAPPY ABOUT THIS PLAN.

LORD OF THE RINGS. IT'S AN EARTH THING.

18

LATER . . .

GD9 is just a blip at first. A small dot of dim light. And then it grows larger, increasing in size—and I hear a gasp, sudden, sharp, growing all around us.

One pirate exclaims, **"IT'S A PLANET!"** while another cries, **"IT'S A SHIP!"** and a third screams, **"IT'S A WEAPON!"**

"It's all three!" Rani barks. "Now silence. You know what to do . . ."

Cannons line the walls, and at every cannon, a pirate. They growl and snarl, eyes narrowed as they stare out at the endless space horizon.

I smell the thick odor of humming electricity. Glowing energy cannonballs are stacked higher than my head.

A few final pirates scurry about, rushing this way and that.
Cannons are aimed. Energy blasters are leveled.

These parapets—these cove walls—**THIS** is the last line of
defense against Krax...

I watch Humphree grip the wall, squeezing so tight that it starts to crack. To my other side is Dagger, a beaming grin on her face. She catches me eyeing her, looks up, and grins even wider.

"Talk about a showdown!" Dagger says. "This is just like something from the old stories my mom used to tell me. Defending castle walls! Breaching!"

"It's like the Battle of Helm's Deep!" I say.

"The huh?" Dagger asks.

"*Lord of the Rings.* It's an Earth thing."

Suddenly, Rani is behind us. "I hope your plan works, Humphree. Because it's time. Come."

We march the length of the wall, passing the pirate army.

Finally, we come to three unmanned cannons. They are aimed outward, pointed directly at the looming GD9.

They look oddly lonely and especially empty amid the hubbub of hurrying pirates.

"These will be yours," Rani says.

I nod. And then I gulp . . .

"No time for second thoughts," Rani says. "Look."

We all turn. Staring out, into the distance, we see it. Massive, huge—and CLOSE.

Krax has arrived . . .

It's quiet now along the outer ring of Pirates Cove—the only sound is the soft hum of energy cannonballs and the nervous breathing of the space pirates.

Rani yanks a microphone from the wall. She addresses the pirates for the final time. The final time, before many of them may perish. Rani says only one word: **"SURRENDER."**

And on that signal, Pirates Cove—and all of its ships—begin to flash the white holo-banners. One massive holo-banner flies above Pirates Cove, pure white.

It's clear what it means. Pure, unconditional submission ...

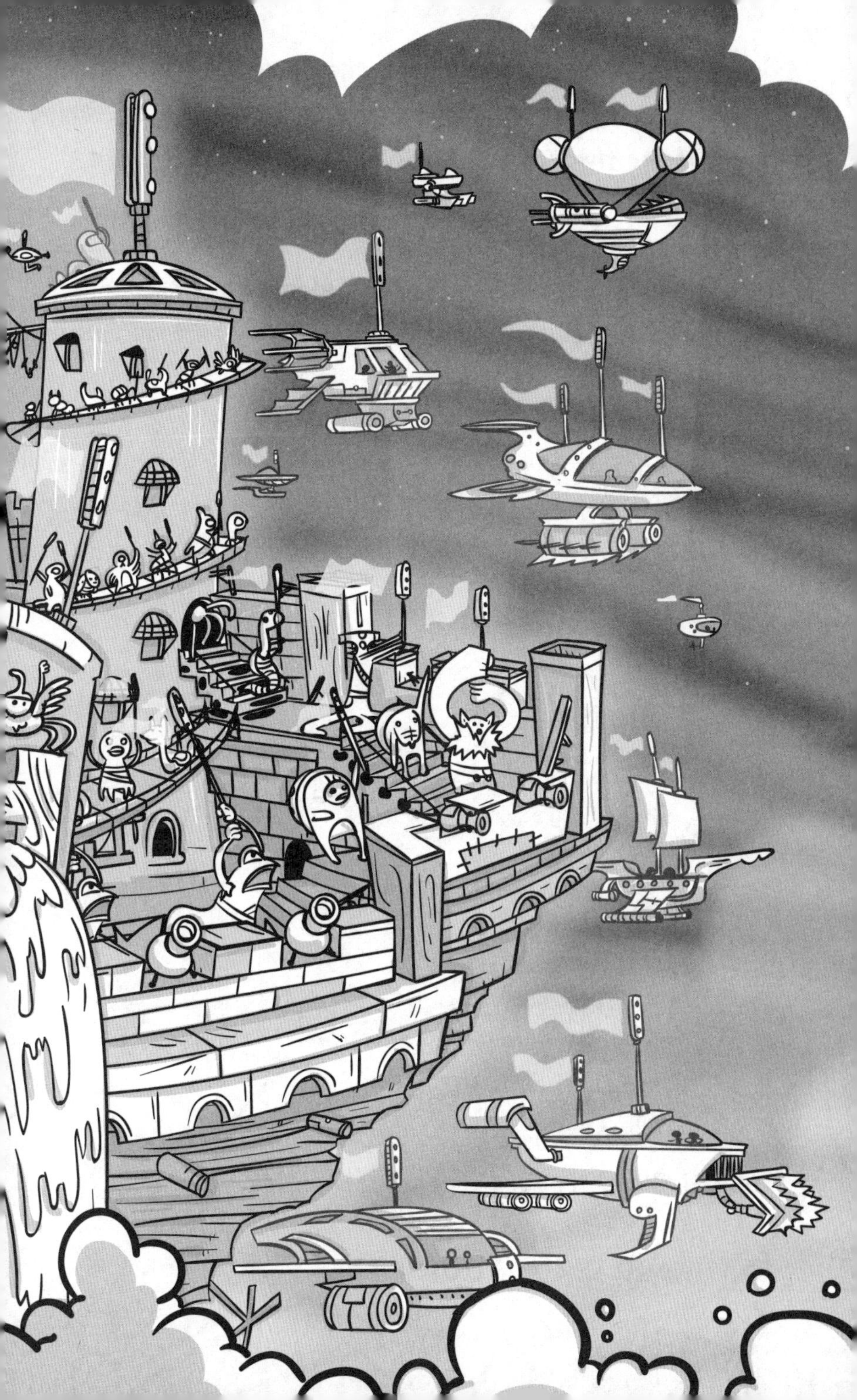

At the sight of the holo-banners, the planet-warship GD9 slows. The sound of the rear thrusters slowing is a deafening boom, cutting through space, ripping through the cove.

One large monitor sits atop the planet-warship. It flickers on, Krax appears, his face huge and hideously punchable on the screen. The familiar—that blasted, doofy bird—is perched on his shoulder.

Another round of gasps cut through the cove. If anyone still doubted that the Coresky King had returned, they doubt it no longer . . .

I SEE YOU HAVE WAVED THE WHITE. SMART. NOW, YOU NEED ONLY KNEEL, AND I MAY SPARE YOU. YOU CAN JOIN AND SERVE YOUR KING.

Rani holds the microphone. She flips a toggle, and there is sudden screeching feedback as she switches the frequency. Her voice now reaches out into space.

"Lower your cannons, General Krax!" Rani barks. "And THEN we will kneel."

I glance at Humphree. A pit forms in my stomach. Not sure if it's fear or anxiousness. Every pirate here is about to fight for their life—and not just for their life, but their WAY OF LIFE.

But me? I care most about getting my friend Goober back.

Krax, on the monitor, roars, "I could devour you!"

"Maybe so," Rani calmly replies. "But still—with your cannons aimed, we will not kneel. It is up to you. Do you want an army of pirates at your service? Or do you prefer to rule over NOTHING?"

Krax thinks this over. Ridiculously unaware, he even chomps at a fingernail—then remembers he's being watched, and snaps back, trying to look authoritative and threatening.

After a moment, he nods. We hear a series of thunderous clicks as the thousands of cannons that protrude from the side of GD9 are pulled back within its walls.

"And now you kneel!" Krax roars.

Rani grins and tosses me the microphone. "Cosmoe, Humphree, Dagger—you got us this far ..."

I grip the microphone, and I shout at the top of my lungs ...

In a sudden instant, every single white holo-banner is turned back around. A hundred ships now fly a hundred different banners.

There are two distinct **BOOMS.** The first, every single pirate ship surrounding the cove opening fire. The second, the cove's thousands of energy cannons, perched along the outer ring firing. A haze of blue steam fills the air.

The battle has begun ...

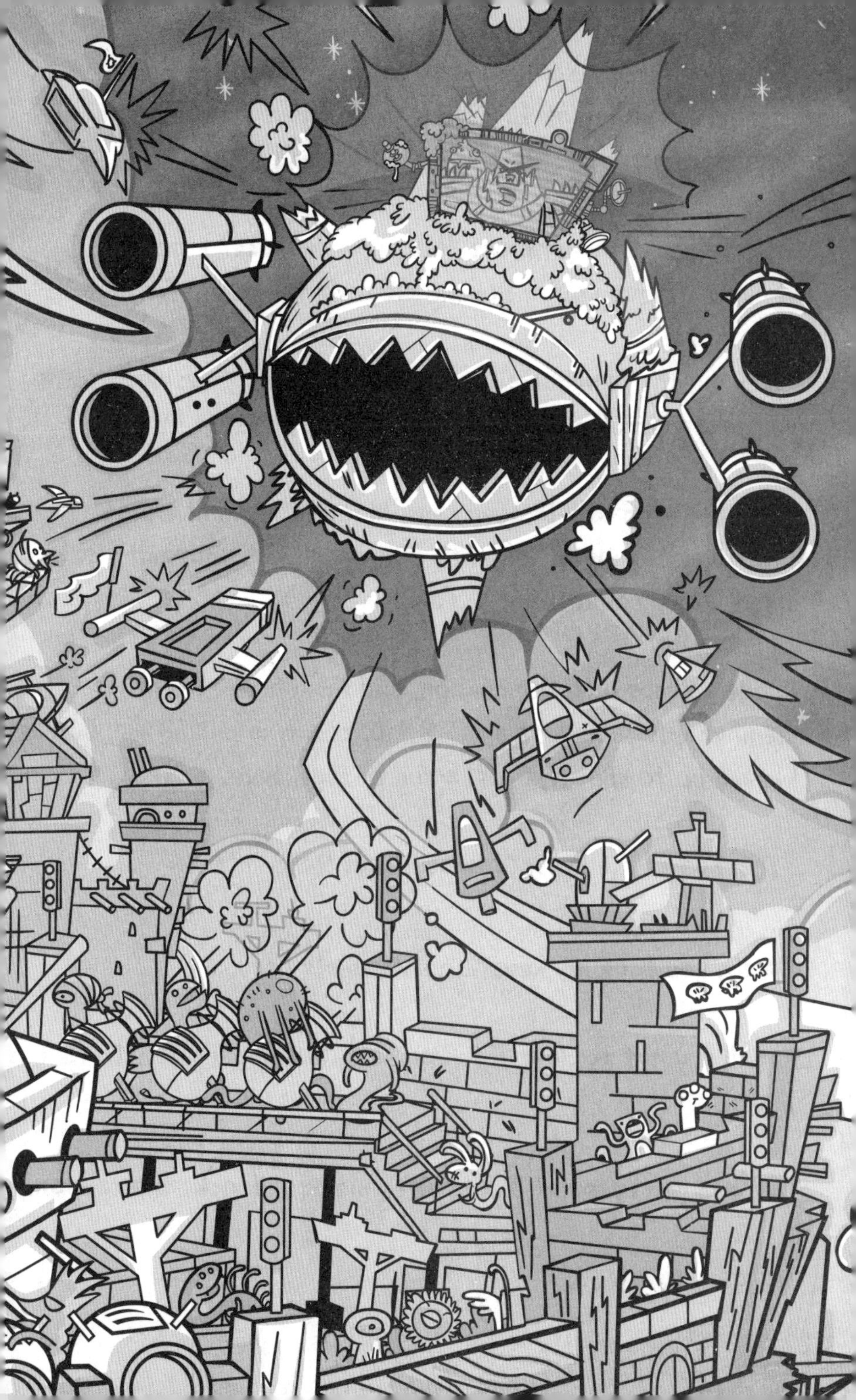

"Come on!" I say, screaming to be heard over the next thunderous volley of fire. "It's time for us to do this thing. And hopefully, it won't be the LAST thing we do..."

Despite the circumstances, Humphree manages a groan. "I can't believe you're making me walk the plank, Cosmoe..."

"Walking the plank was your idea!" I exclaim. "Besides, this is just like a circus stunt—and we're used to those by now."

"Hey, I'm excited!" Dagger says. "I love this plan! We get to climb inside cannons! It's silly and dangerous and might get us killed! What could be more fun?"

Dagger climbs into her cannon, and Humphree into his. I clamber into mine last and F.R.E.D. zooms in behind me. But as I reach up to shut it, I feel a tug at my sleeve.

"Thanks for the keys, Cosmoe," says Rani.

"Wait, you took my keys? The *Wiener!*" I say.

"I will try not to dent it," Rani says, flashing a grin. "I promise."

Before I can respond, Rani stuffs me in and locks the cannon.

No leaving now ...

I'm curled up in a small ball inside the cannon's cold iron barrel. F.R.E.D. bobs beside me.

Outside, the attack rages. Over the booming, earsplitting sounds of battle I hear General Krax. His voice is a dim muted echo, but the words are clear enough:

"OPEN THE MOUTH! DEVOUR THE COVE! EAT EVERY LAST PIRATE AND EVERY LAST SHIP!"

Rani ignites our three cannons. Warmth fills the cannon tube, radiating. Energy sizzles and crackles.

An energy cannonball is forming: a strange, Jell-O—like substance, taking shape around me. It's like being in a small, warm bubble.

The cannon begins to vibrate. My stomach is tight with anticipation—it's like that feeling you get as the roller coaster clank, clank, clanks its way up toward the first big drop, and you know any moment you're about to go over, and you don't have a lick of control over it . . .

And then, at last—after what feels like an eternity but is really only moments . . .

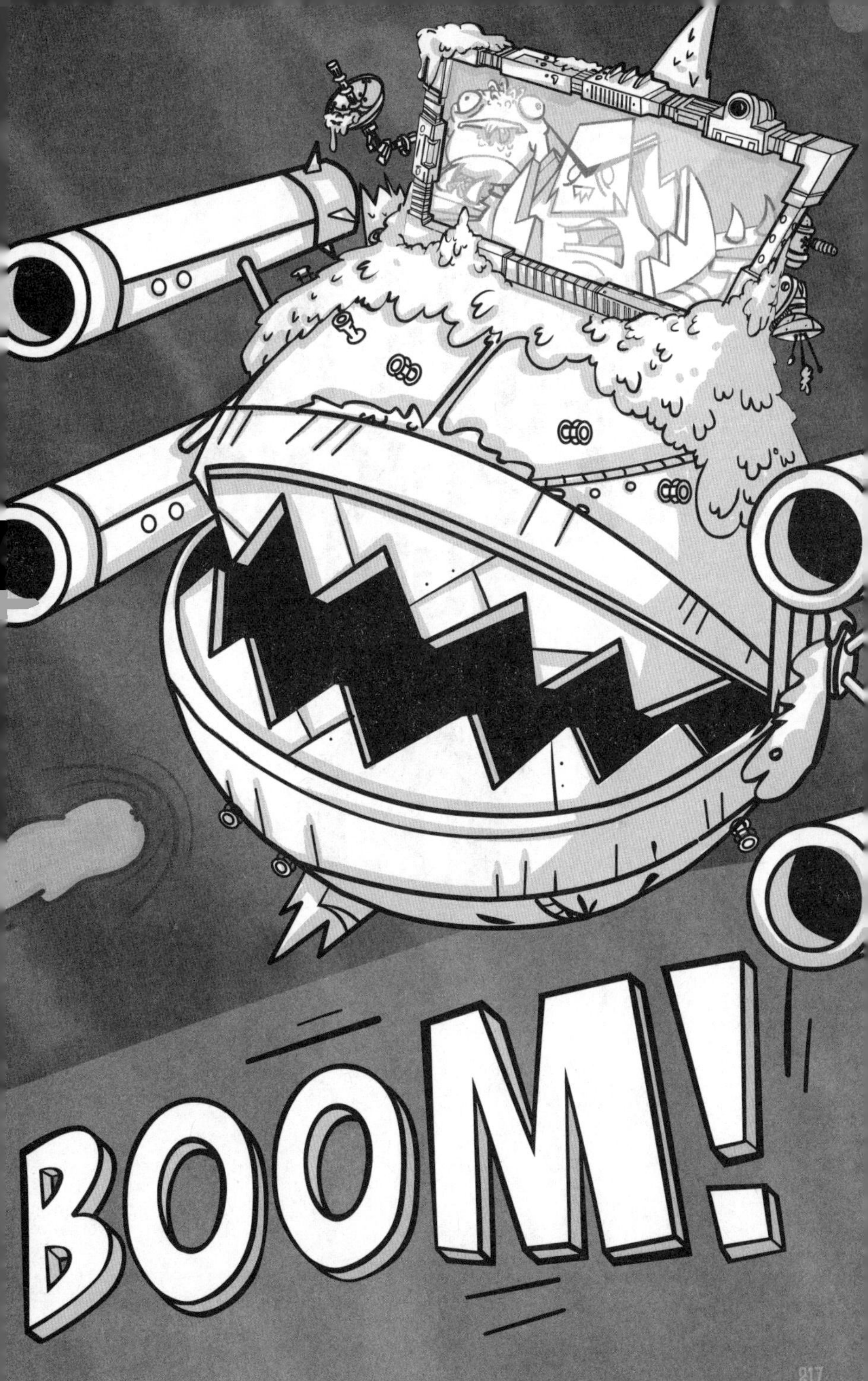
BOOM!

HURL! BUT NOT LIKE A PUKING HURL!

19

I'm **EXPLODED** out of the cannon! Cradled in this tiny, tight ball of energy, I'm soaring through space.

It's a Tilt-A-Whirl on hyperdrive—my stomach flipping, my head spinning, my entire body tumbling and revolving as the cannonball soars toward GD9.

I'm close to barfing inside this thing, which would just be splatterific and extra messy, when—

SMASH!

Seconds after **RIPPING THROUGH THE OUTER WALL OF THE PLANET-WARSHIP,** the energy ball evaporates and I flop onto the floor. Behind me is a sparking, smoking hole.

My ears are still ringing from the cannon blast that brought us here. As the ringing fades, I hear another sound—an alarm, sounding throughout GD9. We've got Krax's attention.

I get to my feet, then immediately fall back onto my butt. I stand again, try to walk, but I'm instead zigzagging this way and that.

"Humphree!" I manage to shout. "Dagger!"

My heart pounds. If those cannons weren't aimed perfectly and properly, my friends will still be spiraling through space— and they won't stop until, well, ever . . .

Apparently they don't get dizzy. Curse their fancy alien inner ear drums. But whatever, 'cause ... "It worked!" I exclaim, rushing forward and bumping fists with my buds.

Glancing around, finally able to see straight, I take stock of our surroundings. We are in a long, curving corridor. The wall is smooth but rough, built from cubes of tightly compacted garbage. The stink of trash isn't as strong here on the outer levels of the ship, near the surface.

The pirate armada continues to pound GD9 with energy cannonballs. The walls are turning to Swiss cheese—but still, GD9 is so **BIG**, the assault is little more than a distraction. A distraction allowing us to get back Goober ...

F.R.E.D. beeps on, informing us he's found the planet's main energy source. "That'll be Goober," I say. "Let's go!"

We charge through the wide halls, moving quickly but cautiously. Rumblers patrol the ship. We catch glimpses of them hurrying back and forth, responding to alarms. Every few moments another energy cannonball blasts through the side of the planet-ship.

"If I get hit by one of those," Humphree grumbles, "I'm gonna find out exactly who fired it and hurl them from the cove."

"Shh," Dagger says, peeking around the corridor wall. "Three Rumblers ahead. I'll handle this ..."

Dagger flashes a confidently evil grin, then strolls around the corner, softly whistling the Dagger family tune. Her twin flash blasters—Fire and Ice—are crisscrossed behind her waist. "Hey, trash robos!" she calls out.

I watch the trio of Rumblers wheel around, raising junk cannons. Dagger holds up a hand. "Whoa, guys. It's cool. I'm Princess Dagger! I'm totally team evil, like you guys."

Confusion flashes across their robotic faces. "You are?" one asks. "PROVE IT."

"Sure," she says, with a shrug. And then ...

"Whoa, Dags," I say. "That was some Clint Eastwood stuff."

"I don't know what that means, Cosmoe," she says. "But I'll take it as a compliment! I AM EASTWOOD!"

"C'mon," I say as we begin racing through the ship. But suddenly, I skid to a stop—I catch a sound: the screaming of an energy cannonball.

"Down!" I shout, and— KRASH!

WHOA . . .

The cannonball rips through the wall and over our heads. Close call. I steal a glance through the smoking hole.

A massive space battle is underway.

Pirate ships weave and dodge as this planet-warship
continues its cannon assault. One is hit by a junk blast, but
manages to steer itself to a rough landing on the cove.

One ship is quicker than the rest: the *Neon Wiener*. I still
can't believe Rani took my keys! The ship swoops and dives,
dodging fire, barely avoiding a cannonball to the gut.

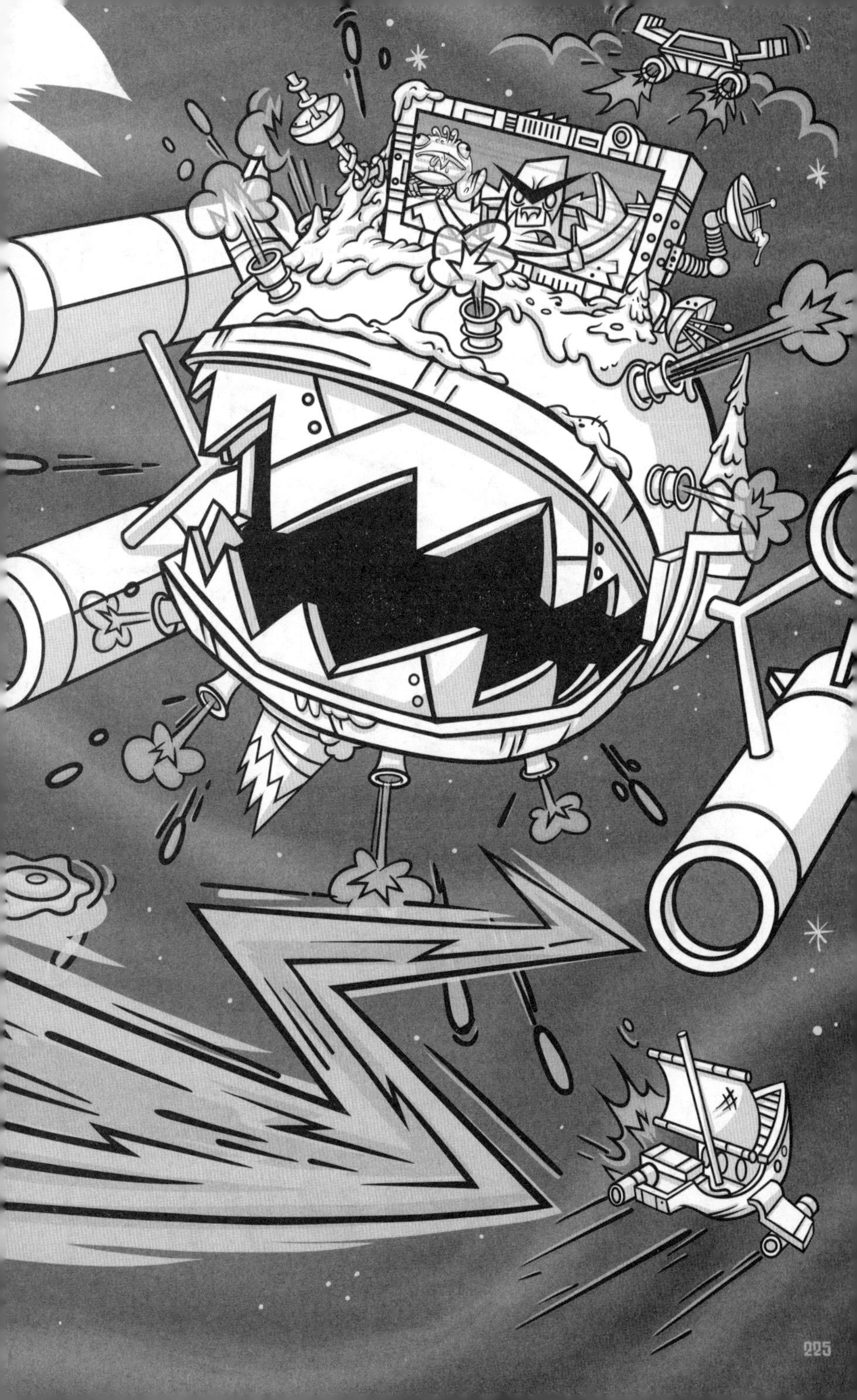

My stomach flips, and I feel the entire planet-ship LURCH. There's a deafening metallic screech and the floors and walls shudder violently.

F.R.E.D. spins, flashing on—showing us Rani behind the wheel of the *Neon Wiener.*

I'M GUESSING *YOU* GUYS FELT THAT. THE MOUTH IS NEARLY OPEN, COSMOE! WE CAN'T LAST MUCH LONGER. **HURRY!**

"We're close!" I shout as we speed ahead.

Around the next corner, I spot a large, spiralizing door. I can sort of SENSE Goober just beyond it. There's something in my symbiotic gut, telling me we're close.

But we're not in the clear yet ... Rumblers.

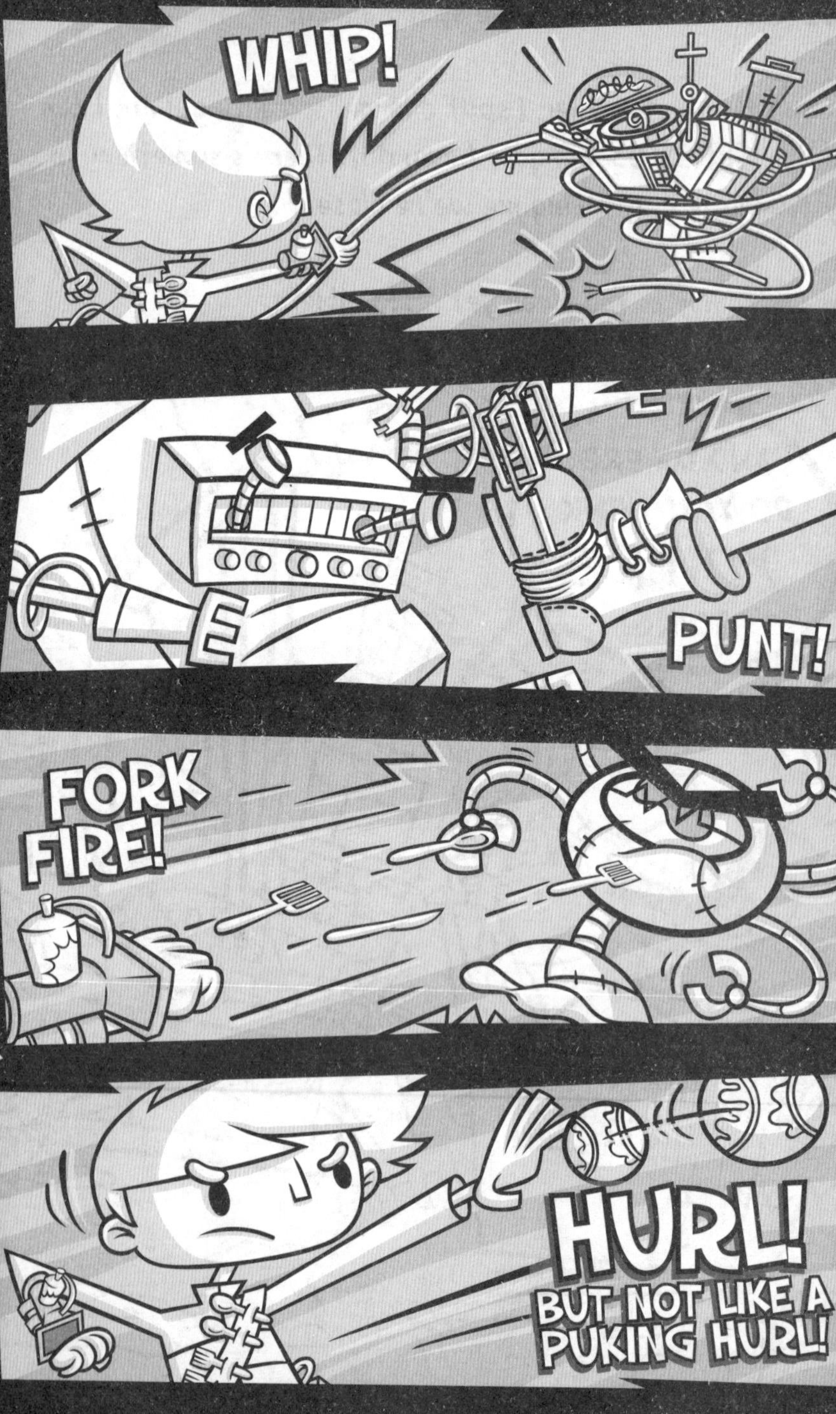
WHIP!
PUNT!
FORK FIRE!
HURL!
BUT NOT LIKE A PUKING HURL!

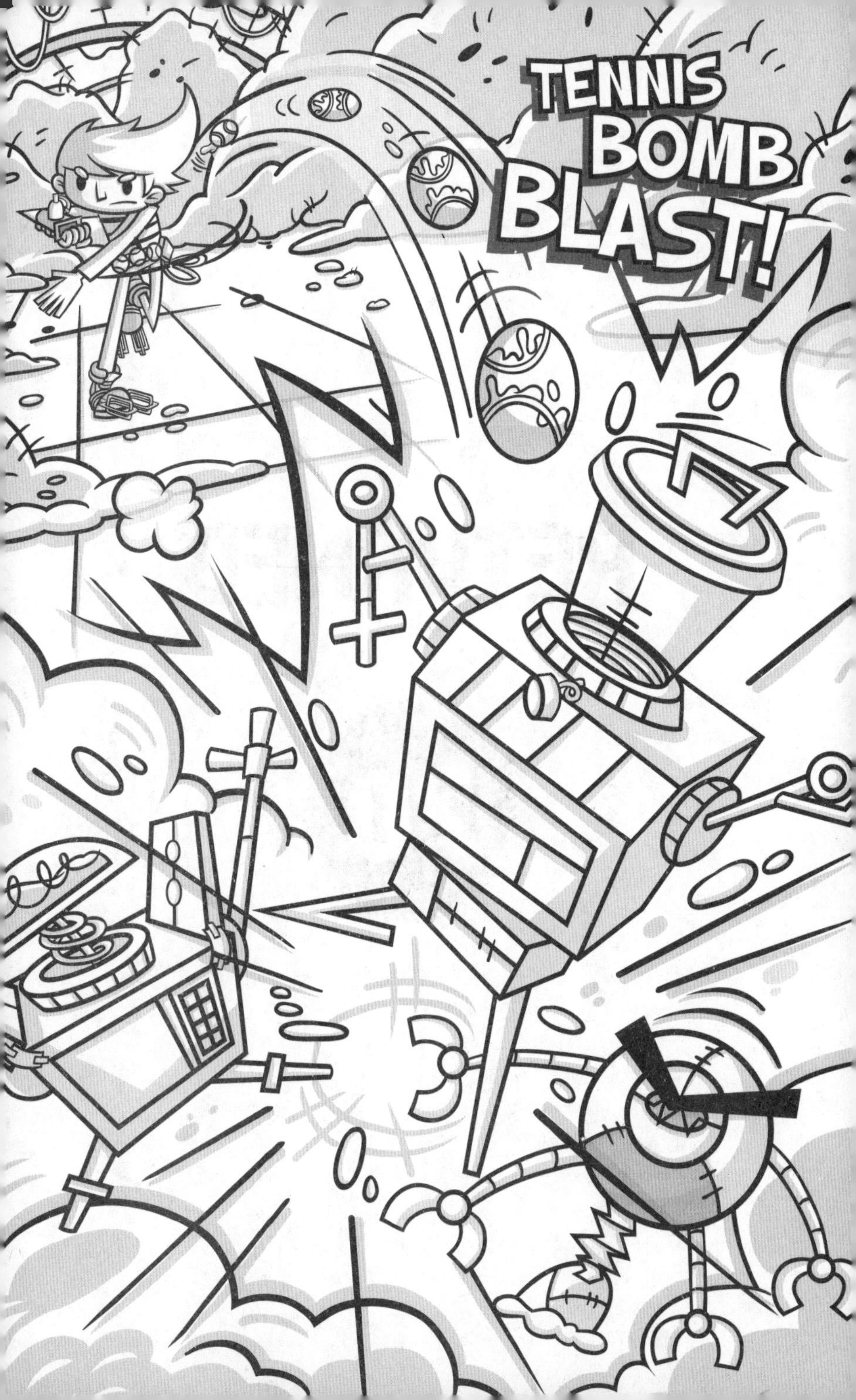
TENNIS
BOMB
BLAST!

RETURNED

I flash Humphree a proud grin. "I call those my Cosmoe powers," I say.

A massive door looms beyond the pile of sparking, sizzling bots. F.R.E.D. zooms toward it. There is a sudden flash of light as he scans the door, and then his hands begin working—small bursts of electricity zapping the door.

Beyond that door is Goober. Beyond that door is the ship's main energy chamber. Beyond that door is our only hope of stopping Krax the Coresky King and saving Pirates Cove . . .

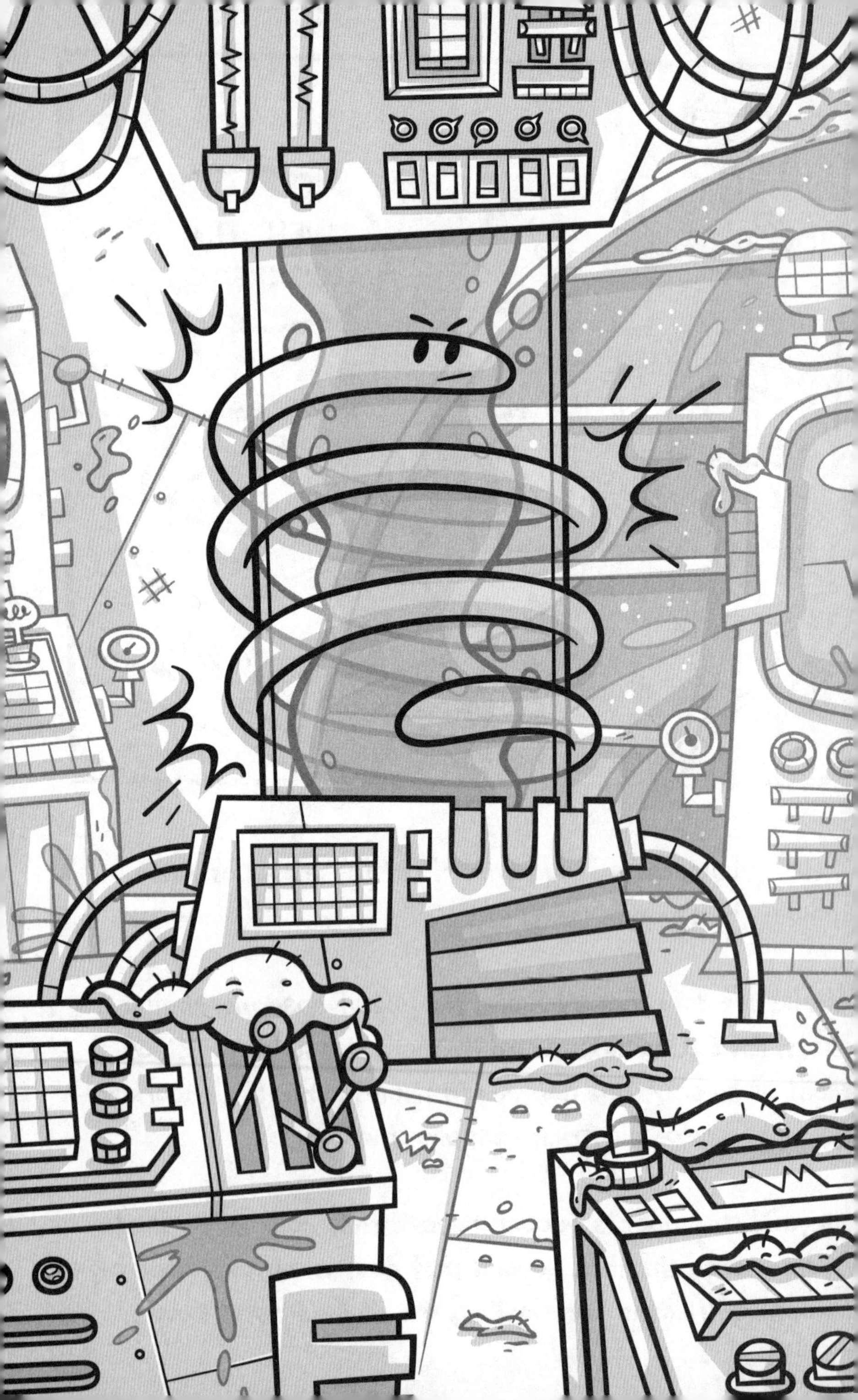

I see my friend. Goober is twisted and coiled around the main reactor ...

I gulp. "He's connected to the planet-warship's main energy reactor. He's **POWERING** the entire ship. And the ship, in turn, is **POWERING** him. It's an endless energy loop."

Suddenly, F.R.E.D. zooms forward as Rani buzzes in—a loud, frightening crackle. **"COSMOE, THERE'S NO MORE TIME!"**

I whirl, looking out a titanic-sized window that overlooks the battle and the cove. Pressing my face to the glass, I can just make out the planet-warship's massive mouth and the junk-built fangs.

Squinting, staring out across open space, I see pirates running for cover. Huge, towering pirates scoop up the younger ones, shielding them.

Other pirates still work the defenses, steadily firing a barrage of cannonballs. Ships continue their futile assault, swooping and diving—but the pirate fleet is being picked apart by GD9's junk cannons.

GD9 continues forward. In moments, the cove will be devoured. Eaten. Chomped in two ...

I feel sick to my stomach. The pirates are doing everything they can, but it's futile. It's MADNESS. They're buying us time—but nothing more.

To win this battle, I need to stop the planet-warship GD9—and that means removing Goober. But how?

Goober encircles the massive, main energy reactor. I could simply reach out and grab him, but there are, roughly, at least 37 gazillion bolts of energy pumping through him.

"There has to be some way to shut off the power so we can remove Goober," Humphree says.

I shake my head. My stomach is heavy. "I don't think so, Humps. Goober feeds the reactor, and the reactor feeds Goober. We can't shut off the reactor without removing Goober. And we can't remove Goober without shutting off the reactor."

Another shuddering shake. Any moment now, Pirates Cove will be done.

I step close to Goober. I look at him. Look at MY FRIEND. I remember that moment, years earlier, when I first reached out to touch him.

And I remember how that changed everything. Can I . . . Can I change everything again?

I don't touch him. I hold my hand just inches away from the reactor. And ever so slightly, he trembles...

"Come on, Goober," I say. "Come to me."

His rubbery, gooey body shivers.

"Buddy, I know this isn't how it usually works. I know that you belong to Krax now. But we're FRIENDS. Come on. Come here..."

The planet-ship rocks. The floor quakes.

"Any moment now," Humphree says. "The planet will chomp into Pirates Cove."

I try not to listen. I need to focus on Goober. I need to focus on getting him to come to me.

But that's about to become very hard to do . . .

"Cosmoe?" Dagger says. "If it doesn't work—what do we do?"

I whirl around. There is the **KLANG** of a door opening, and heavy, metallic footsteps as Krax enters.

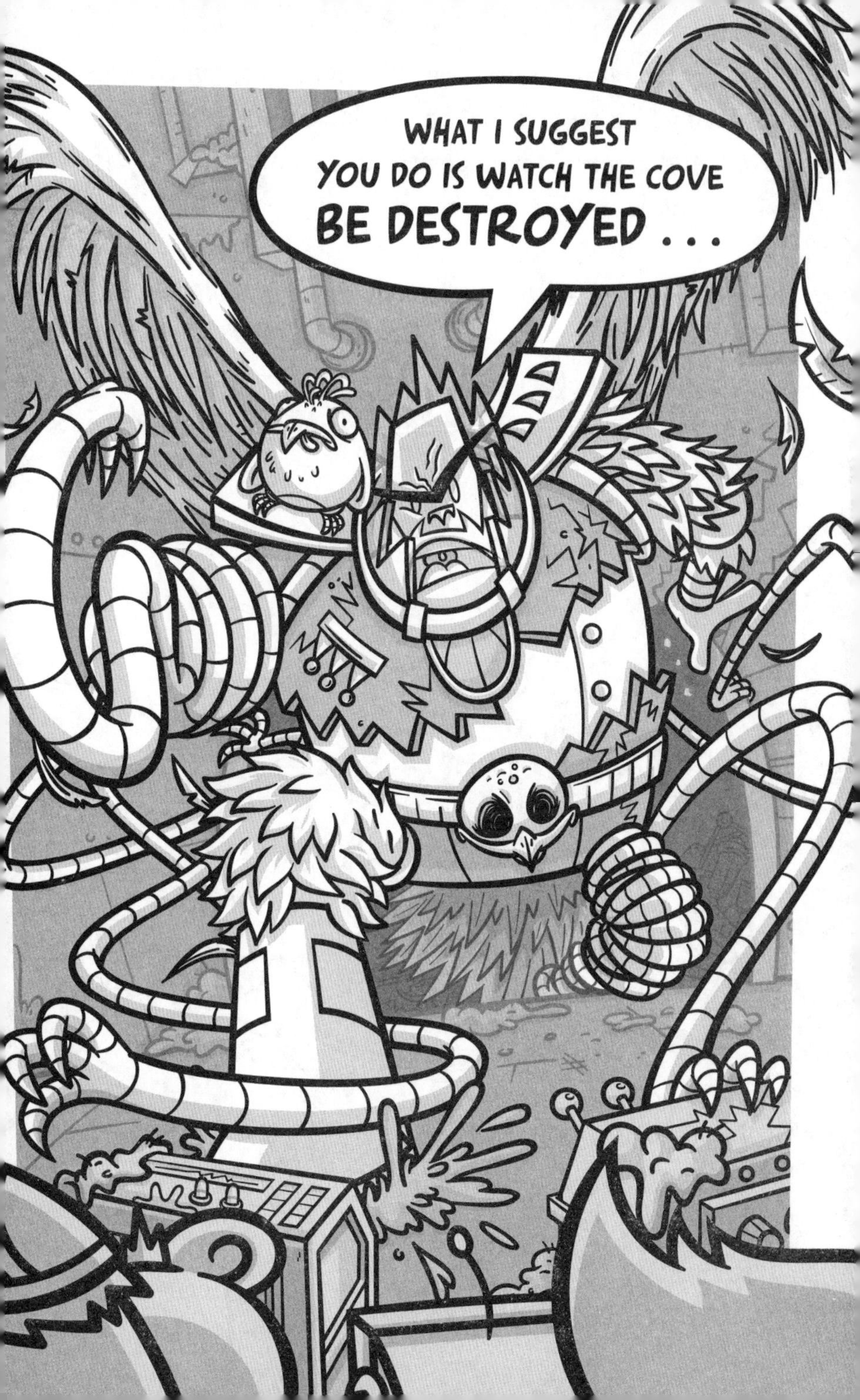
WHAT I SUGGEST
YOU DO IS WATCH THE COVE
BE DESTROYED . . .

"You are too late," Krax says. "In moments, the cove will be devoured. The pirates will be swallowed. My power will grow. And any remaining pirates will pledge their loyalty to me—or die."

He giggles. "I mean, am I villainous or what, huh?"

Krax's mouth, a cruel smile at first, turns into a wide, fanged thing. The familiar, perched on his shoulder, hops from foot to foot.

Krax sees me eyeing the bird. He taps the thing, and it hops around his back—keeping any of us from getting to it. The familiar's power cannot be understated.

"Guys," I say softly to Humphree and Dagger. "I need more time. I'm CLOSE."

Humphree rolls up his sleeves. "We'll hold him off."

"Hold 'em off?!" Dagger says. "Forget that. It's clobberin' time!" Combat comes hard and quick and fast. I try to tune the sounds out. It is a final knock-down, drag-out fight with General Krax. Furious, fist-flying action . . .

"Goober," I whisper. "Ignore all that. And come to me. Because if you don't—everyone on Pirates Cove will be destroyed . . ."

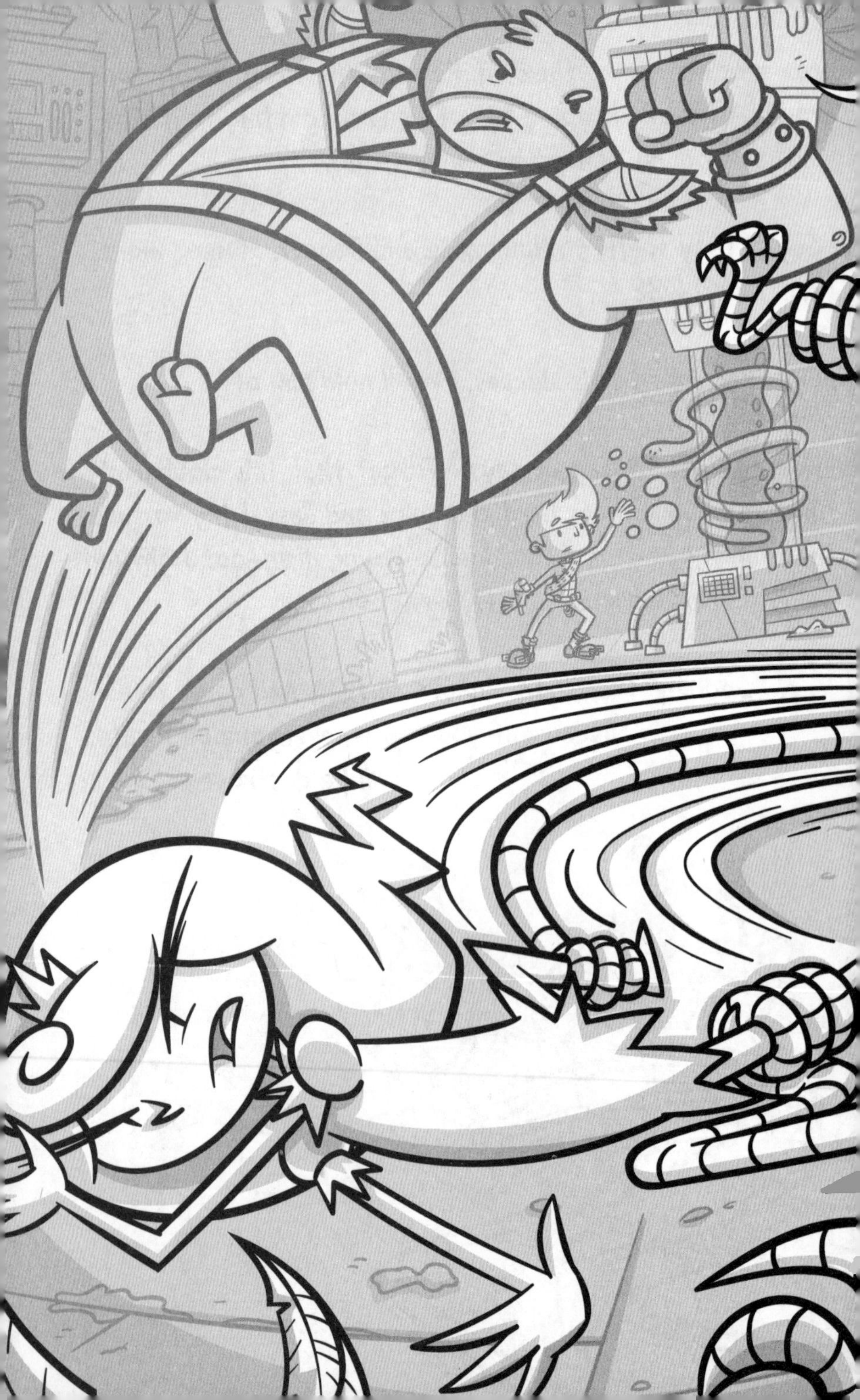

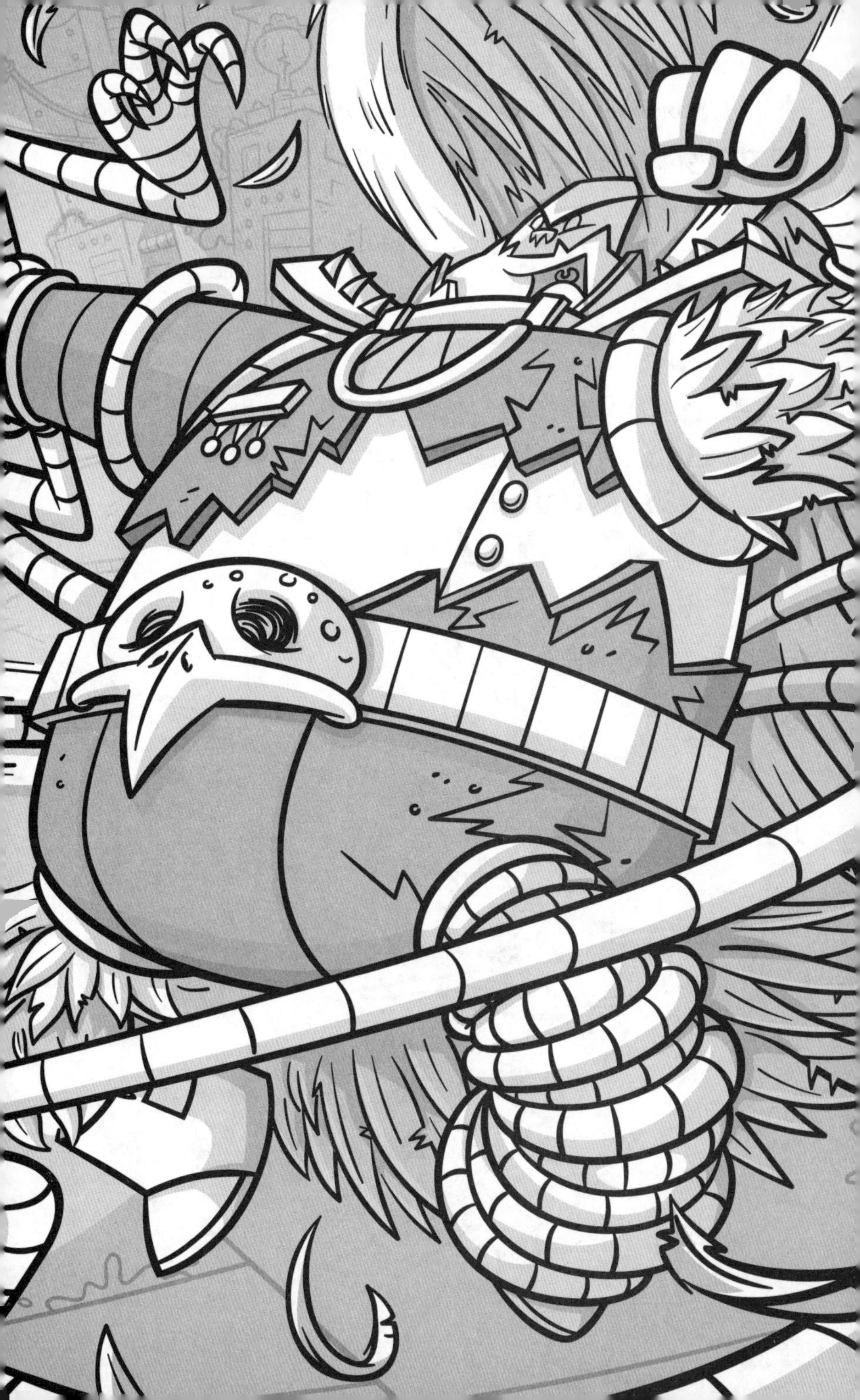

The sounds of battle outside are deafening. The sounds of fists hitting flesh inside are frightening. They cause Goober to tremble, recoil, and hug the energy rod tighter.

"Goober, just pay attention to me," I say softly. "Don't pay any attention to—"

I tune out Dagger.

I focus.

I feel my symbiotic buddy.

I feel the pain from when he was separated—from when he was removed. My eyes close.

And finally ...

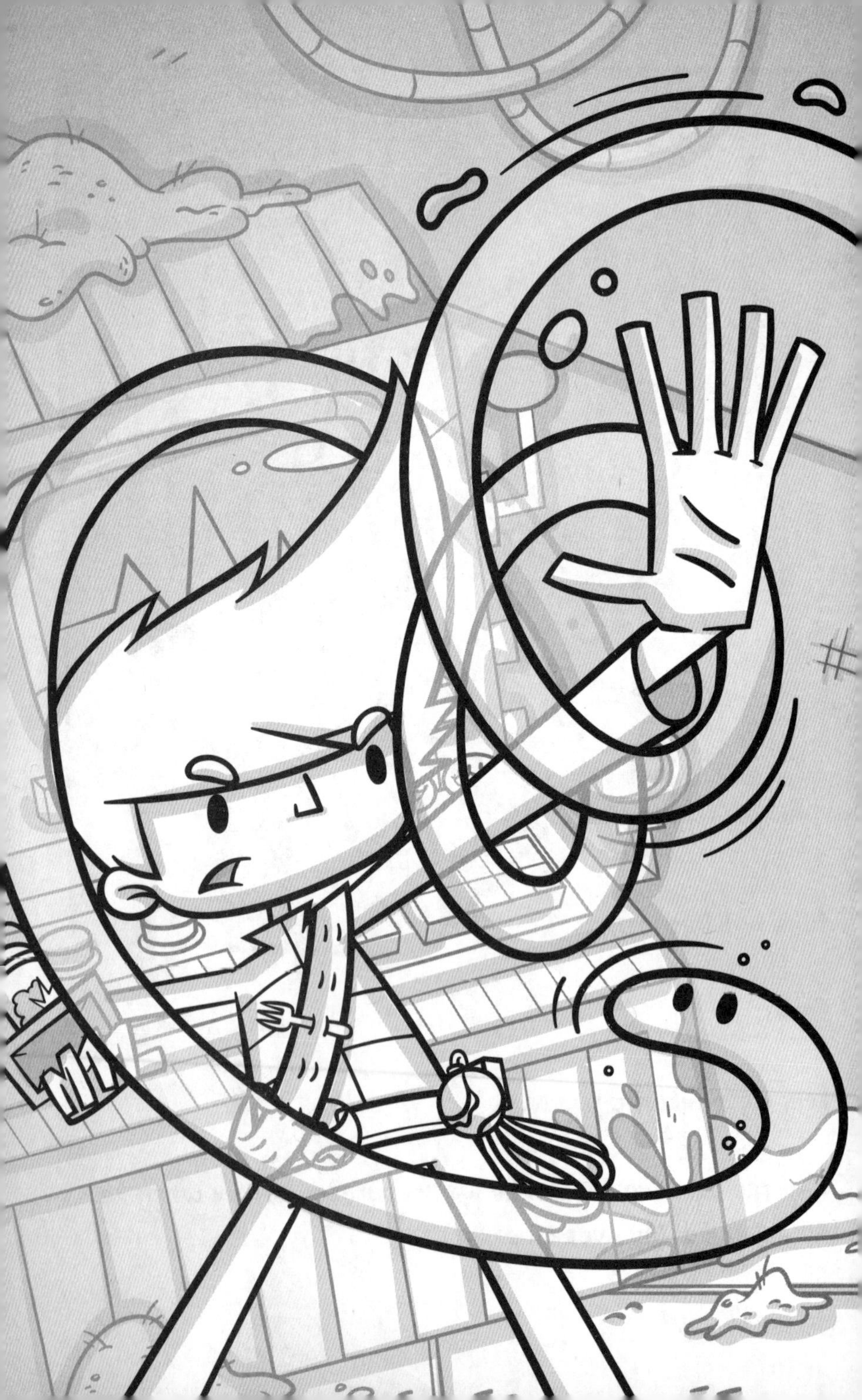

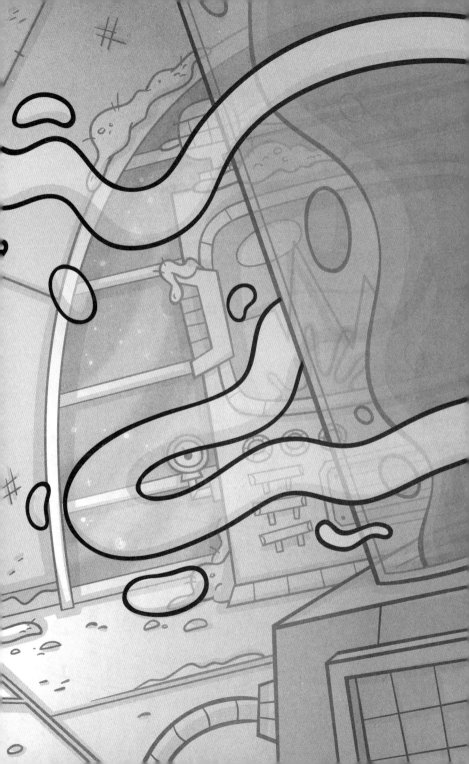

Goober is there. Attached. BACK. **RETURNED.**

I feel whole again. And at the moment he separates from the energy rod, the power dims. Flashes. And then goes out.

There's a deafening screech as the massive, monstrous mouth of GD9—only moments from devouring Pirates Cove—is halted.

We have **STOPPED** it. Entirely, completely.

I can hear what's happening outside, far below, on Pirates Cove ...

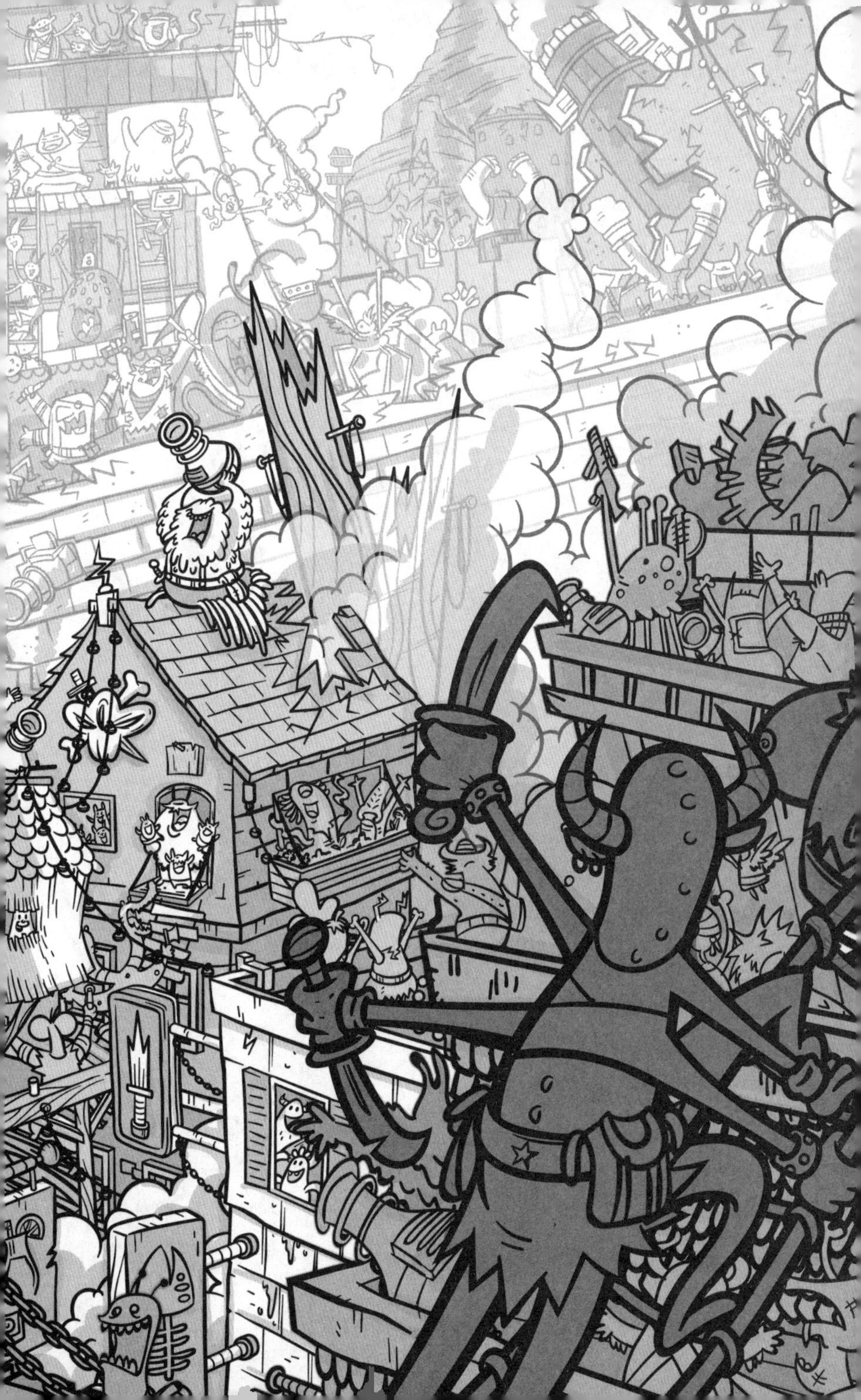

Unfortunately, our triumphant moment lasts for—well—only a moment.

I see Dagger and Humphree on top of Krax, covering him. Pounding. Trying to subdue the villain.

But then Krax roars, super-powered, and—

Krax's face is a cruel smirk. "You have not defeated me."

He raises the electro-zap bat. He points it toward me. I glance at my friends. They both lie on the ground, rising slowly.

Too slowly . . .

And then—

MIGHTY MEGATON ZAP!

BZZZZT!

ENERGY ASSAULT!

PAIN. SO. MUCH. PAIN.

Energy rushes through me, mixing with electric agony, like I'm suddenly being pounded by a billion bolts of lightning.

My mouth snaps open, my lungs eager to scream, but I cannot...

My legs are weak. I would collapse, but the hard, pumping, streaming energy is keeping my knees locked in place. Stiff and tight.

The lights in the room flash. Goober shakes. EVERYTHING shakes.

I manage to turn my head. Through the blinding, white-hot pain, I see Krax. I see fury on his face.

The generator—what little energy in it remains—sparks and sizzles. Energy rushes from it, filling the room. Filling the walls, the floors, filling everything.

The room trembles.

Everything is shaking, quaking, building to a furious crescendo.

I turn to Humphree and Dagger.

GUYS, BRACE YOURSELVES . . .

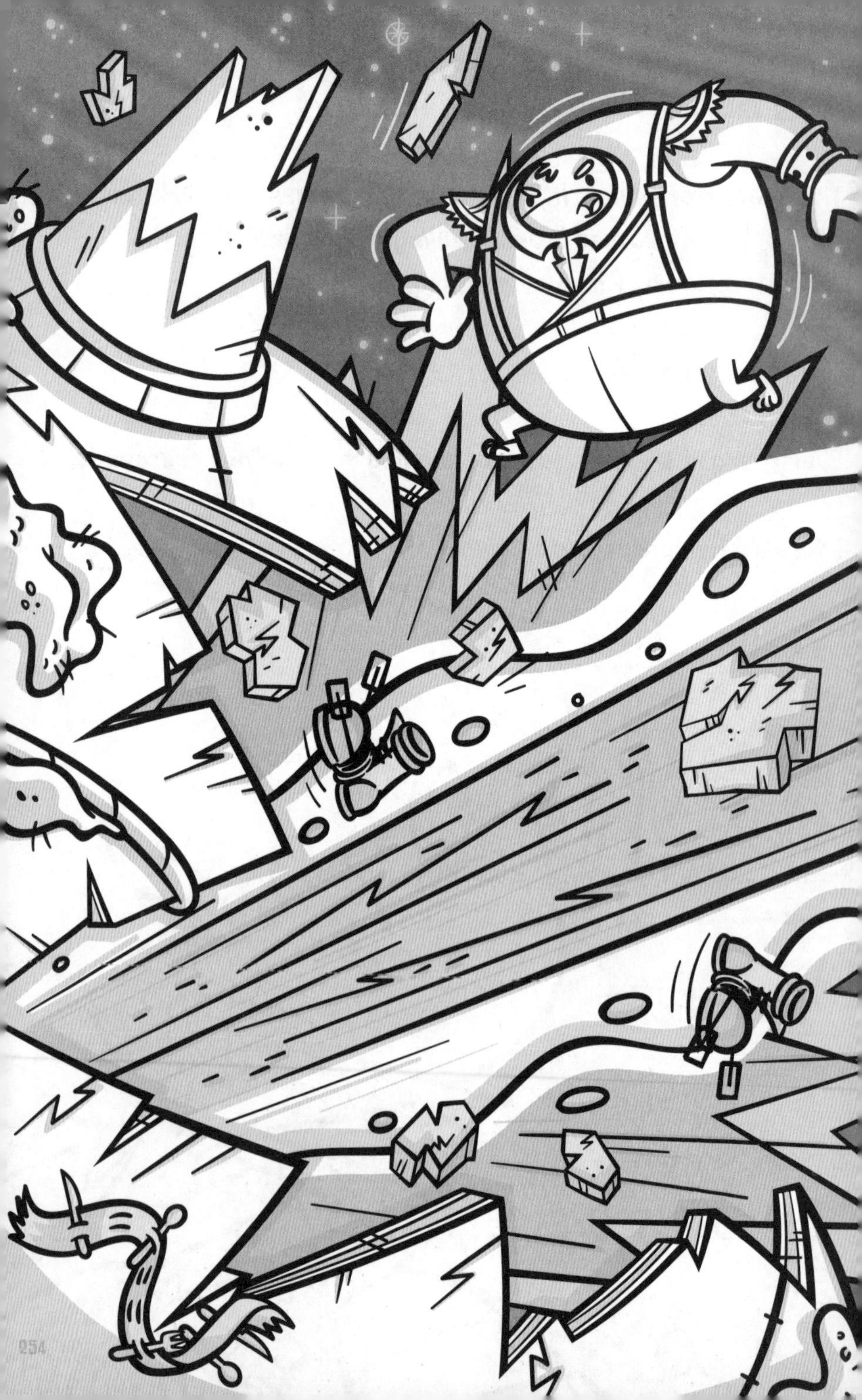

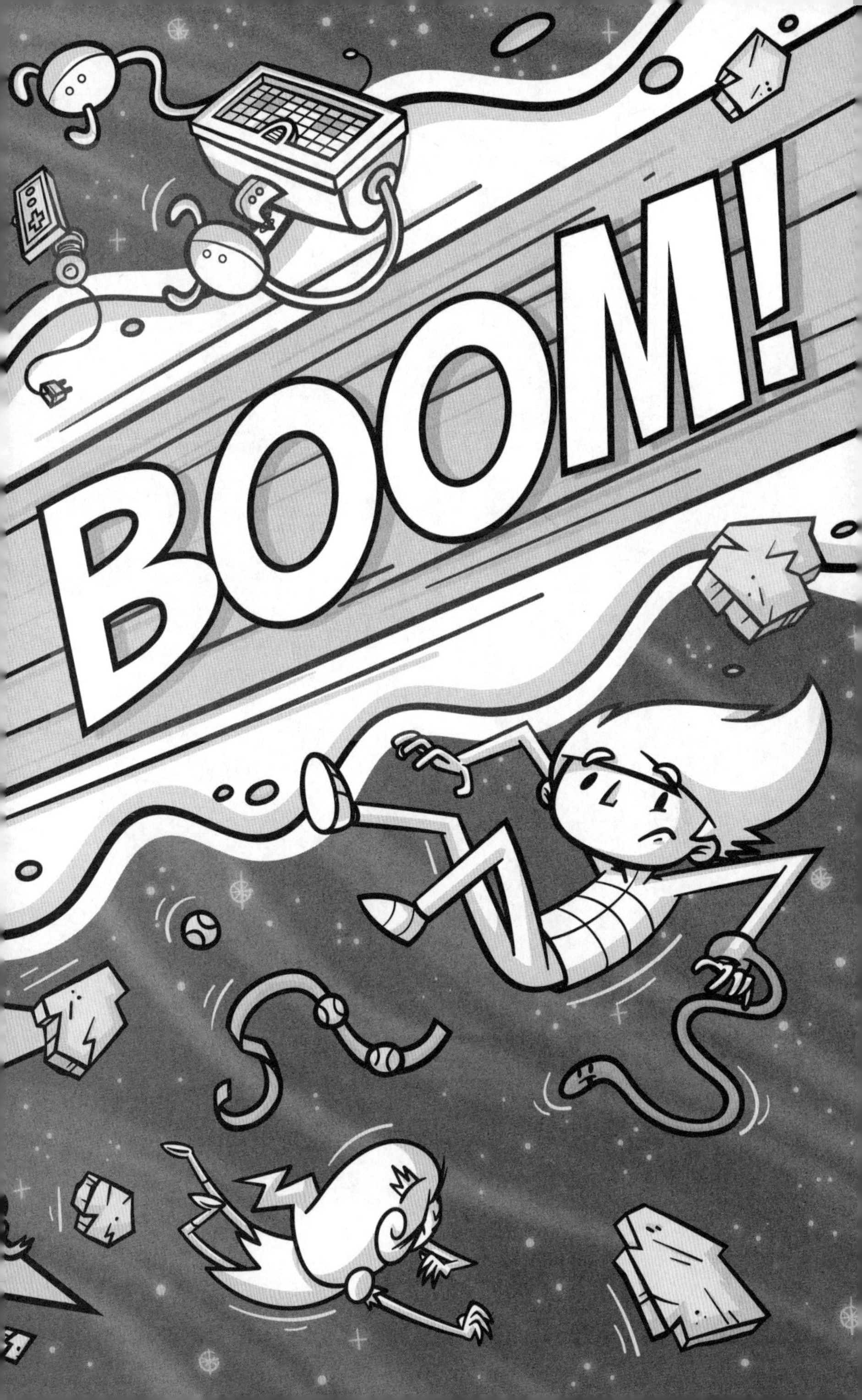
BOOM!

FINAL FORM!

21

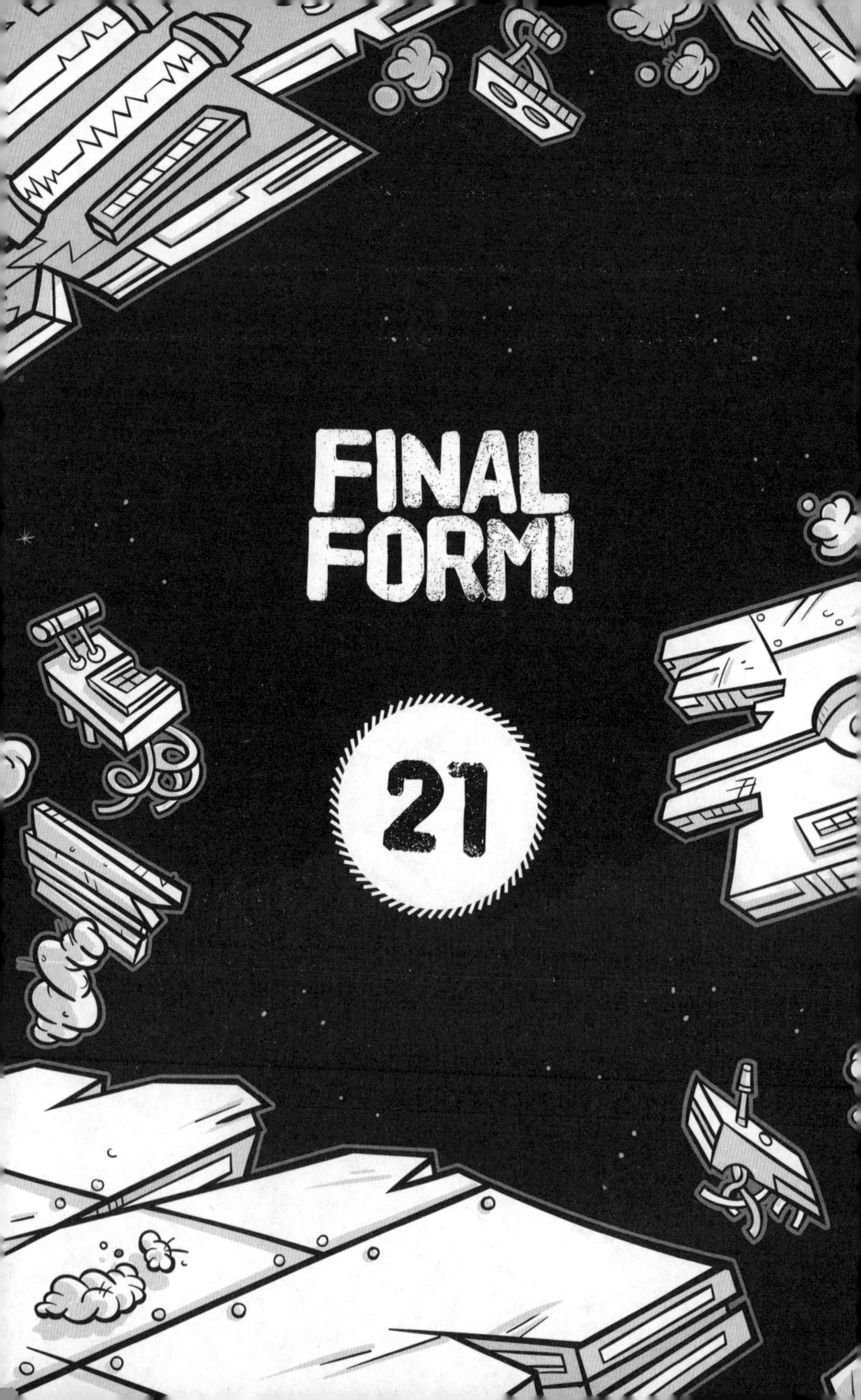

I am exploded from the ship. Hurled into space.
My body spirals and somersaults.

For a long moment, I see only white. Bright, bright white.
My eyes burn.

And then, for the briefest instant, I see things unfold . . .

I see my friends, tumbling through space . . .

I see the *Neon Wiener.* I see Rani, piloting it, speeding toward Humphree and Dagger.

I see the ship's rescue arm unfolding, and I see her saving them—pulling them inside.

I see white light, radiating everywhere. But my friends are safe.

Or are they? From the smoldering wreckage of GD9, I see something else.

A massive hand. Godzilla sized. Mutated and fiery. Reaching out, gripping the *Neon Wiener.* And suddenly, hurling it, off into the distance...

What **WAS** that?

Krax?

But Krax is not **THAT** powerful. Not that **LARGE.**

Unless the explosion ... the sudden burst of energy ... Could it have transformed his familiar? Transformed him? Given him more power than ever before?

A shattering sound comes from the smoking hole in the side of GD9. Something is emerging from the wreckage. Floating outward. Growing in size.

It's him ... in his ...

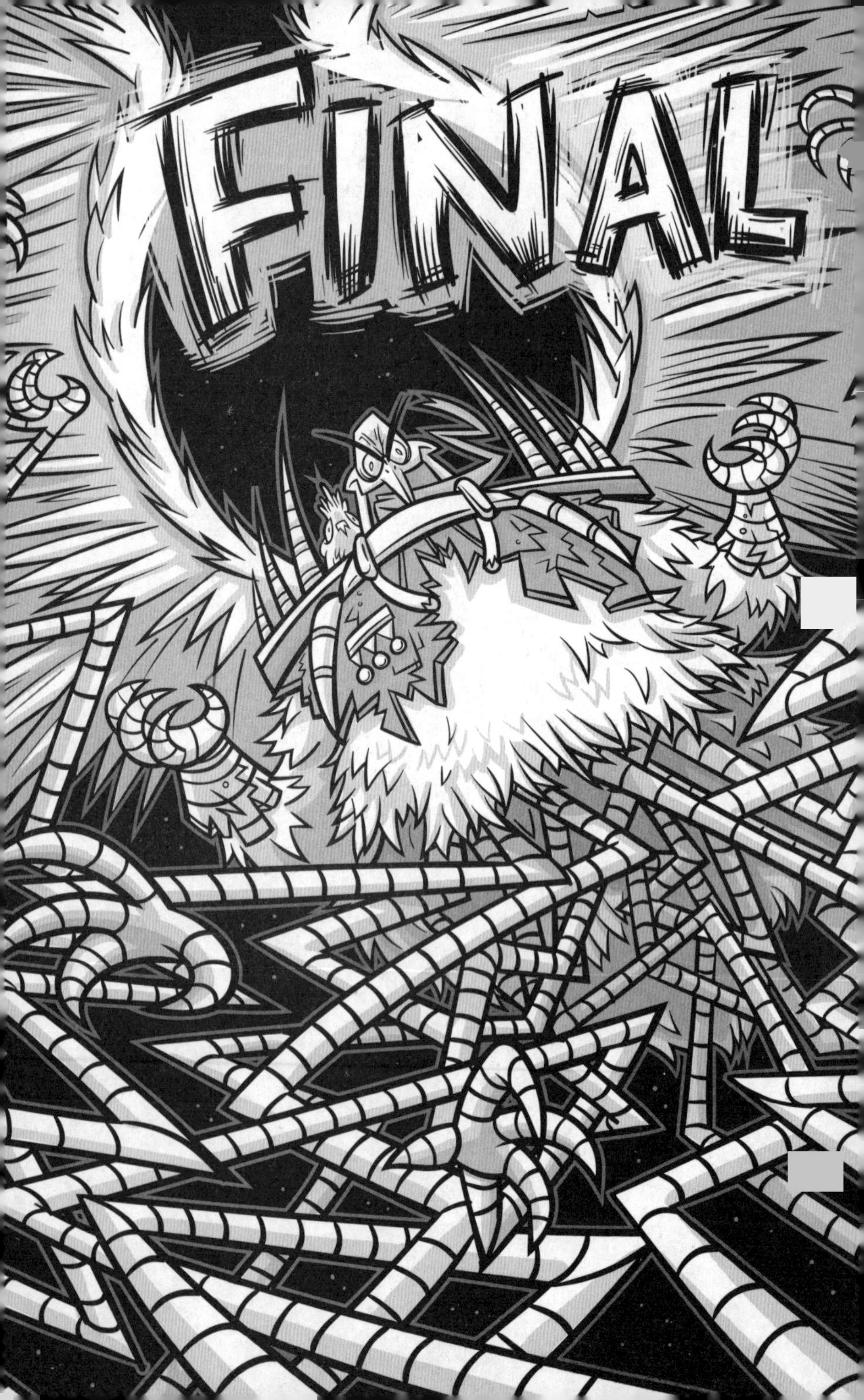
FINAL

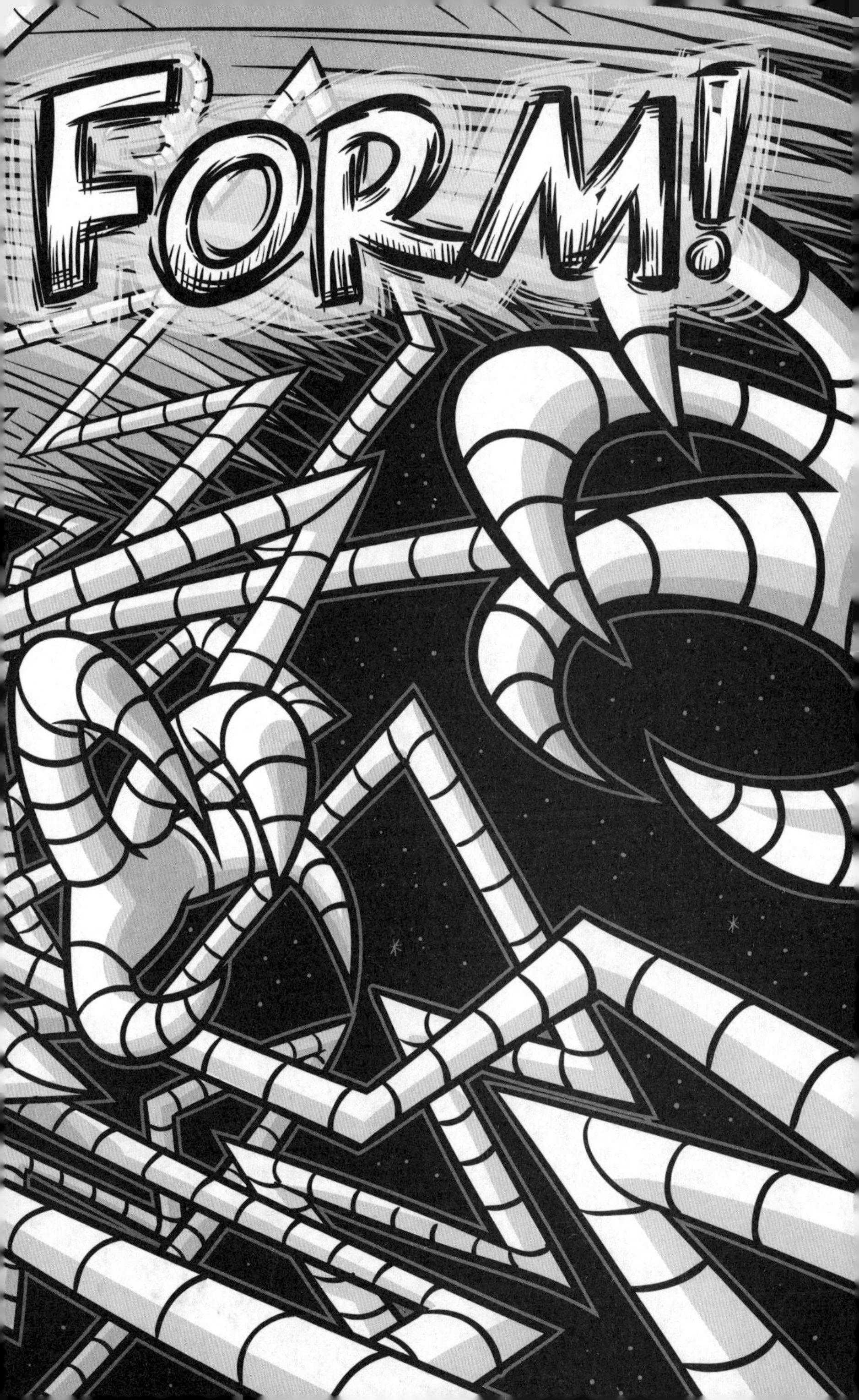
FORM!

Seeing that massive monster Krax, I gasp.

Wait.

No. I don't GASP.

I WANT to. I TRY to. But I can't. I open my mouth, but I get nothing. There's no air. Nothing to breathe. I'm a human being—and human beings can't breathe in space ...

PANIC! Panic like I've never felt before. My heart begins slamming in my chest, blood pumping like old-school Reeboks.

My chest is swelling. I try for breath. Wish for breath. Beg for breath. But none will come. I'm drowning in space. Not a fun way to go. But this might be the end of it all...

I'm floating, helpless, useless. The *Neon Wiener* and my friends have been hurled into the far reaches of space...

And what can I do?

Nothing?

I'm floating amid wreckage and rubble.

My eyes shut. Everything goes to black...

BECAUSE I'M COSMOE THE EARTH-BOY AND I'M A RADICAL GALACTIC HERO!

22

HELLO, COSMOE.

Who's that?

IT'S ME.

Who's me?

YOUR BUDDY! GOOBER!

Goober?

SURE!

Wait—what? You're talking? What is this? Some sort of dream?

I DON'T KNOW. YOU TELL ME.

How should I know?

I THINK YOU WOULD KNOW BETTER THAN ME!

But, Goober, you can't talk.

I GUESS I CAN.

Goober, I'm floating through space. Alone.

YOU'RE NOT ALONE. YOU HAVE ME!

Oh. Right. But, Goober—I'm cold. Like freezing.

IT'S COLD IN SPACE. DIDN'T YOU TAKE A SCIENCE CLASS WHEN YOU WERE A LITTLE KID?

Yes. But it's like really cold.

TRUE. I'M A LITTLE CHILLY MYSELF.

Goober, you're a weird rubbery blob. And I love you.

COSMOE, YOU'RE A WEIRD FLESHY HUMAN. AND I LOVE YOU!

Goober, I can't breathe in space.

I KNOW.

So what happens now?

I'M NOT SURE.

I didn't get to say good-bye to my friends. I didn't get to say good-bye to Humphree or Dagger or F.R.E.D. Good-byes are not fun.

NO, THEY AREN'T.

I never got to say good-bye to my parents. Just one day—
poof—gone.

I KNOW THAT.

You do?

**SURE. I WAS THERE, WHEN YOU WENT BACK
TO VISIT THE OLD CIRCUS TRAIN. AND I'M
HERE, ALWAYS, WITH YOU. IN YOUR HEAD.**

Well, it's not fair. Now I don't get to say good-bye again?
Now I'm the one who's just—poof—gone?

YEAH. IT STINKS.

It's getting colder out here, Goober. And darker. I didn't
know there was anything darker than black. But there is. It's
hard to describe. It's just like—black-black.

YEP. IT'S REALLY DARK.

You can see the darkness?

SURE!

Goober, what are you?

I DON'T KNOW. I WAS MADE IN A
LABORATORY, A LONG TIME AGO. BUT I'M
NOT THERE ANYMORE. NOW I'M HERE.
WITH YOU.

Okay.

REMEMBER, IN THE FIELD, ON EARTH—WHEN
YOU REACHED DOWN AND GRABBED ME?

Yes.

THAT WAS AWESOME.

You thought so?

YES.

Goober, it's even colder now and blacker now. I'm sleepy.

THAT'S OKAY.

Should I go to sleep?

THAT'S UP TO YOU.

If I go to sleep, what happens to you?

I'M NOT REALLY SURE. I WAS STILL MYSELF WHEN KRAX TOOK ME AWAY. BUT I DIDN'T LIKE MYSELF THEN. I LIKE MYSELF WHEN I'M ON YOUR WRIST.

Goober, you're weird.

I KNOW. SO ARE YOU.

I know. Goober?

YEAH?

I'm so tired and cold.

YOU CAN GO TO SLEEP IF YOU WANT.

I don't think I want to at all.

SO DON'T!

But I'm in space. And I can't breathe in space. And I can't move in space. And it's too cold in space for me.

LET ME SEE WHAT I CAN DO ABOUT THAT.

Sharp pain as I swallow. The final few ounces of air in my lungs are nearly gone...

But, despite the icy chill of space, I feel warmth! Warmth, on my arm! I look down. And through the darkness of space, I see light...

Goober—he's DIFFERENT. He's glowing neon blue and radiating heat.

My rubbery friend begins oozing up my arm, growing larger, changing, surrounding me, enveloping me. Over my mouth, my face—I'm able to see through the strange face, and his body becomes endlessly slithered, thin, so that I can see through it.

Without realizing it, I inhale. And—and—I breathe! Goober's symbiotic power has allowed me to breathe in space.

Goober wraps himself around me, again and again and again. It's like stuffing an entire packet of Big League Chew into your mouth, then wrapping it around your finger, over and over and over ...

He's not just protecting me—he's turning himself into full-on rubber armor—a GOOBER SUIT ...

"Thanks, Goober," I say.

But he doesn't respond. He doesn't speak now. I don't hear him anymore.

Rolling, tumbling in space, my body revolves—and I see Krax. GIANT KRAX.

And we may have stopped GD9. But now?

Now Krax is using the wreckage, the garbage—to DESTROY Pirate's Cove . . .

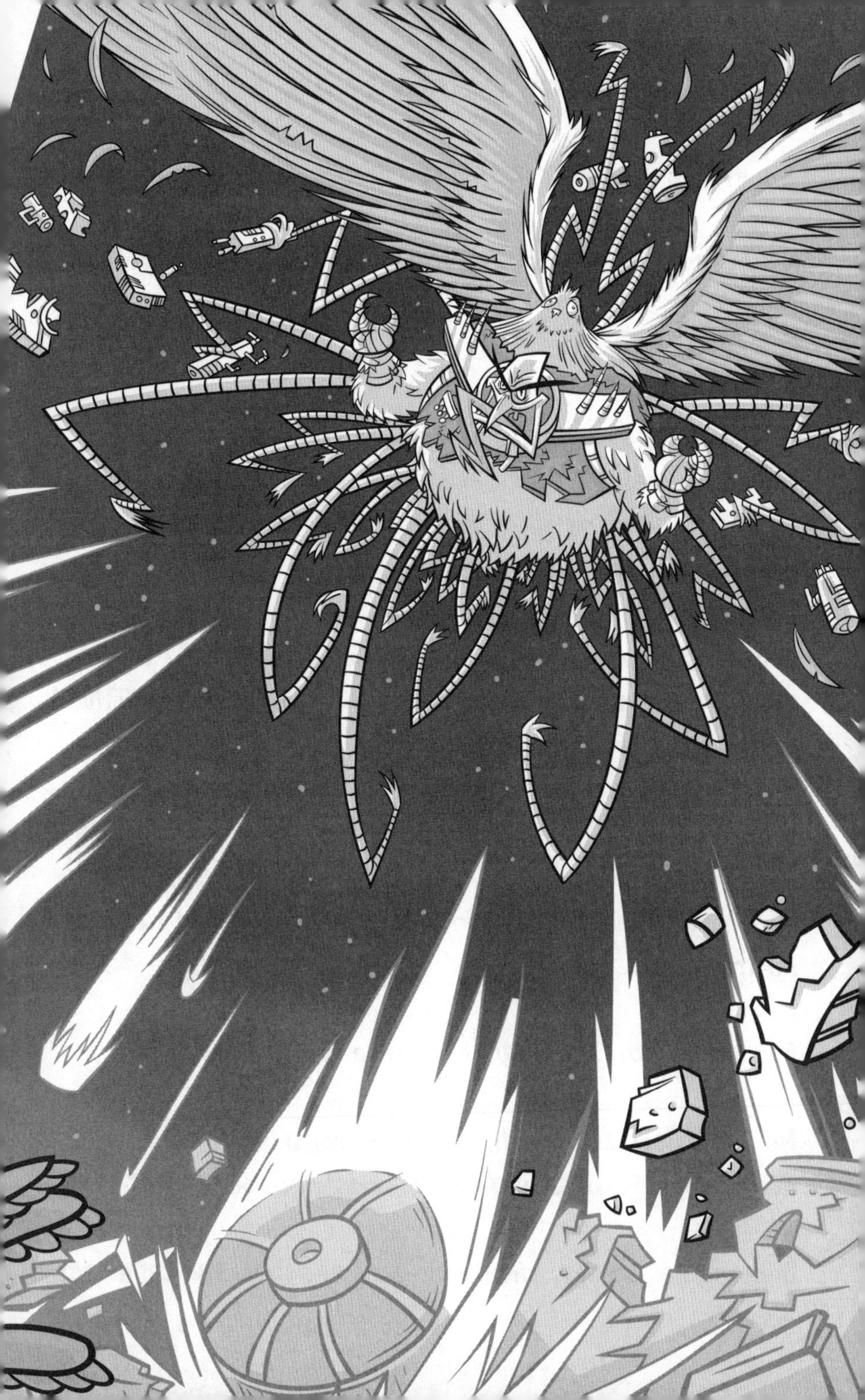

I manage to right myself, get myself UP.

It's not an easy feat in space.

No, in fact, it should be AN IMPOSSIBLE FEAT IN SPACE.

But it's not.

I think about stopping, slowing, and I do. I feel a strange sensation near my feet—and I realize it's Goober, moving ever so slightly—but his slight movement is just enough to allow me to move, shift, and direct myself.

I think about moving forward, like Superman-style soaring, and I do. And suddenly, without realizing it, I exclaim, "This is amazing!"

Krax.

Oh, Krax. I almost feel sorry for you. You wanted to destroy Pirates Cove.

But I think not. No. Now I'm coming for you.

No more back and forth. No more exchanging blows. I will destroy you now, Krax. And I will destroy your planet-ship . . .

Because I'm Cosmoe the Earth-Boy, and I'm a radical galactic hero . . .

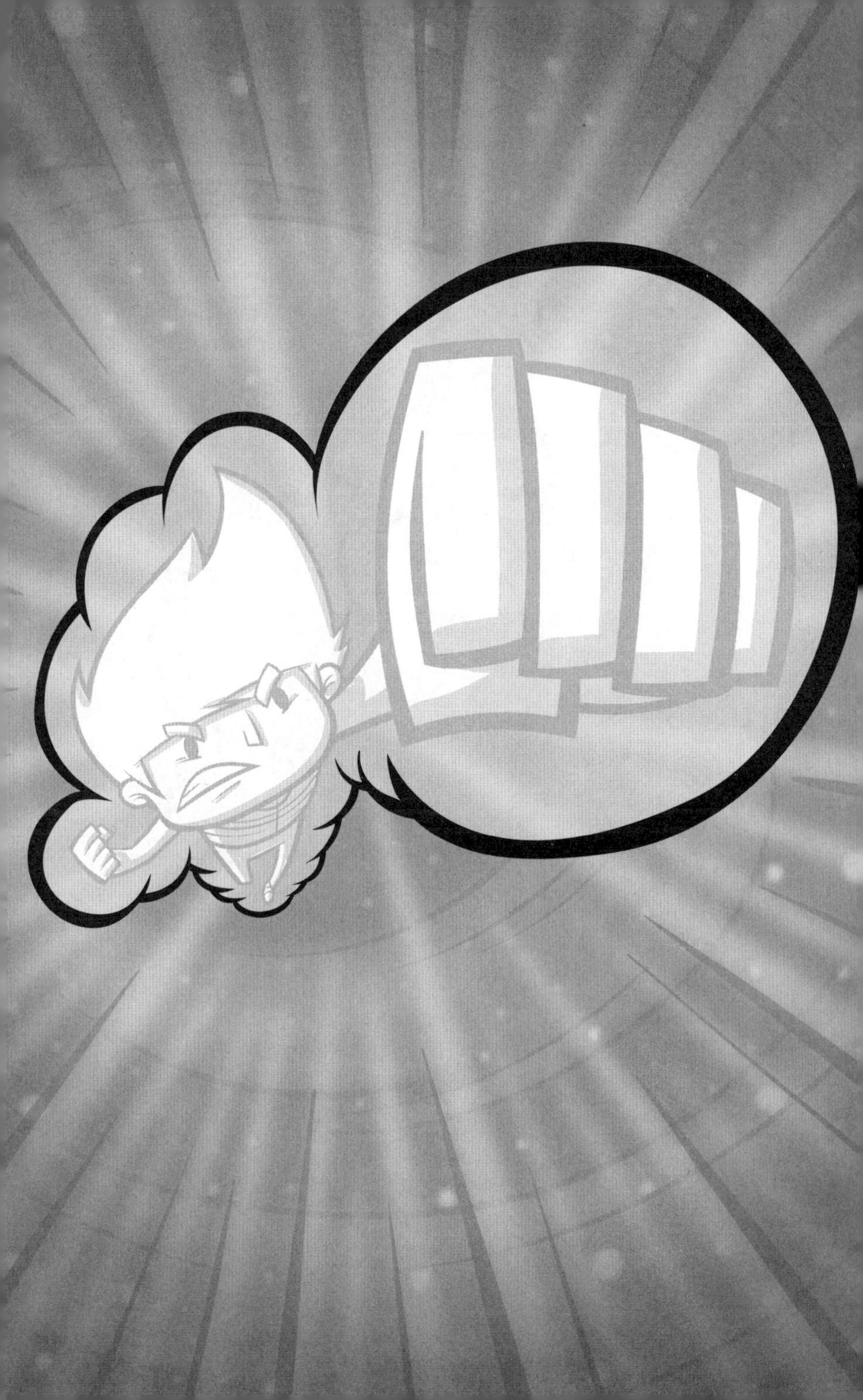

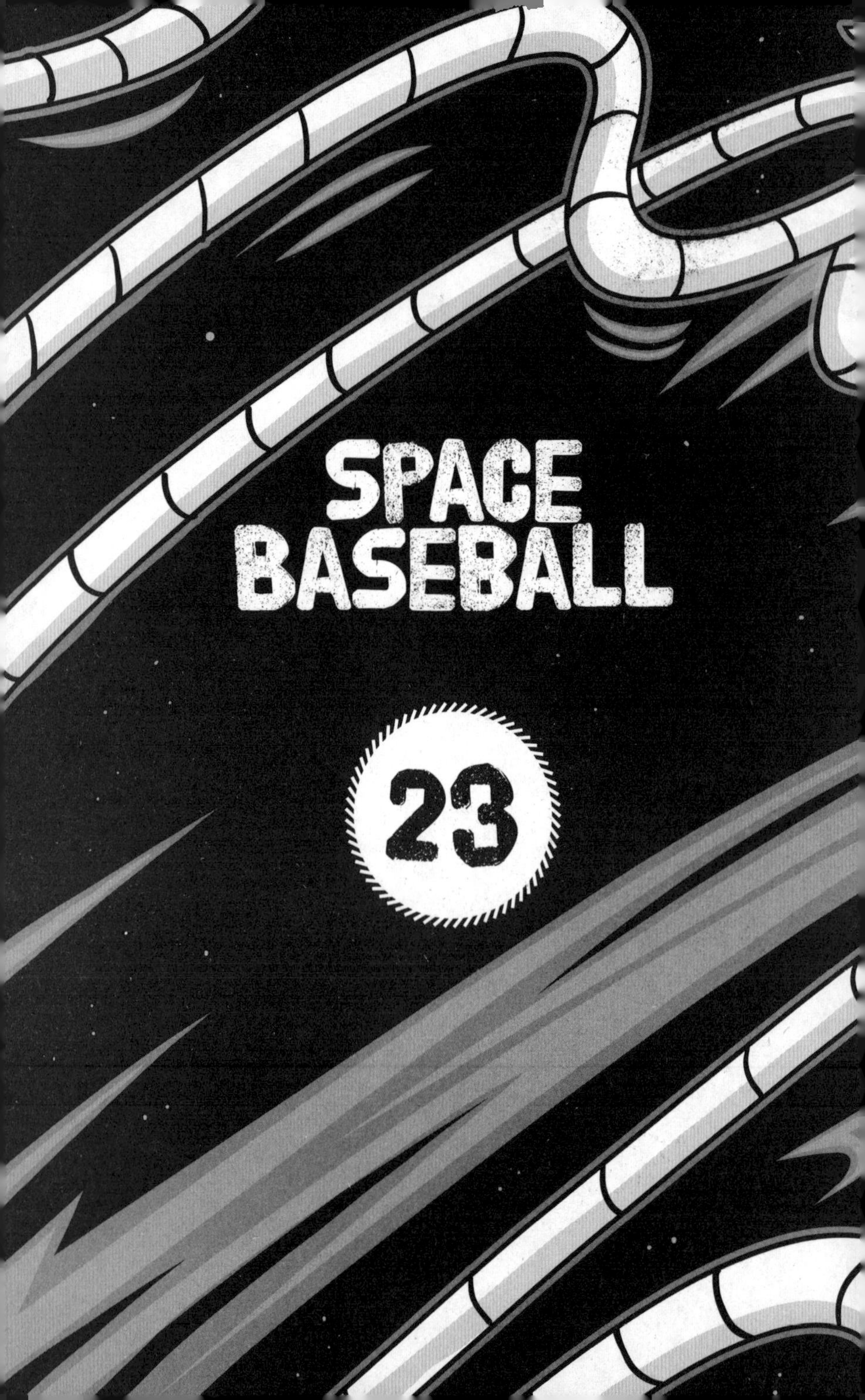
SPACE BASEBALL
23

I slam into Krax's massive, ginormous frame—
my Goober-covered fist hitting him in the gut.

I'm tiny, compared to Krax—a mosquito. But tiny
mosquitos can be HUGELY ANNOYING.

I unleash a flurry of fists, punching and pounding away. Krax
roars, looks down. He swings at me.

"Sorry, too slow!" I shout as I zip away, speeding around his
back. I feel alive, happy—I feel a grin spreading across
my face.

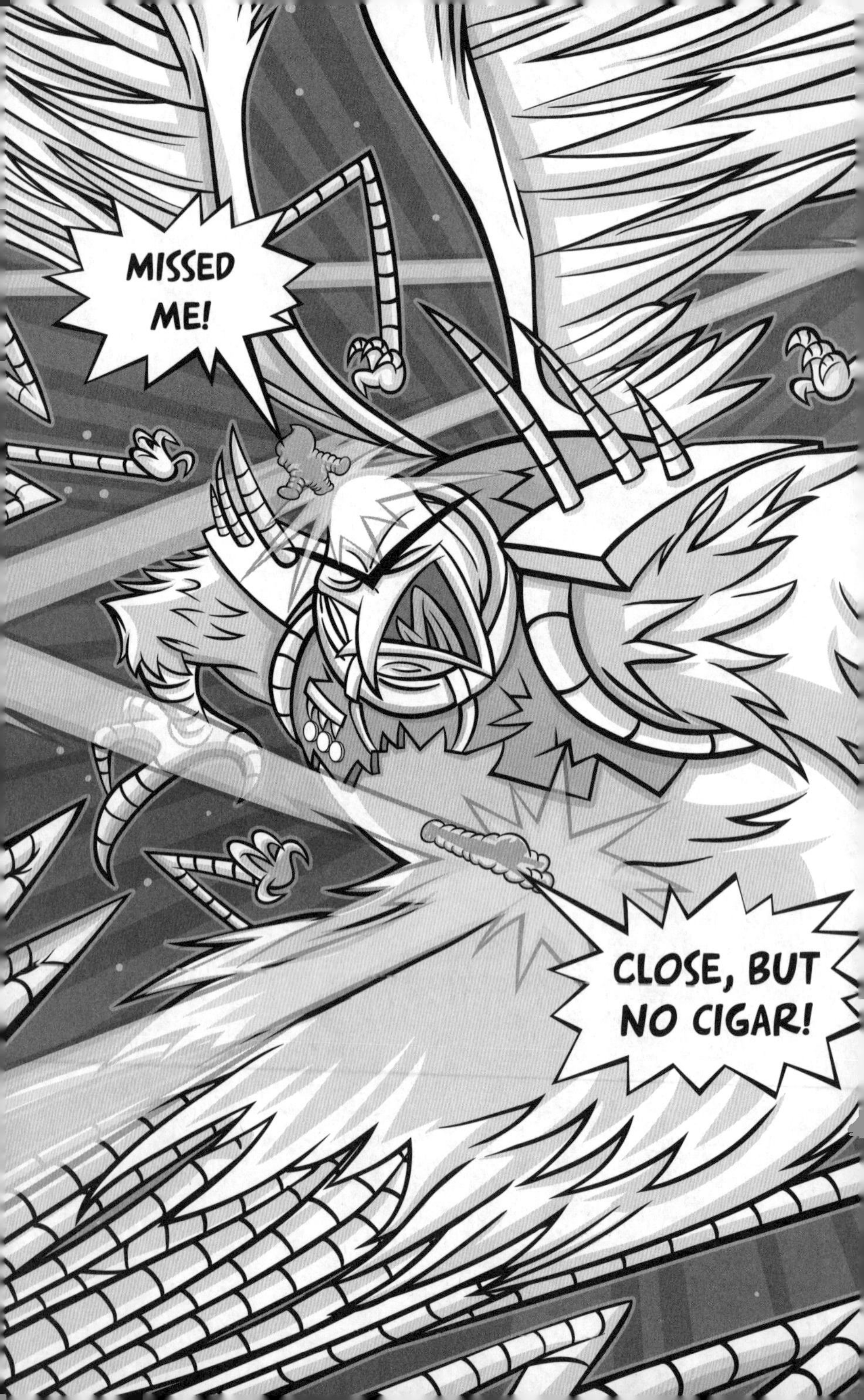
MISSED ME!
CLOSE, BUT NO CIGAR!

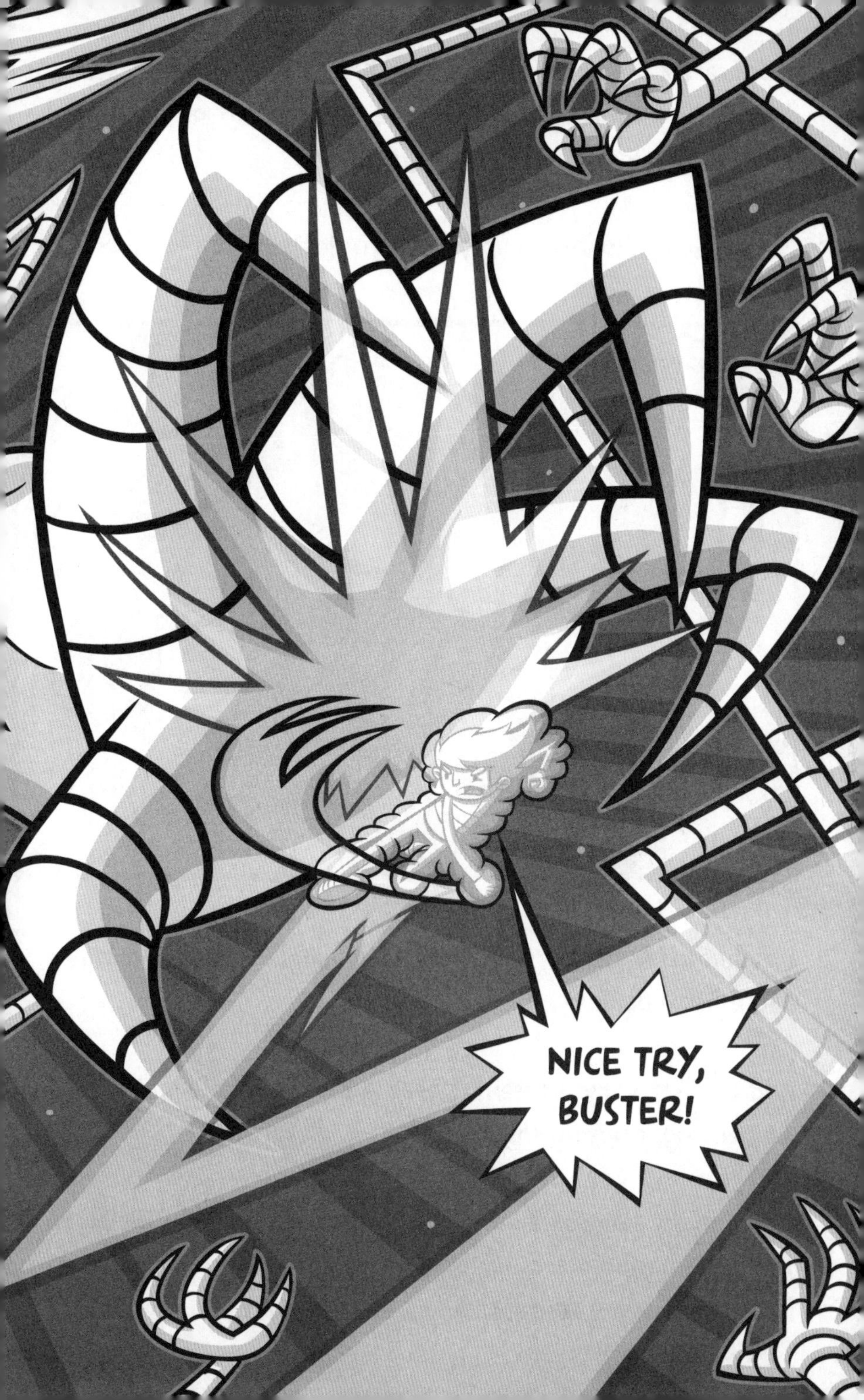
NICE TRY,
BUSTER!

A powerful punch to the base of Krax's skull causes his armor to fracture further, and I see the pulsing spot on his back. I see the familiar—that strange, evil bird.

It's glowing. Now—I simply need to destroy the familiar . . .

I pound away, but it's not quite enough. I'm close. If I only had a little backup . . .

And at that very moment, I hear a sound—my favorite sound. A speeding, cruising ship.

Krax howls, swiping at me, but I dodge—spinning, swirling in the air. Swooping around, ducking one hand, I come twisting back, and I see a fantastically welcome sight.

"Dags!" I shout. "**WONDERFUL** to see you. We need to knock out the familiar. Can you guys handle that?"

"On it!" she calls.

Suddenly, from below—screams and cries. I glance down at Pirates Cove. Tendrils of smoke rise up. "Whoops. Gotta take care of something real quick!" I say. "Be right back!"

And then I dive, rocketing toward Pirates Cove. I burst through its weak atmosphere, spiraling above the streets.

Breezing, rocketing above their heads, I see what Krax has done. He's pelting the cove with hunks of his garbage planet. The ground is cratered. Storefronts are blown apart. Smoke snakes up.

But that's not the real problem.

The real problem is the Black Mast. He's broken the tip, and it's tumbling, falling, about to crush hundreds of pirates.

"I got it!" I cry out. "Have no fear, pirate dudes!"

I dive low, my Goober-powered hands scooping up the gigantic tower, catching it a quick instant before it falls.

I hear an eruption of thankful pirates. "All in a day's work!" I cry out.

And then a moment later—I'm speeding back toward Krax. It's time to end this. It's time to play a little space baseball...

I spot the *Neon Wiener* rolling, dodging a swipe from massive Krax.

I speed up, zooming alongside it.

Atop the *Neon Wiener*, Dagger shouts, "Hey, Krax, I have a message from Rani. Deal's off! You can take back your spaceos!"

The space air erupts. A huge explosion and a glittering sparkle as coins—every last spaceo that Krax paid Rani days earlier—are launched through the air.

Time seems to stand still. But only for a moment. Krax turns, trying to brace himself, but it's too late...

SPACEO BLAST!

The familiar is destroyed! Krax's armor begins to disappear.

And I race ahead, lifting the tip of the mast, cocking it back, and then—

"Good-bye, Krax."

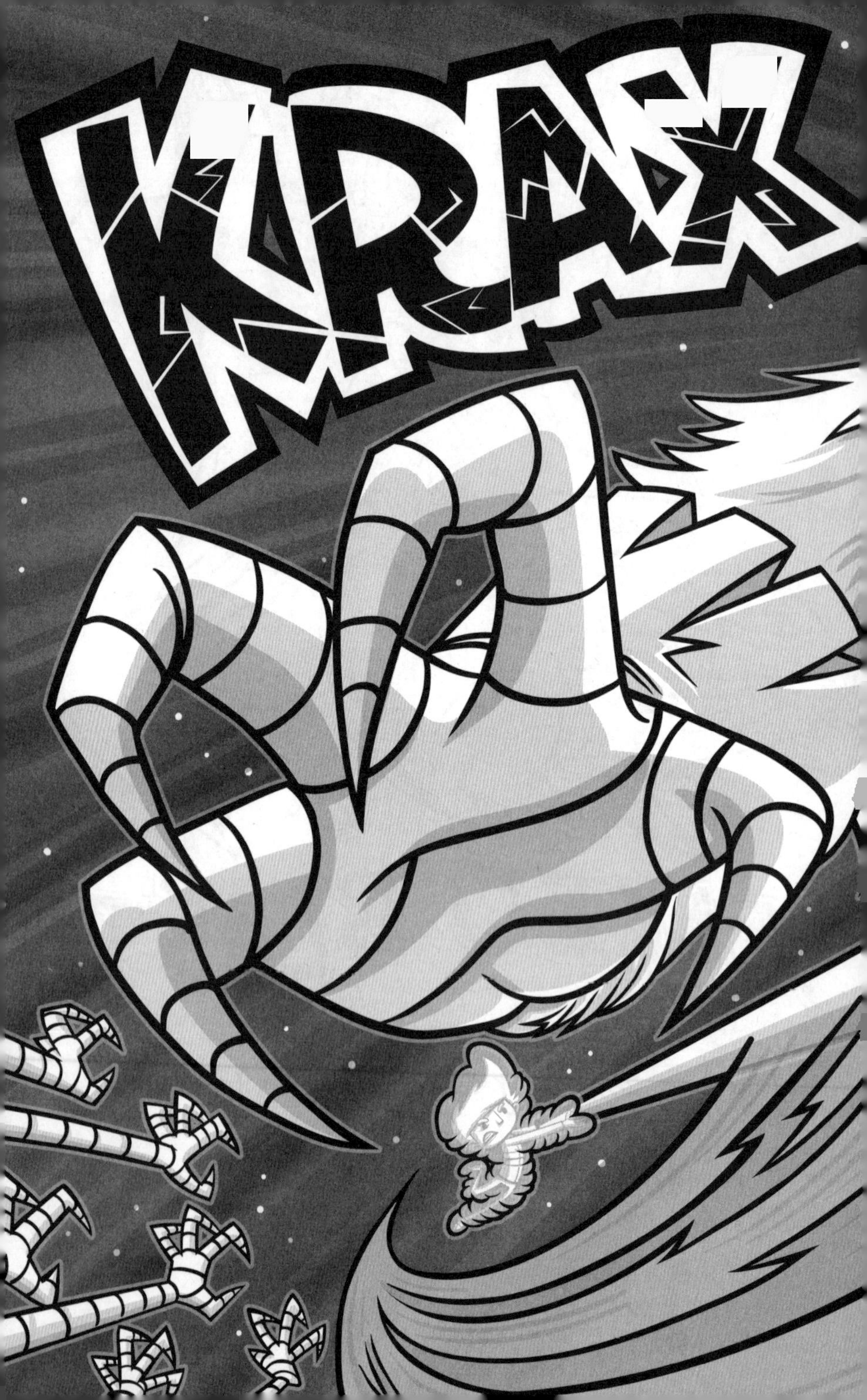

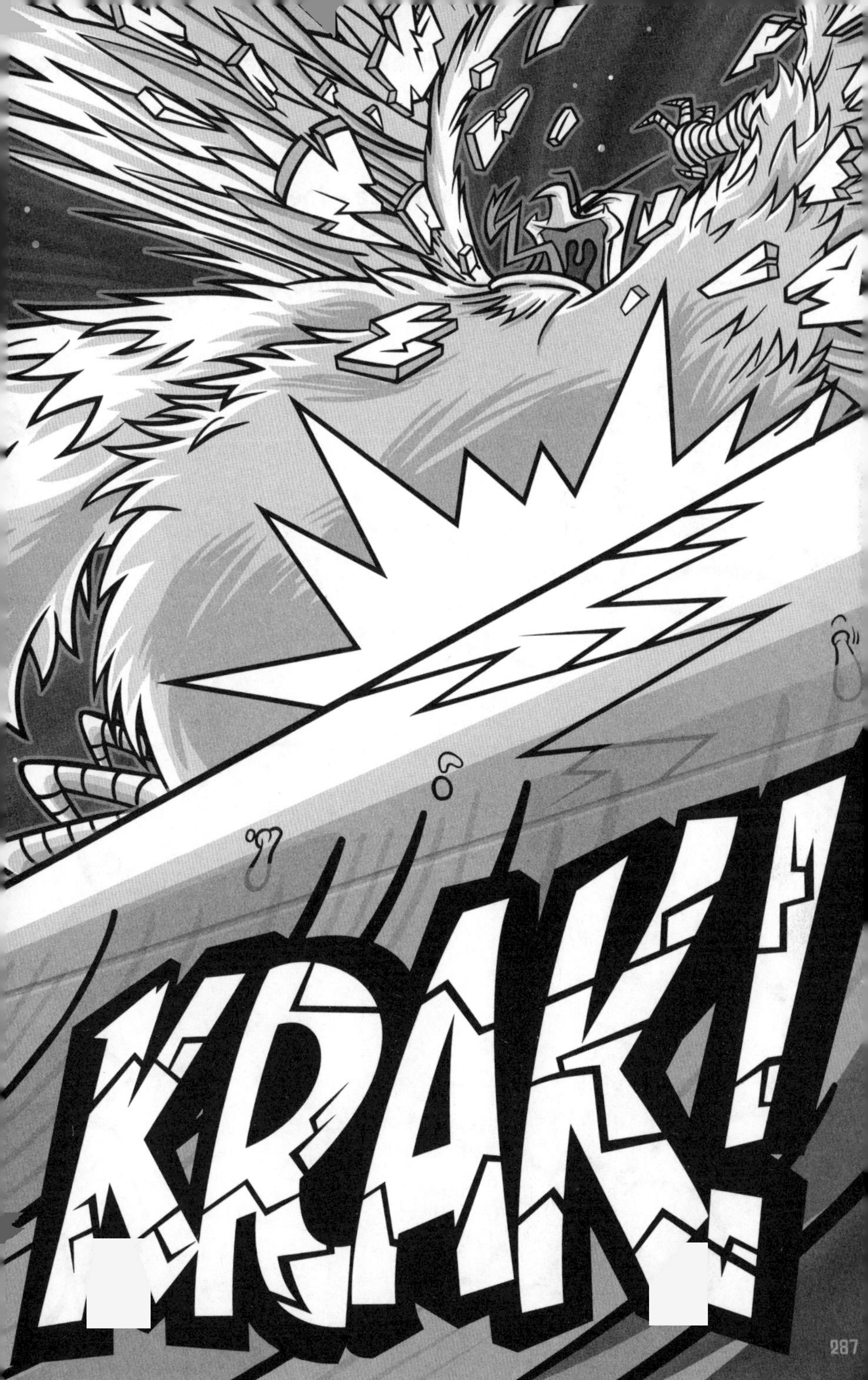
KRAK!

I catch a final glimpse of Krax's enraged face as he slams into the mouth of GD9.

There's a wave of energy. The force—the tremendous, space-shattering force of the mast's blow—sends the planet-ship rocketing through space. Disappearing into the distance.

The Coresky King is no more ...

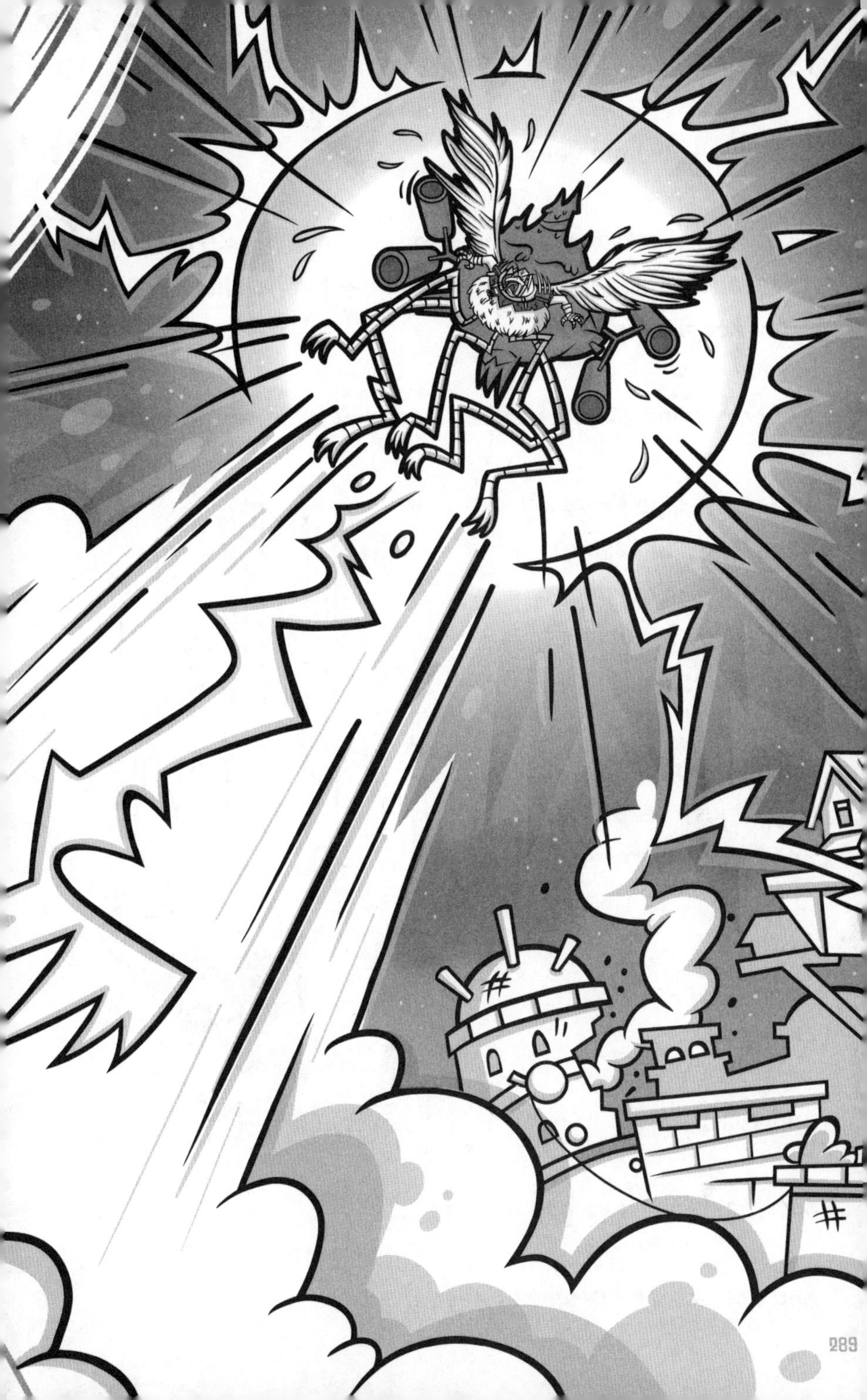

I smile.

But only for a moment.

Goober is weakened, fading, used up, thin. Thin from powering the planet-ship. Thin from helping me battle that villain. Thin from keeping me alive.

Goober fades away, receding from my body, my face.

The mast slips from my hand, and I'm falling. I'm tumbling through space, down, toward nothingness . . .

Without buddies to save me, I'll just keep floating and falling, forever.

And ever.

And ever.

And ever.

But thankfully, I've got buddies . . .

And they catch me when I need it most . . .

Moments later, I'm resting in the *Neon Wiener's* hangout room. Rani is steering the ship down toward the cove.

"So is everyone good?" I ask. "Everyone still alive?"

Humphree and Dagger grin. "Yep."

Humphree leans in close. "Short pants, when you were out there—floating, alone, in space—we thought we were going to lose you."

"Yeah, dude," Dagger says. "What happened?"

I think about that for a moment. And then I just shrug.

I COULDN'T TELL YA. ASK GOOBER.

UNTIL WE MEET AGAIN . . .

That night, there are fireworks over Pirates Cove. Pirates—
and those in their care—celebrate. A cool wind whips off
space.

When we defeated the Ultimate Evil, I felt elation. When we
stopped Crostini's circus, I felt RIGHT.

But now—now the feeling is different. There's something
gnawing at me.

It's like that feeling after you wake up from a bad dream,
and even though you can't quite remember the details—you
just feel off.

Comfort food. That's what I need. The same way I needed it, years earlier, when I felt lost aboard the *Neon Wing*.

I leave the celebration and make my way through the winding streets, toward the *Neon Wiener.* I grill up two dogs, then take them to the farthest edge of the cove—leaning on a railing, staring out at space.

I look down at Goober. "Buddy," I ask. "Were you really talking to me before? Out in space? Or was that just like a dream?"

Goober looks up at me. He doesn't react. He certainly doesn't SPEAK. He's back to regular old Goober.

And then—for a quick instant—I think I see him wink.

"Hey! Goober! You winked! Did you wink? Buddy, talk to me!"

But before I can get any answers, I'm interrupted . . .

"Hey, short pants!"

I turn to see Dagger and Humphree striding toward me. "What are you doing out here all alone?" Dagger asks.

"Just looking for a little peace and quiet," I say.

Humphree nods. "We can do that."

We stand there for a long while before, suddenly, I realize what was bugging me. "Wait!" I exclaim, whirling around. "Dagger, back when I was on GD9, you guys said a deal was made. A deal to rescue me."

Dagger swallows. Humphree looks at me for a moment, then turns away.

"Well?" I ask. "Is that right? You made a deal?"

"Yes, a pirate deal. And a pirate deal cannot be broken."

It's Rani's voice. I spin around to see her stepping out of the shadows.

"What PIRATE deal? Wait, did someone sell my soul?" I say. "I did not authorize anyone to sell my soul. No soul selling."

Dagger shakes her head. "The deal was for me."

That hits me like a slug to the stomach. "Wait—for YOU?"

Dagger nods. "I'm going to be a crewmate on the *Looting Star*," she says. "Well, the *Looting Star* got eaten—but whatever Rani's next radical ship is. I'm going to be a crewmate on **THAT!**"

"Rani . . . THAT'S why you agreed to rescue me?" I bark.

Rani leans against a metallic tree. "Don't be angry at me, Cosmoe. It was not my idea."

I turn to Dagger. "You? You . . . you mean . . . you want to leave? You don't want to be friends anymore?"

Dagger's chin is trembling. She sets it, and smiles in a sad sort of way. "Cosmoe, you helped give me what I never had. Friendship. Real, non-evil friendship. You and Humphree gave that to me."

"So why do you want to leave?!" I exclaim.

Dagger opens her mouth to speak, but her lip begins to quiver, so instead . . .

Stepping back, Dagger wipes a tear from her chin. "Because I need to. I need to learn and junk! I need to see **MORE**. The galaxy is so big. I want to try new things," she says.

"But we can!" I say, fighting back tears. "We can do whatever you want! Anything! Any stupid thing you ever wanted to do we can do it, together, I swear!"

Dagger shakes her head. "Cosmoe, it's okay! Really. I'll be back. It's just temporary!"

Humphree squeezes my shoulder. His eyes are warm and kind. And I look down at Goober, back on my wrist, as always. He's smiling.

Rani steps forward. "Cosmoe, I never should have taken you from Earth. But if I hadn't ... well, I think it's clear. You being in space? You've made these two beings' lives much better. You've given them meaning."

Dagger nods. She opens her mouth again, but she doesn't say anything. So she simply touches my hand, squeezes, then walks away ...

Rani looks Humphree up and down. "We're even," she says. Then she flashes a sly grin and turns, following Dagger.

For a long while, Humphree and I don't say anything. The fireworks come to an end, and we hear laughter and fun from the square.

SHORT PANTS,
YOU CAN GO BACK TO THE PARTY.
BUT I DON'T BELONG HERE. I'M NO PIRATE.
I'M JUST A HOT-DOG SLINGER.

SO AM I.

Humphree chuckles and lets out a deep sigh. "So it's just the two of us again, huh?"

F.R.E.D. suddenly whirs over. "NO, IT IS THE THREE OF US. AND I AM TIRED OF BEING FORGOTTEN."

"Of course, F.R.E.D., my friend," I say. "So whaddya think, guys? Time to blow this cove?"

"Yep. Time to be getting on. What now?" Humphree says.

"Somewhere, in this galaxy, someone's in need of a hot dog. And it's our job to feed 'em ..." I say.

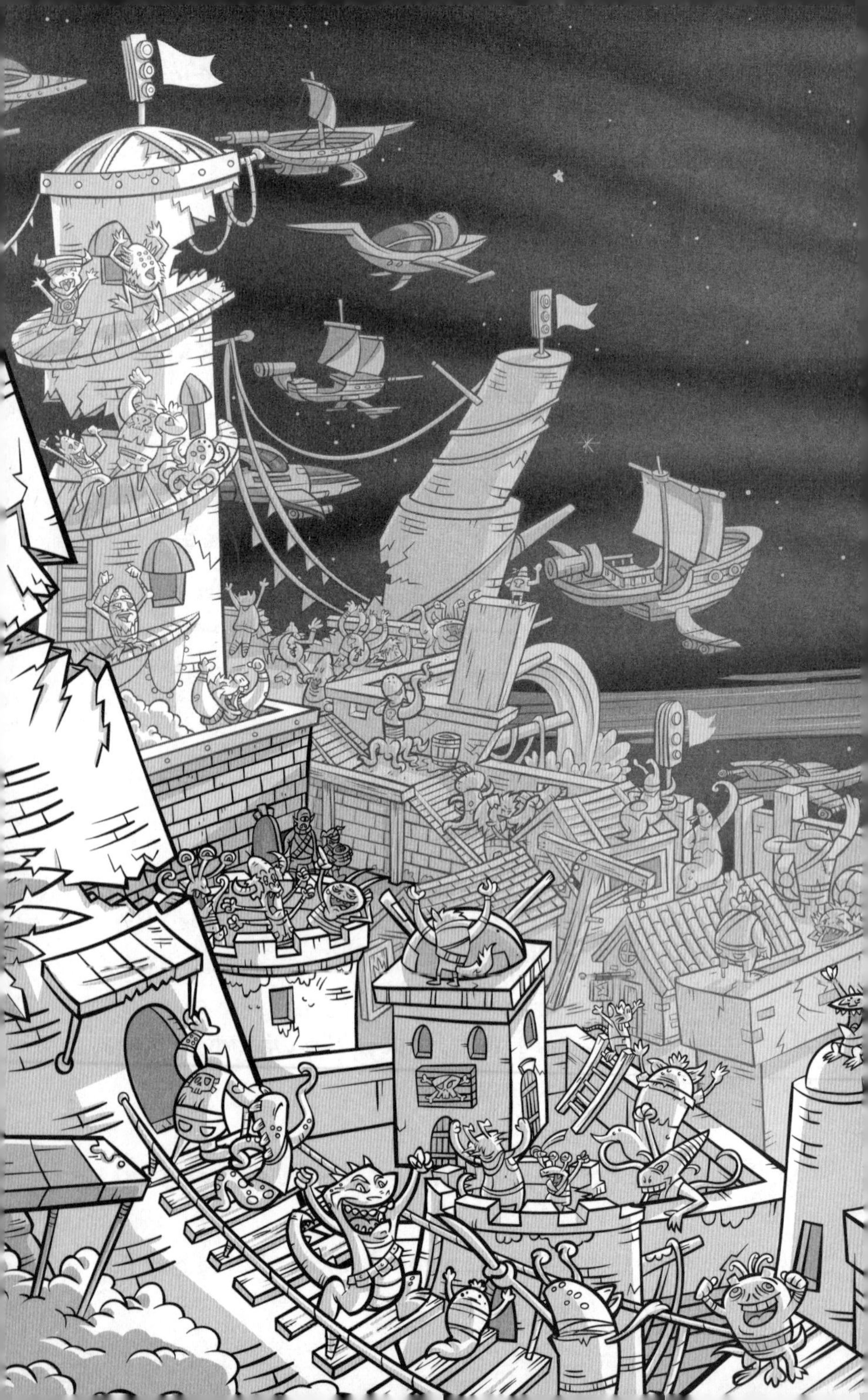

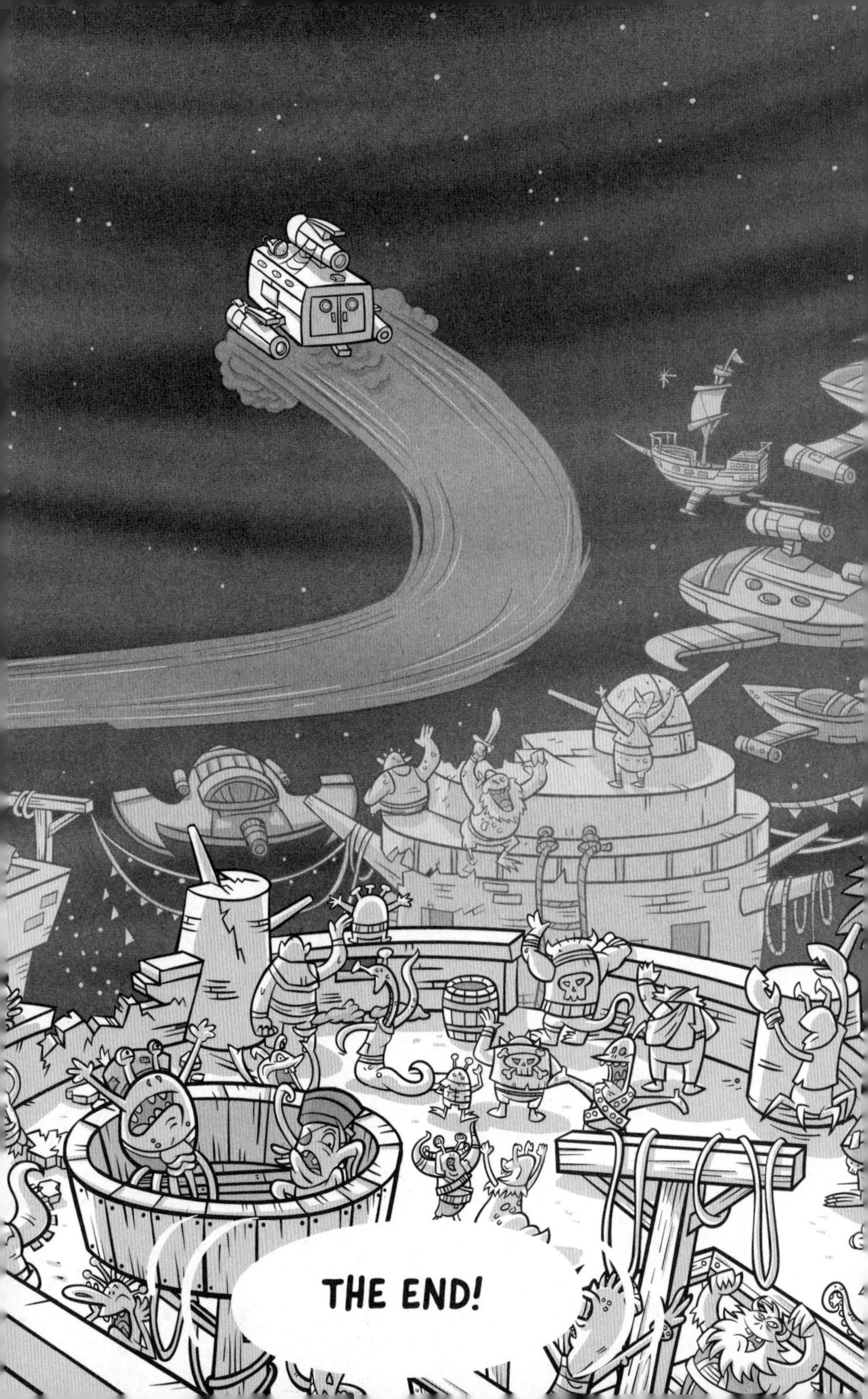
THE END!

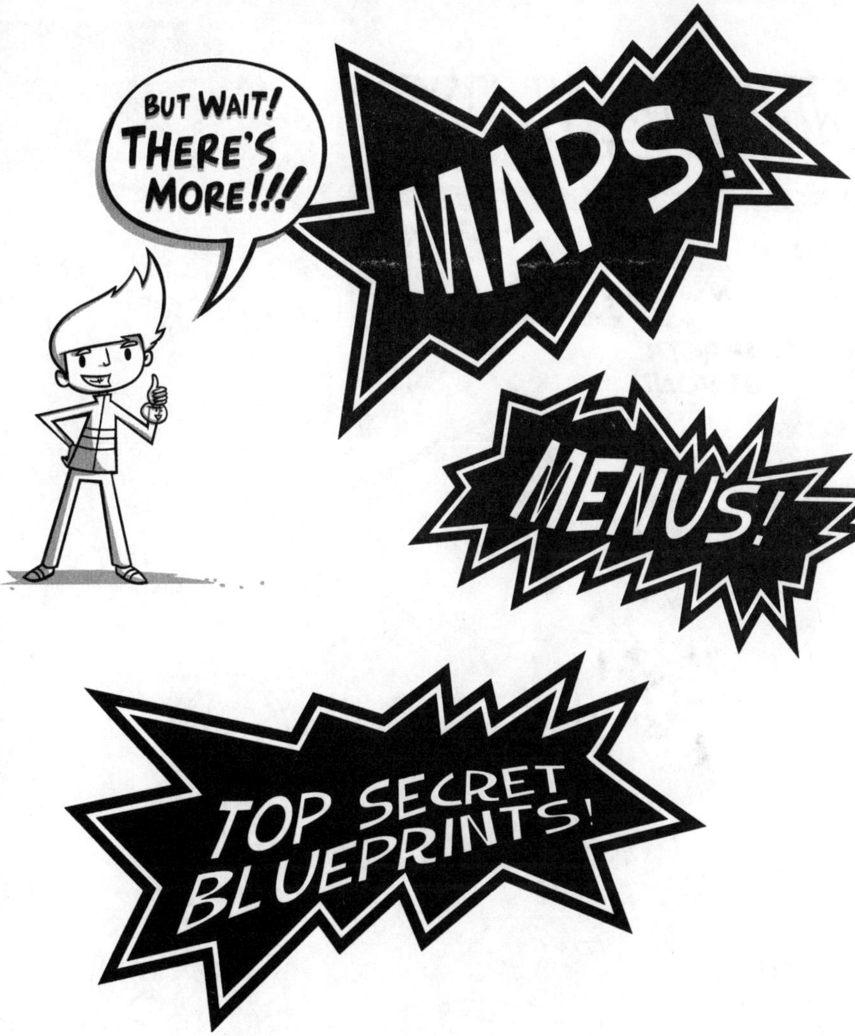
BUT WAIT! THERE'S MORE!!!
MAPS!
MENUS!
TOP SECRET BLUEPRINTS!

THE GALAXY

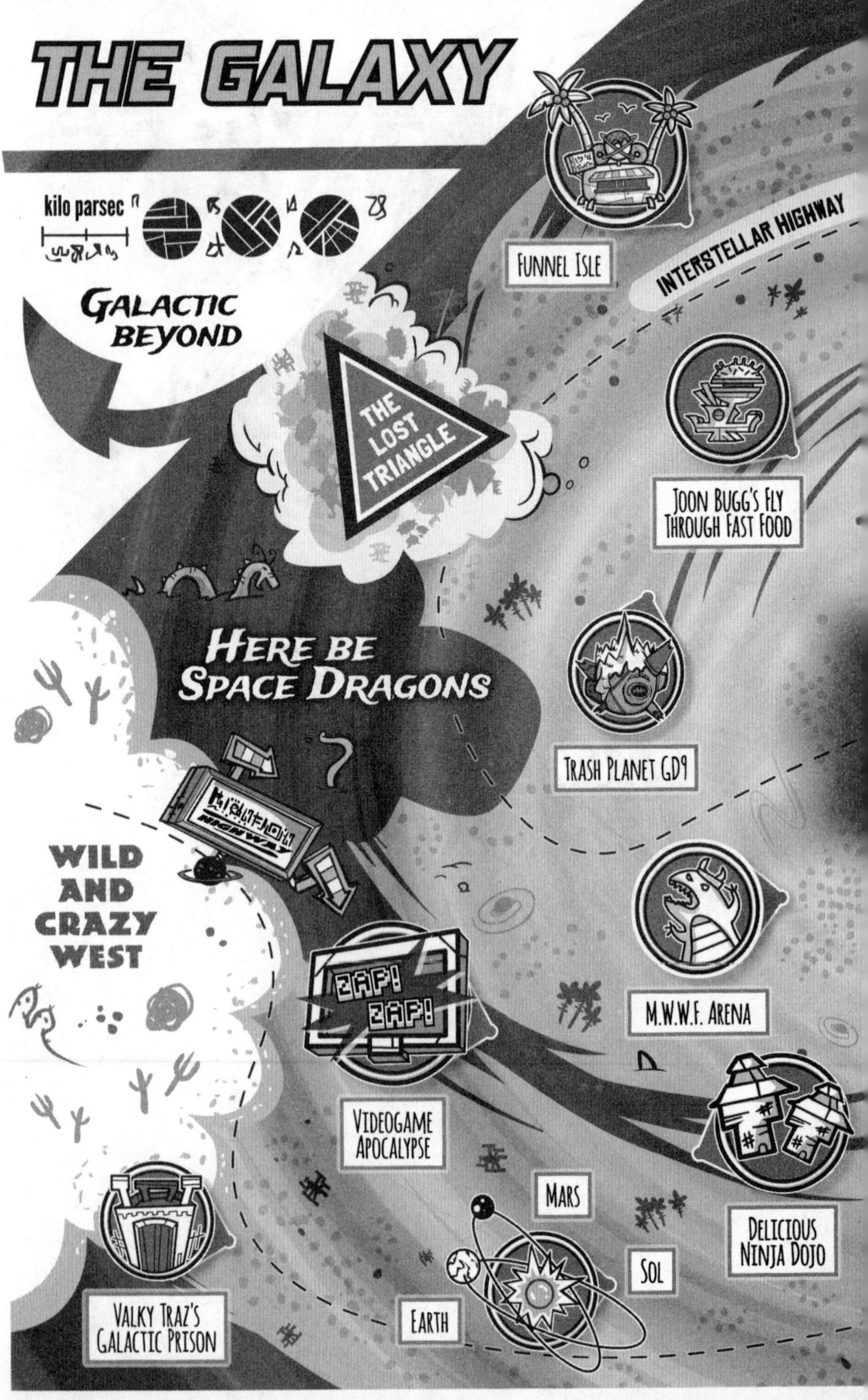

kilo parsec
Galactic Beyond
The Lost Triangle
Funnel Isle
Interstellar Highway
Joon Bugg's Fly Through Fast Food
Here be Space Dragons
Trash Planet GD9
Wild and Crazy West
M.W.W.F. Arena
Zap! Zap!
Videogame Apocalypse
Delicious Ninja Dojo
Mars
Sol
Earth
Valky Traz's Galactic Prison

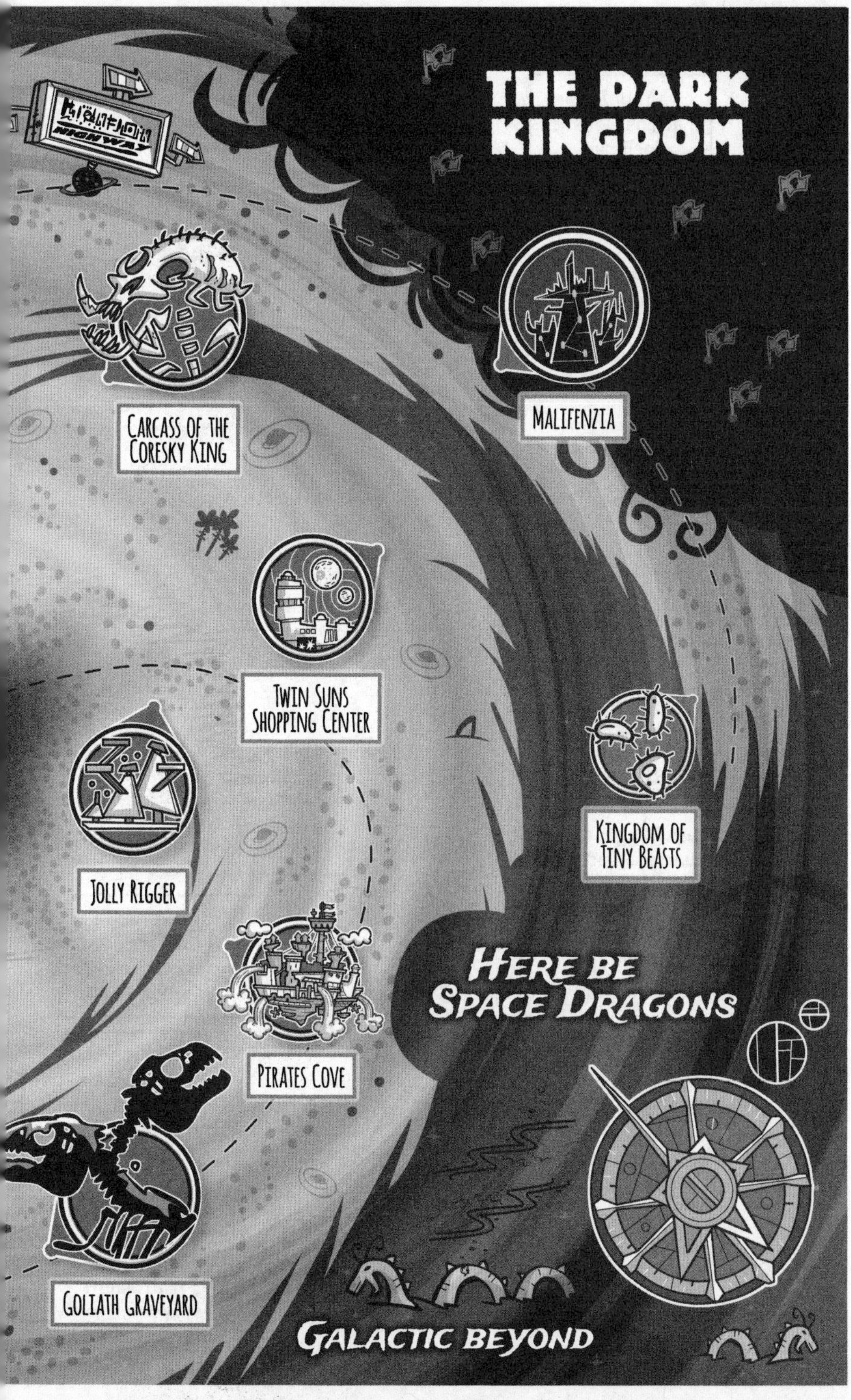

THE DARK KINGDOM
HIGHWAY
CARCASS OF THE CORESKY KING
MALIFENZIA
TWIN SUNS SHOPPING CENTER
JOLLY RIGGER
KINGDOM OF TINY BEASTS
HERE BE SPACE DRAGONS
PIRATES COVE
GOLIATH GRAVEYARD
GALACTIC BEYOND

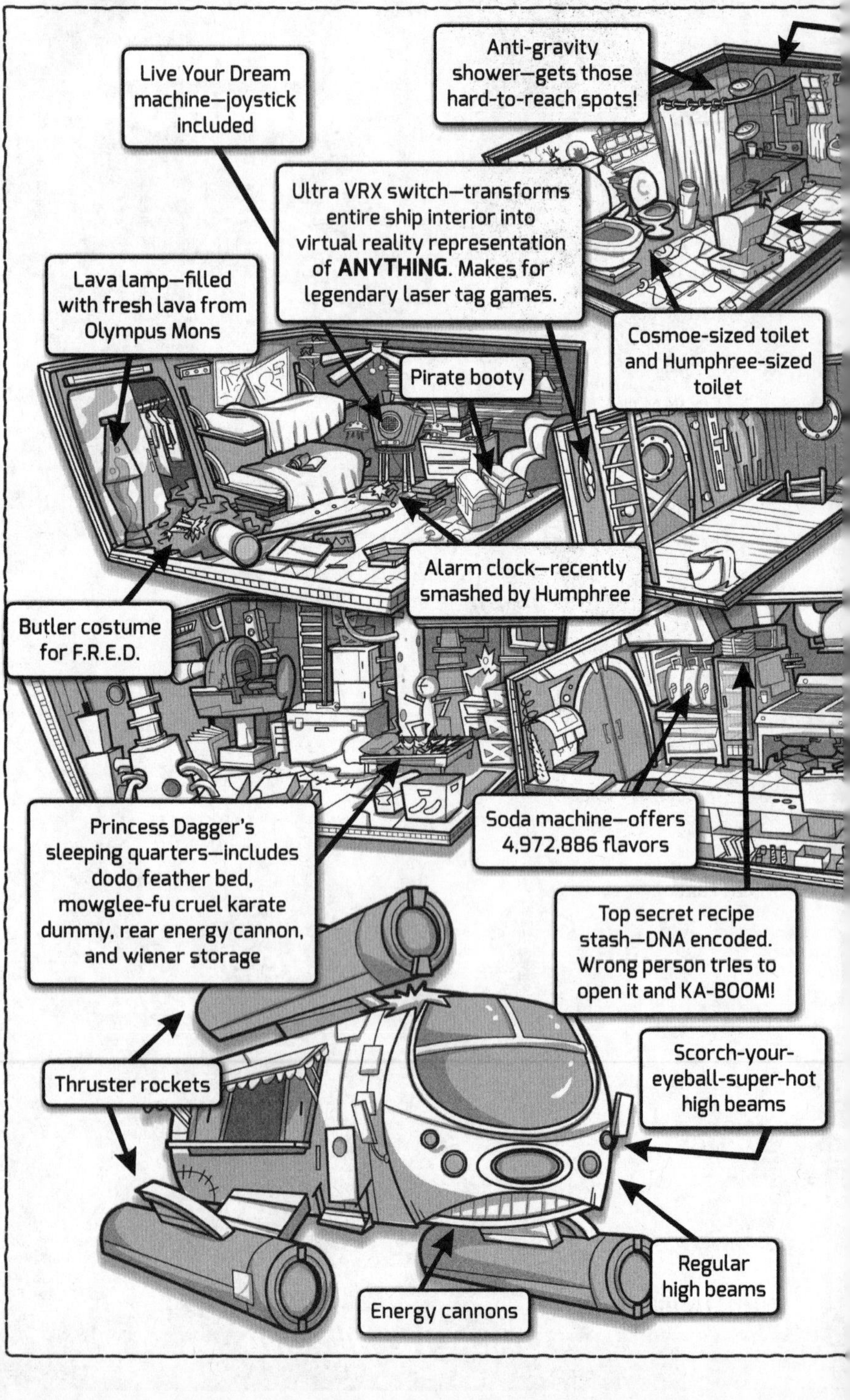

Live Your Dream machine—joystick included
Anti-gravity shower—gets those hard-to-reach spots!
Ultra VRX switch—transforms entire ship interior into virtual reality representation of **ANYTHING**. Makes for legendary laser tag games.
Lava lamp—filled with fresh lava from Olympus Mons
Cosmoe-sized toilet and Humphree-sized toilet
Pirate booty
Alarm clock—recently smashed by Humphree
Butler costume for F.R.E.D.
Princess Dagger's sleeping quarters—includes dodo feather bed, mowglee-fu cruel karate dummy, rear energy cannon, and wiener storage
Soda machine—offers 4,972,886 flavors
Top secret recipe stash—DNA encoded. Wrong person tries to open it and KA-BOOM!
Scorch-your-eyeball-super-hot high beams
Thruster rockets
Regular high beams
Energy cannons

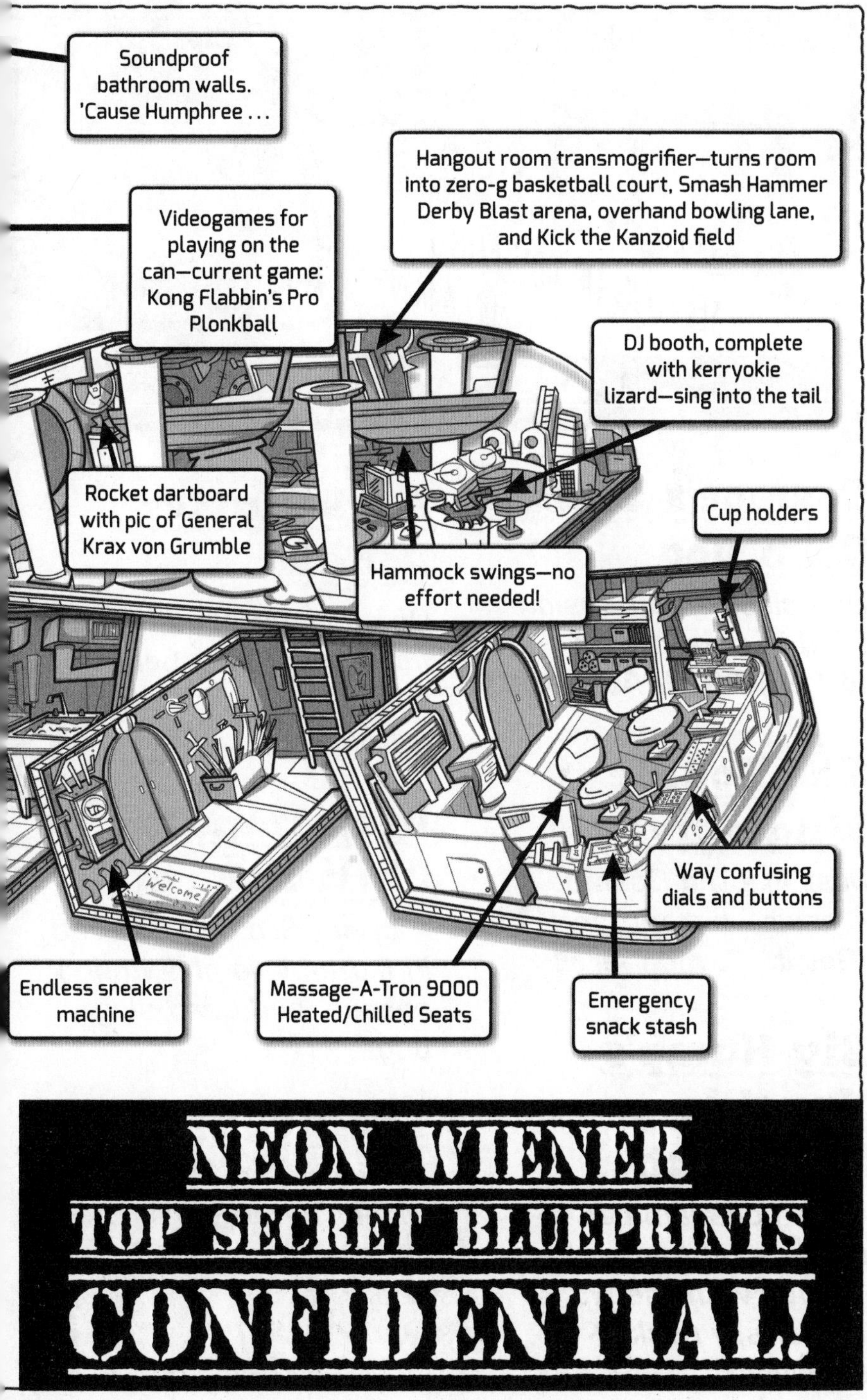
Soundproof bathroom walls. 'Cause Humphree . . .
Hangout room transmogrifier—turns room into zero-g basketball court, Smash Hammer Derby Blast arena, overhand bowling lane, and Kick the Kanzoid field
Videogames for playing on the can—current game: Kong Flabbin's Pro Plonkball
DJ booth, complete with kerryokie lizard—sing into the tail
Rocket dartboard with pic of General Krax von Grumble
Cup holders
Hammock swings—no effort needed!
Welcome
Way confusing dials and buttons
Endless sneaker machine
Massage-A-Tron 9000 Heated/Chilled Seats
Emergency snack stash

NEON WIENER
TOP SECRET BLUEPRINTS
CONFIDENTIAL!

GALACTIC HOT DOGS ™

— SERVING UP ADVENTURE ... ON A BUN —

Official Galactic Hot Dogs

T-shirts

#5

WIENERS

Cosmoe's Classic Corn Dog

One classic dog, fusion-fried in cake batter. **NO NASTY SPACE BUGS!**

The Double Whammy

Just like the Cosmoe Classic—but meteor! (Get it . . . meatier?!)

Big Hump's Knuckle Sandwich

Eight dogs jammed inside a fat loaf of dough. Topped with the works and crispy nuckto knuckles.

Dark Matter Doggie

One dog wrapped in fudge fur, served on a bonbon bun, topped with cocoa crawlzacs.

Deep Impact Chili Dog

A crispy fire dog covered in frozen lava chili, moon cheese, and bean slug-bugs.

The Mega-Dog

The legendary 498-pound wiener entered into the Intragalactic Food Truck Cook-Off. **OUT OF STOCK**

Prices may vary by star system.

TOPPINGS

Moon Rock Relish
Seyfert Sauerkraut
~~Humphrees' Hot Hot Sauce~~

NO LONGER SERVED ↗

Raw Arakzid Legs
Lime Moon Cheese

HAD SOME ISSUES ...

MILKY WAY SHAKES

Buzzberry Shake

Buzzberry ice cream, blotto berries, and Doug Adams' apples.

The Black Hole

Clandaapoo cocoa ice cream, chocolate creepy-crawlies, and nostromo nougat.

Blue and Cream

Inkskyn blue milk swirled with shaved Jeerjeer ice.

Princess Dagger's Royal Pain

Lavenberry ice cream whirled with Dark Kingdom kandy krystals

SNACKS and SWEET TREATS

Crater Tots
Bradbury Cream Egg
Onion Orbitals
Arthur C. Clarke Bar

Acknowledgments

Rachel, Nichole, Steve, and Ryan—thanks for bringing this world to vivid, fantastic life. Much thanks to Jeff Faulconer and Dena Bachman, Stephen Connolly, and the entire Sandbox team. Liesa Abrams—you rule, simple as that. Dan Potash, Mara Anastas, Jon Anderson, and every wonderful person at Simon & Schuster—thank you! Dan Lazar, Cecilia de la Campa, Victoria Doherty-Munro, and all the folks at Writers House. Bob Holmes—the calmest of the calm. And above all, my parents, my sister, and my darling wife and daughter.
—M. B.

The art for this illustrated novel came to exist (on deadline nevertheless!) because of the following: Max Brallier for his continued writings, Steve Young and Ryan Young for invaluable excellent artistic skills and fearlessness in jumping into a project headfirst, Jeff Faulconer and Dena Bachman for project managing prowess, Bob Holmes and Dan Potash for art direction, Liesa Abrams for editorial direction, the lovely folks at StoryArc Media, and of course the crew from Simon & Schuster.
—R. M. & N. K.

About the Author

Max Brallier is the *New York Times*, *USA Today*, and *Wall Street Journal* bestselling author of more than thirty books for children and adults. His books and series include Galactic Hot Dogs, The Last Kids on Earth, Eerie Elementary, Mister Shivers, and *Can YOU Survive the Zombie Apocalypse?* Max lives in New York City with his wife and daughter.

About the Illustrators

Rachel Maguire is an artist armed with a whimsical drawing style and a Wacom pen living in a realm south of Boston. She has designed characters, props, and backgrounds on Emmy award-winning PBS programming *WordGirl* and *SciGirls*, colored comics for BOOM! Studios, and worked for The Oil Painting Conservation Studio. She holds a BFA in Illustration & Animation from Massachusetts College of Art & Design and currently teaches art full-time.

Nichole Kelley has worked professionally as an animator, illustrator, and designer. This combination has allowed her to work on a variety of awesome projects, including web animation, casual games, console games, board games, and children's illustration. In her free time she enjoys video games, board games, toys, crafting of all sorts, and sleeping.

Steve Young is an illustrator, writer, and hotshot stunt pilot. He's previously worked in the worlds of comics, children's books, and animation. He resides in the sunny little hamlet of Weymouth, Massachusetts, with his wife and three adorable sons.

Ryan Young is an illustrator who has worked in print, on the web, and on several animated television shows. He works in both traditional and digital painting styles. In his spare time he enjoys drawing, music, films, and sports. A native of Massachusetts, he currently resides in North Carolina.